ABOUT THE AUTHOR

Katharine Lillico, after working for many years in different sectors of the criminal justice system in England, is now a full-time writer. Her novels reflect her interest in issues of criminal behaviour and justice.

Her debut novel was *A Lethal Bequest* (2019).

Katharine Lillico lives in rural Cambridgeshire.

A
TRIANGLE
OF
CIRCLES

Katharine Lillico

Matador
9 Priory Business Park,
Wistow Road, Kibworth Beauchamp,
Leicestershire. LE8 0RX
Tel: 0116 279 2299
Email: books@troubador.co.uk
Web: www.troubador.co.uk/matador
Twitter: @matadorbooks

ISBN 978 1800461 475

British Library Cataloguing in Publication Data.
A catalogue record for this book is available from the British Library.

Printed and bound in Great Britain by 4edge Limited
Typeset in 10.5pt Adobe Garamond Pro by Troubador Publishing Ltd, Leicester, UK

Matador is an imprint of Troubador Publishing Ltd

To the memory of DGH

One

'For heavens' sake, Sophie,' exploded Joanna, 'just *tell* me! What's bugging you this morning?'

She looked her friend steadily in the eyes. Somewhat taken aback, Sophie's face reddened, and an air of uncertainty replaced her usual composure.

'What do you mean, Jo?' she asked, hesitantly.

'Oh, come on Sophie, give me some credit,' retorted Joanna rather sharply, 'there's clearly something on your mind, and you're not sure whether or not to tell me about it. That's right, isn't it? We trust each other, so what's the problem?'

By the time Sophie had finished explaining what was bothering her, Joanna's mind was in turmoil, but she was determined not to show this.

* * *

Theirs was an unlikely friendship in many ways, as Joanna and Sophie had little in common. They had met one Sunday morning at Blakesford Golf Club, where their husbands were members. They discovered that they belonged to the same gym, so they agreed to meet up one Saturday for a workout and coffee. This soon became a regular arrangement. Otherwise, they rarely saw each other, as their interests and lifestyles were very different.

Sophie was in her forties and seemed to have everything… an expensive and immaculate house (or so Joanna imagined it from Sophie's comments), a high-achieving daughter soon to go to university, a husband who was devoted to her, and seemingly no financial worries. She invariably wore designer clothes, even to the gym.

Joanna was ten years younger and felt more at ease in cheap denims and a casual top, when not at work. And yet she sometimes perceived an air of discontent in Sophie. Nevertheless, in spite of their differences, the Saturday meetings had gradually become important, and something was missing if either had to cancel occasionally.

* * *

Driving home from the gym today, though, Joanna was finding it impossible to come up with an innocent explanation for Sophie's revelations.

Could Sophie have invented the whole scenario? But why would she do that? Sophie had nothing to gain by telling a malicious story about Steve and potentially causing trouble between them. And anyway, that would be completely alien to Sophie's character.

Joanna was churning it all round and round in her mind.

So, had they mistaken someone else for Steve? Notwithstanding the candlelight in the restaurant, that really seemed unlikely. Marcus and Steve knew each other from the golf club. But who was the chestnut-haired young woman having an intimate dinner with Steve, holding his hand across the table?

Joanna racked her brains, trying to recall any new colleagues or acquaintances Steve might have mentioned recently. She wished that she generally listened to him more attentively.

But new colleagues don't hold hands by candlelight, do they? she asked herself.

She was beginning to fume.

And why that restaurant of all places? That was their *special restaurant, the one they chose for celebrations and special occasions. What the hell was Steve doing there with another woman?*

Joanna's anger was increasing, but thankfully she had a week to think everything over, as Steve was away in Scotland working. Furious as she was, she was loath to come to any conclusions immediately. But the more she thought about what Sophie had said, the fewer acceptable interpretations of Steve's behaviour she could come up with.

And who could this young woman be? she wondered.

By the following Thursday Joanna felt no further forward, but she made one decision. She would leave a message for Sophie, saying that she couldn't go to the gym on Saturday.

She needed more thinking time, alone.

Two

At times of personal crisis Joanna missed her older sister, Zoe. As young girls they had wanted little to do with each other, but after their mother died suddenly, when they were in their late teens, the sisters had become closer. Their father had died of cancer when Joanna was seven, so now she and Zoe had become a family of two.

A couple of years later, Zoe gained a scholarship and went off to university. The following year, Joanna left home too, to study at a different university. But they kept in regular contact, partly to deal with the practicalities of the family home.

After graduating, Zoe moved to Montreal to continue her studies, researching a little-known French-Canadian novelist. She and Joanna had talked many times about the move, and they agreed to keep in email contact. They also decided to sell the family home.

So, when Zoe departed for Canada, Joanna initially felt alone in the world. But, being a generally positive person, she determined to regard this as an opportunity to carve out her own direction in life.

* * *

In her final year at university, Joanna fell deeply in love with Steve Hearnden. He was in his mid-twenties, the epitome of charm, with mapped-out career ambitions. In Joanna's view, he was an amazing catch! She couldn't imagine why he had also fallen for her. She didn't recognise her own emotional vulnerability, nor the attraction of her substantial financial assets since the sale of her family home. Egged on by her university friends, some of whom envied her, Joanna married Steve after a whirlwind romance. It was a quiet, registry office wedding, which Joanna told Zoe about a week or two later.

The following year, they were invited to Montreal to attend Zoe's marriage to Jean-Pierre Le Saux. Joanna and Steve stayed on for a couple of weeks, and this was Zoe's first opportunity to get to know her brother-in-law. Her impressions were not entirely favourable, but she didn't say this to Joanna. His manners were impeccable, she thought, even slightly old-fashioned, but Zoe had an uncomfortable feeling that there was something disingenuous about him. She felt uneasy when alone with Steve, even though he gave her no identifiable reason to feel this way. But Joanna appeared happier than Zoe had known her for a long time. She persuaded herself that she was worrying unnecessarily. She shared her concerns with Jean-Pierre, though. He thought that Zoe was simply being over-protective of her younger sister. Jean-Pierre found Steve good company on the golf-course.

* * *

But that was all several years ago. Zoe and Jean-Pierre now had two children, Armand and Delphine, who were the focus of their lives. Communication between Joanna and Zoe had become less regular, but they still contacted each other when there were particular highs or lows in their lives, and they were quickly on each other's wavelength again.

So, after Sophie's story about Steve and the mysterious young woman, Joanna emailed her sister for advice.

Zoe can be relied on to make sound judgements, she thought.

But Zoe resisted the temptation to tell her sister that she had always had reservations about Steve… Joanna didn't need to hear that right now.

Over the next few weeks, Zoe supported Joanna through the traumas of confrontation with Steve, of unravelling truths from lies, of disentangling all the emotions which surfaced, of facing pain and humiliation, and of coping with everyday life at the same time.

There was now no doubt that Sophie and Marcus had been right in their suspicions.

But, wondered Joanna, *is this just the tip of an iceberg?*

Three

A hundred miles away, in her classroom in Hadley St Giles' primary school, Marie Wilkinson was gathering up her papers and books. The children were rushing out into the playground, eager to be in the sunshine. Just one girl lingered.

'What can I do for you, Chelsea?' asked Marie. Ten-year old Chelsea Smithson would usually have been among the first to head for the classroom door.

'Look, Miss,' she said, with tears in her eyes, and carefully rolled up her cardigan sleeve. Marie looked at the child's arm and asked, 'How did that happen, Chelsea?'

Marie saw a movement in the corridor and noticed a colleague peering through the glass panel in the classroom door. She beckoned her into the room. Celine Martin joined Marie and quickly took stock of the situation.

'Mrs Martin,' said Marie, 'as one of our first aiders, would you please have a look at Chelsea's arm and see what you think needs to be done? It looks a bit nasty to me. I was just asking Chelsea how it happened.'

Mrs Martin listened with Marie as Chelsea told her story. She'd been messing about at home yesterday evening, she said, and her mum got crosser and crosser. In the end her mum said she had to learn a lesson and stabbed at Chelsea's arm with her lighted cigarette, then again, and again. 'It really hurt,' wailed Chelsea.

While Mrs Martin took care of Chelsea, Marie went and informed the headteacher, Mrs Lassiter, and a phone call was made to the local children's safeguarding team.

* * *

Back at home that evening, Marie was thinking about Chelsea Smithson. She knew that Chelsea could behave in an annoying way, as she occasionally did in the classroom, but nothing could excuse deliberately burning a child's arm.

How could any mother treat her child like that? she asked herself. *The poor girl must've been in agony.*

Marie had been a teacher for more than a decade, and she loved her job. Only once before had she experienced one of her pupils being abused, and that was a very different story from Chelsea's. But it had remained in Marie's mind, continuing to trouble her whenever something prompted her memory… as now.

Like Chelsea, Louise Purvis-Brown had waited near Marie's desk after the lessons had finished. She had tentatively asked if she could speak with her teacher. This was the first time Louise had approached her, and Marie immediately gave the child her full attention. Louise stared at the floor. She clearly had something on her mind, but she suddenly said, 'Sorry, Miss Wilkinson, it's nothing really,' and she ran out of the classroom.

Marie was left feeling concerned but with no idea what Louise's problem was. She decided to keep a special eye on her over the next few days.

The following day, though, Louise didn't come to school. Her father phoned Mrs Lassiter to say that Louise was unwell. A week later she'd still not returned to school, but her father had phoned twice to report on Louise's continuing illness. Marie wondered if

Louise had simply felt unwell when she'd asked to speak with her, and perhaps there'd been no other problem after all. She still had an uneasy feeling, though.

A few more days passed, and Louise still hadn't reappeared at school. Marie became increasingly worried and decided to share her concerns with Mrs Lassiter at lunchtime.

On arriving at the head's office, Marie was surprised to see two other people there, whom she didn't recognise. They introduced themselves as police officers, and the reason for Louise's recent absence quickly became clear. About two weeks ago, the officers said, Louise had made some serious allegations, which the police were investigating. They asked whether Louise had given any hint of personal problems to Miss Wilkinson. She recounted her pupil's request to talk to her after lessons one day, just before she was off sick, but Louise had then changed her mind. Marie didn't know what she'd wished to talk about.

Louise didn't return to the school. Marie was told that her father had decided to move the family to another part of the country.

Four

The months leading up to the divorce were stressful and acrimonious. Joanna and Steve had each been advised by their lawyers to continue living in the marital home until all the negotiations had been finalised. At times Joanna felt sorely tempted to change the door locks while Steve was out, purportedly playing golf, but good sense prevailed, and the tense waiting continued.

It gradually emerged that the chestnut-haired young woman, whom Sophie and Marcus had seen, was not the only one being wined and dined by amorous Steve. Such assignations had apparently been happening for some time.

And, thought Joanna, *all this must have been costing him a considerable amount of money.*

Initially Steve scoffed at suggestions that he was being unfaithful to Joanna, but as the evidence mounted up, his tone and demeanour changed.

Joanna now slept in the spare bedroom, and she'd moved most of her personal belongings there too. But twice she suspected that an item of jewellery had disappeared, the first of which was her engagement ring. She searched everywhere, while Steve was out of the house, but couldn't find it. Then it was a gold bangle, which Steve had brought back for her from a work trip to the Far

East. Again, it was nowhere to be found. Sinister thoughts began to form in Joanna's mind.

Could this be Steve's doing? Was he really a despicable thief?

She didn't want to believe this… after all, she'd once been desperately in love with this man.

Should she confront him about it? The atmosphere between them was far too strained for that, she decided.

But one day, on impulse, Joanna looked at their online joint bank account. She didn't usually bother about it, but she now had a nagging suspicion that perhaps Steve might be using it for his own benefit. It had been earmarked for mutually agreed purposes only. She stared at the screen, as there was virtually nothing left in the account. It had been drained systematically over the past few months.

Joanna was furious. She'd been paying money regularly into the joint account, while Steve had been syphoning it off elsewhere. She vaguely recalled a conversation, during which Steve had told her not to worry about the account, as there was nearly enough to pay for a luxurious holiday. And she'd trusted his word.

She felt like an idiot. She'd been unaware of Steve's dates with other women, she was possibly living with a common thief, and she'd been duped out of thousands of pounds.

What the hell else has he been up to? she asked herself.

* * *

A few days later, Joanna decided to broach the subject of the bank account with Steve. She had naively hoped that the conversation would be civil, but within minutes Steve felt cornered, and he aggressively went onto the offensive. How dare she imply that he'd stolen the money? It was obvious that he'd moved it elsewhere to earn more interest. He did it for *her* benefit! And now the stupid cow had spoiled the surprise. He demanded an apology!

Steve's manner was threatening, and Joanna began to feel scared, in a way she never had before in his presence. He fixed her with his eyes and shook with anger. Joanna didn't dare mention the ring or the bangle. In fact, she didn't respond at all. This seemed to infuriate Steve still further, and he lunged at his wife, grabbing her tightly on the upper arm and landing a vicious punch on her face.

Suddenly, Steve seemed to realise what he'd just done, and he crumpled to the floor, apparently sobbing.

'I'm so sorry, Jo,' he mumbled quietly.

Joanna was in shock, and the pain in her face was acute. Steve had hit her with a clenched fist, and she wondered if her jaw was fractured. She made for the door, but Steve grabbed her leg and demanded to know where she was going.

'I'm going to the loo,' she said, and, to her relief, he released his grip.

After locking the bathroom door, Joanna felt safer... for the moment. But her phone was in another room.

She sat on the floor, leaning against the side of the bath, trembling and in agonising pain. She found some painkillers and took a couple. Several minutes later, she heard the front door slam and the sound of Steve's car being revved and reversed out of the driveway. She cautiously unlocked the bathroom door and went into her bedroom to find her phone. Her head was still throbbing and she couldn't think straight. She was frightened.

Should she drive to the hospital to have her face checked out? she wondered. *If she did, how would she explain the injury? Should she ring the police? That would certainly make matters worse between her and Steve. But could they get any worse? And where was he now? When would he come home again?*

She simply didn't know what to do.

Five

Joanna was unable to sleep much following Steve's assault. She was in excruciating pain, but she was also scared, and she started nervously at every sound which might be Steve arriving home. She lay awake, her mind going round and round in circles about what she should do. The assault had put a new perspective on their already doomed relationship.

What was stopping her from reporting Steve to the police? she asked herself. *That was surely the best thing to do, wasn't it?*

Joanna knew, though, that she was petrified of the consequences of doing that. Steve had hit her behind closed doors, with no witnesses. As far as she was concerned, it was a completely unprovoked attack, so what was to stop him from doing it again? It was just his word against hers, and he would deny everything. He controlled the situation, and Joanna felt powerless.

Eventually, she decided to pin all her hopes on a rapid divorce and a complete break from Steve.

My physical injuries will heal before too long, she tried to persuade herself, *although the mental scars might take longer.*

In the meantime, she hoped that he would stay away from their home... but she suspected that this was probably a vain hope.

* * *

Joanna phoned her boss at the library, Tony Stoneman, and apologised that she wouldn't be at work today. She told him that she'd fallen downstairs yesterday evening and hit her face hard on the bannisters. Her shoulder was badly bruised too. She'd had some dizzy spells, so she felt unable to work, but she assured him that she'd return to work tomorrow.

Lies didn't usually come so easily to Joanna, but she still felt thoroughly shaken up by Steve's violence, both mentally and physically. She had never thought him capable of such actions. But she'd never envisaged him having clandestine dates with other women... or being a thief.

A reddish-purple bruise was developing on the left side of Joanna's face, and there was swelling around her eye. She held a packet of frozen peas against the swelling, hoping that this might reduce it. There was also a large bruise on her upper arm, and marks around her lower leg, where Steve had grabbed her tightly.

A long-sleeved top and trousers will hide those bruises, she thought, trying to be practical, but the marks on her face were more of a problem. *I'll just have to wear more make-up than usual,* she decided.

* * *

There was no sign of Steve over the next couple of days, and Joanna had no texts or calls from him either. She returned to work, laughing off the questions from colleagues about the bruising on her face, and blaming her own clumsiness. That seemed to satisfy their curiosity, much to Joanna's relief.

On the third evening, she returned home, and Steve's car was still not on the driveway.

Where is he? she wondered. *What's he playing at?*

But she was annoyed with herself for wasting energy even speculating about it. She needed time and space to think about her own future, and if he'd decided to disappear, that was fine by her.

It became evident, though, that Steve had been into their home, while Joanna was at work, and taken away some of his clothes. She wondered what else he'd taken, but concluded that she didn't care. She didn't want him or his possessions there. Her only wish was to get out of the marriage without being assaulted again, as soon as possible.

Joanna noticed a dog-eared envelope on the work surface in the kitchen. It was addressed to Mrs J. Hearnden. She opened it and found £500 inside. There was no note or explanation. Momentarily Joanna felt scared again, but she didn't know why.

It's obviously from Steve, she reasoned, *but what the hell's it all about? Has he actually got a guilty conscience about emptying the bank account? I don't buy that at all! And why the stupid formality?*

Joanna put the money back into the envelope and replaced it on the work surface. She didn't want it. If it was a peace-offering of some kind, Steve could take it away again. He would see that she'd opened it and rejected it. He wasn't going to regain control of her, or of the situation, by giving her money.

The more she thought about it, the angrier Joanna felt. But some of her anger was directed at herself.

How on earth did I misjudge his character so completely? she asked herself, over and over again. *How did I manage to be so deluded?*

* * *

A few days later, Joanna had two sturdy bolts fitted on the inside of her bedroom door. She now had one secure room to retreat into, if ever she heard Steve come into the house… or so she hoped.

But, as time went by, there was no communication from him. The divorce was being handled by their respective lawyers, who were fuelling acrimony unnecessarily, in Joanna's view. She sometimes thought that she and Steve could have sorted everything out between themselves, without all the vitriol… until she recalled his violence.

The envelope containing the £500 still lay untouched in the kitchen. If Steve had been in the house again, he'd ignored it. Occasionally Joanna was tempted to go out and spend it all on something frivolous, but her better judgement told her to wait until all the divorce formalities were completed.

Her Saturday mornings with Sophie continued, except on the day when her face had been badly bruised. But Joanna kept quiet about Steve's abuse, and about the divorce. In fact, she told no one what she was going through, not even her sister, at first. When she eventually disclosed it all to Zoe, Joanna was relieved to have her support. She was surprised, though, by Zoe telling her that she'd always had misgivings about Steve. Her first impressions of him, she told Joanna, had been of a smooth-talking charmer, who perhaps wasn't all he seemed to be. Zoe had hoped then that she was misjudging her new brother-in-law, and anyway, she hadn't wanted to burst Joanna's happy bubble.

But now she felt powerless to help her sister, who was so unhappy… and so far away.

Six

Celine Martin was on duty at the school gates in Hadley St Giles. The headteacher, Mrs Lassiter, was insistent that all children should be collected by a known adult at the end of the day.

On this particular occasion, Mrs Martin noticed someone she didn't recognise among the usual throng of parents and grandparents. She kept her eye on the casually-dressed young woman, who seemed to be trying to engage some of the parents in conversation. It seemed to Mrs Martin that she was making occasional notes of what she heard. After being approached, the parents talked animatedly in little groups and nodded their heads towards the young woman. Mrs Martin wondered what this was all about and beckoned to a couple of the mothers whom she knew well.

By the time all the children had set off home, there was no sign of the young woman. Mrs Martin went to see Mrs Lassiter and explained that there had been a reporter circulating among parents at the school gates, asking about Louise Purvis-Brown and trying to elicit sound-bites from them. The reporter had claimed to be researching some background to the forthcoming trial.

It was several months since Louise had transferred to a school in Dorlingsworth. Mrs Lassiter decided to contact the local police for more information and advice. She didn't want any other media people snooping around the school.

* * *

It was only by chance that Marie Wilkinson found out when and where the trial of Louise's alleged abuser was to take place. She had walked hurriedly into the staffroom between lessons, having forgotten to take an important book with her to the classroom. Mrs Lassiter was in conversation with the school nurse, who happened to be visiting. Marie heard Louise's name and looked enquiringly at Mrs Lassiter, who confirmed that she knew when the trial was to be held.

As it was during the school holidays, Marie decided to go and listen from the public gallery. She didn't mention her intentions to Mrs Lassiter.

* * *

Marie hadn't been to a court hearing before, and she found the courtroom and proceedings rather daunting.

But how much worse must it be for poor Louise, she thought.

Louise gave her evidence by video-link from another room, so people like Marie, in the public gallery, couldn't see her. She sounded tearful and tentative, scarcely audible at times, and the judge encouraged her to speak up.

There's something different about Louise's manner, thought Marie.

She listened to the whole trial and wished she could talk to Louise. Occasionally she looked around at the other people in the public gallery, but she didn't recognise anyone. There was one man, though, who appeared to be completely absorbed by the trial, particularly while Louise was giving her evidence. He seemed to be silently urging her on, and Marie wondered if that was the girl's father.

She also noticed a young woman in the Press seats, listening intently to every word and making copious notes. She wondered if that was the reporter who'd been hanging around near the school gates.

Trying to make a name for herself at the expense of other people's misery? Marie thought cynically.

After two days of deliberations, the jury was unable to come to a unanimous verdict. Eventually, the judge accepted a majority decision, and Gregory Mortimer was convicted of sexual offences against a ten-year old girl. Throughout the trial he had consistently denied the allegations. He looked dazed and bewildered on hearing the verdict, and slowly shook his head. He was led down to the cells, having been told to expect a prison sentence. Until then, he was to be remanded in custody.

Marie left the court feeling confused. She'd always had confidence in the criminal justice system previously, but today she had gnawing doubts about whether she'd witnessed a just outcome.

* * *

In contrast, unbridled elation was felt by Frank Purvis-Brown when the "Guilty" verdict was announced. He immediately jumped up from his seat in the public gallery, punched the air with his fist and shouted jubilantly, 'Yes, you bastard!'

He was quickly escorted out of the court by an usher and a security guard. He later regretted not seeing that scumbag Mortimer walk down the steps to the cells. But the victory had been won. Mortimer was a convicted paedophile, and life would be very hard for him from now on. No more abusing children while posing as a caring choir master. He was a pervert, and everyone knew that now. He was a marked man.

From Purvis-Brown's perspective, the sentence, when he later learned of it, was far too lenient. He was definitely a "hang 'em and flog 'em" man, although he never admitted that to his work colleagues. No sentence was long enough for paedos, who wormed their way insidiously into children's lives, and then abused them. The many suspects he had interviewed in the course of his duties were poor physical specimens of men, in his view, with personalities oozing inadequacy. But, in his job, he had to keep such opinions to himself.

No sentence would ever be harsh enough for sodding Gregory Mortimer, he thought.

* * *

As Marie was waiting for a bus outside the court buildings, the young woman reporter came and stood beside her.

'What did you make of the verdict?' she asked Marie quietly.

At first Marie thought she must be speaking to someone else or on her mobile, but the reporter was looking straight at her.

'What do you mean?' she asked guardedly, taken aback by the woman's question.

'Well, just off the record,' she replied, 'do you think the jury got it right?'

Alarm bells started ringing in Marie's head. She now felt sure that this must be the reporter whom her colleague, Celine Martin, had seen talking to parents outside the school. She wondered what the woman's interest in the case really was. Marie decided not to get drawn in.

'By the expression on your face, you weren't too sure,' the woman prompted Marie. 'Am I right?'

'I have nothing to say to you,' replied Marie. 'I don't know what you're talking about,' and she turned her back on the reporter.

'Well, in case you have second thoughts, my name's Lucy Flynn, and here's my card,' she said. 'I had some doubts, too, so get back to me. It's not good to witness injustice, is it?'

The reporter thrust her card into Marie's hand and walked off.

Marie looked at the card she was holding. She was in two minds. Was Lucy Flynn genuine in thinking that the verdict had been wrong, or was she just interested in pursuing a potentially lucrative story?

Marie had no way of knowing.

Seven

On the day the divorce was finalised, Joanna took herself off to a nearby stately home, which had converted one wing into an exclusive health spa. She indulged herself in all the treatments she could fit into one visit. She had chosen this spa in the hope that she wouldn't meet anyone she knew. She wanted to be alone with her thoughts.

What a massive relief, she smiled to herself, as she lay contentedly in a seaweed bath, *thank heavens that's all over.*

* * *

The initial euphoria at ridding herself of *that rat of a husband,* as Joanna now thought of Steve, and severing all ties with him, gradually began to wane, though. She was facing a new reality. But she was relieved that she had managed to continue working in the library throughout the months of turmoil and trauma. Her boss, Tony Stoneman, was oblivious of Joanna's personal troubles, and she was determined that he would remain so. Her job was her only source of income now.

With the help of a substantial mortgage, Joanna bought a "compact apartment", as the estate agent described it, on the top floor of a recently completed development on the outskirts of Blakesford, several miles away from her previous home. The apartment had expansive views over rooftops to the parkland beyond. It was the views that Joanna had fallen for, as they gave the illusion of space and freedom. She had sold most reminders of her previous home and started afresh, and she was pleased with her efforts. As time went by, though, she began to realise just how "compact" her new home really was.

There's no outside space, she grumbled to herself, *not even a small balcony.*

Joanna was feeling increasingly dissatisfied with other aspects of her new life too. Her job at the library was beginning to have frustrations. One day, nothing seemed to be going right, and Joanna's spirits were steadily sinking. For the third consecutive week an elderly library user, Mrs Booth, had made a point of seeking Joanna out and inquiring if she had discovered any more books by Myfanwy Treddle. For the third time, Joanna patiently explained that Ms Treddle had only written two novels, and she had died fifteen years ago. But Mrs Booth urged Joanna to keep looking, promising to return next week to see if there was any progress. Joanna smiled at Mrs Booth, but cursed under her breath.

At lunchtime she had more reason to feel despondent. An email was circulated to all staff, stating how pleased Head Office was that Tony Stoneman's anticipated move to Chester would not be going ahead. Joanna failed to understand how this news was pleasing to anyone. She had convinced herself that Tony's job was hers for the taking. She'd even been thinking about how to spend her significantly increased salary, and a more spacious home, plus a reliable car, were top of the list. How dare Tony undermine her plans!

After work, Joanna trudged through the rain to the carpark, only to find that her car had a flat tyre. It was then that she remembered having taken the spare tyre to the garage for repair a couple of weeks earlier… and she hadn't yet collected it. Trying to put conspiracy theories out of her mind, Joanna strode off to a nearby shop, bought a magazine and some self-indulgent, expensive dark chocolate, and waited in the rain for a bus.

She arrived home, soaked through, longing for a hot shower and a lazy evening in front of the television. She collected her mail and walked up the stairs to her apartment. After a shower and a microwave meal, Joanna slumped contentedly on her sofa and thumbed through her mail. Most of it was junk mail, but one envelope caught her eye. She knew the handwriting immediately.

'How the hell has he got hold of this address?' she screeched. 'How dare he contact me?'

Joanna tore open the envelope and pulled out a card. "Welcome to your new home", it read. The card was not signed.

She was shaking, and she looked nervously around the room, half-expecting to see Steve there… but he wasn't.

Her mind was in turmoil. She thought she'd been so careful about who she'd given her new address to.

So who has told him? she wondered. Then a more frightening thought struck her… *or has he been stalking me?*

Eight

A week passed and Joanna was still fuming about the card from Steve.

How dare he intrude in my new life? she constantly asked herself, annoyed that he came into her thoughts so often too.

She resolved to make changes but was indecisive about how. She had settled into a 'prematurely middle-aged routine', she complained to Sophie, of evenings spent reading or watching television, with a take-away meal on her lap.

It was an unexpected phone call which spurred her into action.

'The bloody cheek of it!' she exploded, when she ended Steve's call. 'The patronising bastard,' she seethed, 'how dare he infiltrate my life again and think he has a right to know how things are going for me? And then to suggest we should meet for a drink sometime… it's just unbelievable!'

But Joanna felt she had dealt with the call remarkably well. The coldness of her tone and responses had hopefully given Steve an unequivocal message.

'I don't wish to see you or hear from you again. Get lost!' she had shouted. A more subtle approach was clearly going to make no impact.

Something at the back of her mind, though, was telling her

to be careful. Since the unprovoked assault, Joanna had an ill-defined fear of antagonising Steve. She was angry with herself for this, as she recognised it as handing power to him, but she had these feelings, nonetheless.

But now it's crunch time, she told herself. *I've got to get rid of him, but it's got to be on my terms, not his. I'll get a new mobile tomorrow and be careful who I give the number to. And I'll set up a new email address.*

Joanna was still at a loss to know how Steve had discovered her address. Could Marcus have heard it from Sophie, and told Steve? Or had he followed her home?

Well, she thought, *I can't change my address quickly, but I can guard my phone number and emails.*

Or so she hoped.

* * *

Thinking about Steve's call, Joanna knew that her pride had been hurt. He clearly suspected that she was leading a reclusive, uneventful life, and, damn it, he was right. This realisation touched a nerve in Joanna.

That settles it, she told herself. *I shall go out one evening next week, by myself, somewhere, anywhere. I refuse to be a hermit any longer, and I don't want that bastard's phoney pity!*

Joanna also decided not to tell Sophie about Steve's phone call, and she would wait until after her evening at the local theatre before telling Sophie about that.

Much to Joanna's relief the company was performing a well-known comedy, and this was just what she needed. Apart from the interval, when Joanna felt self-conscious queuing at the bar for a glass of wine, and even more so when she stood alone drinking it, she enjoyed the evening. She was pleased that she had broken through a self-imposed barrier or two. In the foyer she'd seen a few people whom she recognised as regular library users, and they had exchanged smiles. Joanna also picked up a leaflet about forthcoming productions and resolved to go to some.

* * *

She enjoyed going to the theatre, and the occasional concert, and she was pleased with herself for doing it. She also began to acknowledge that, apart from her Saturday workouts with Sophie, her social life was still very limited. Looking back, it dawned on her that all her friends and acquaintances were actually in Steve's social circle and mainly linked to his work. He had never wanted to socialise with any of her friends or colleagues, and he'd subtly discouraged her from doing so either. So, her friendships had faded.

How could I have been so stupid? she asked herself. *I just didn't see it at the time. He was controlling me even then… and I let him do it! What an idiot I've been!*

But knowing this didn't make it any easier for Joanna to overcome the situation. Somehow, life was more daunting as a singleton, than as half of a couple.

Sophie was bewildered by Joanna's dilemma. She had always thought of her friend as capable and outgoing. All this was quite alien to Sophie's experience, ensconced as she was in a secure family life, which seldom required her to face situations alone. But Sophie soon discovered that any suggestions she made to Joanna about broadening her social horizons were summarily dismissed, so she was hesitant about making any more.

Sophie had felt brusquely rebuffed by Joanna a week ago. She'd suggested that Joanna might like to join her and Marcus at a forthcoming party for the opening night of a prestigious new exhibition at the art gallery. Sophie also mentioned that they'd invited Sean, one of Marcus' golfing friends. She explained that Sean's wife had been killed in a water-skiing accident whilst on holiday a few years ago, and he was struggling to rebuild his life. Joanna immediately heard alarm bells ringing in her head.

Sophie is actually trying to bring Sean and me together... it's a sort of blind date, she realised with horror. *I'm sure Sophie means well, but no thanks! I don't want a man with problems. And he's from the same golf club as Steve! I want nothing more to do with bloody Blakesford Golf Club!*

So, Joanna declined Sophie's invitation, as tactfully as she could.

* * *

One Saturday, Joanna was more upbeat than recently, as work was going well at last. Tony Stoneman had finally agreed to Joanna implementing some new systems, which she had suggested to him several weeks before.

'It's really only a bit of streamlining,' she'd told him, but in reality, the changes involved levels of innovation which were difficult for Tony to comprehend.

'Don't worry,' Joanna had said, 'I'll take the blame if it all goes pear-shaped,' knowing that her boss would take the credit if it worked out well. But Joanna could live with that. For the next few weeks, she had her own project to focus on.

Sophie seemed genuinely pleased that life was looking up for her.

'But don't you miss not having a man around?' she asked tentatively. 'I don't know how I'd manage without Marcus dealing with all the paperwork and doing odd jobs around the house. And he's always there to talk to.'

And he brings in a nice fat salary, Joanna chuckled silently.

'Not really,' she replied. 'I think my experience of men is probably a bit different from yours. If someone comes along, that's fine, but I've no intention of going out looking for a man.'

As it happened, she didn't need to.

Nine

The only words which registered with Gregory Mortimer, when the judge sentenced him, were "heinous abuse of trust" and "imprisonment". Then there was the sinister walk, under escort, down the steps to the cells beneath the court, into an unknown world controlled entirely by strangers in uniforms. Greg was in a daze, responding unthinkingly to instructions, facing a bewildering future, for which he had not prepared himself.

He had resolutely believed that somehow justice would be done, but at his trial the jury's majority verdict was "Guilty", and today he had been sentenced accordingly. The nightmare continued.

Greg needed time to take in what was happening to him, but the official procedures went ahead relentlessly, and he was just the next in line. Eventually he was taken to the waiting prison van and secured in his cubicle. Other prisoners were being less cooperative, and the van resounded to abusive shouts, cursing and threats. Greg was beginning to experience the realities of incarceration as a sentenced prisoner.

As the van left the court precincts, cameras were held up to the small window above Greg's head, and flashes of sudden light lit up his cubicle. He could hear hostile shouts of "filthy paedo", "pervert", and worse, from outside the van and loud, angry banging on its sides. It was dawning on Greg that his individuality and privacy were being stripped from him. He was now defined by the nature of his conviction, and the future looked bleak.

In a hurried conversation in the court cells, Greg's lawyer had suggested that all was not lost, and Greg should appeal against his sentence. But he was far from reassured. He sat in his cramped cubicle in a state of shock and despair. He had little faith in the lawyer's views. This was the same man who had repeatedly tried to convince Greg that he should plead guilty to the charges, in the hope of a lighter sentence. And this advice was in the face of Greg's steadfast and consistent denial of all the charges. If his own lawyer wouldn't accept his protestations of innocence, why would a court believe them? Why would a judge be persuaded to give him a lesser sentence?

Greg had never experienced mental turmoil like this before. He was used to feeling in control of his actions. Over the past few months, though, all aspects of his life had spiralled out of control, and he was in constant confusion about what was happening to him.

The girl's allegations had come completely out of the blue. He had only wanted to be kind and support her, as she was clearly unhappy for some reason. And as a consequence, here he was now, a man in his forties whose reputation was irrevocably in tatters, whose friendships had seemingly melted away, whose word was no longer believed, whose integrity had been publicly torn to shreds, whose career had been destroyed.

Greg felt scared of the immediate future. How could he cope with life as a convicted sex offender? He felt utterly empty and powerless.

Is life worth living any longer? he asked himself.

Ten

It was the rush-hour when Joanna set out for home. She had spent the day at a conference which Tony Stoneman had asked her to attend. It had proved to be a mixture of conference and bookfair, and Joanna had capitalised on opportunities to network with other librarians and pick up new ideas. It had been a useful and enjoyable day.

It was a few minutes before the train was due to leave, and Joanna was relieved to find a corner seat as the carriage filled to over-capacity with fellow passengers.

How can people bear to do this every day, she wondered, *and why on earth do they have to ring their partners constantly to report on their progress home?*

Gradually the train disgorged its occupants as they reached their destinations, and eventually Joanna found herself sitting in an almost empty carriage, able to relax for the remainder of the journey.

Only a few more stops, she thought. *I'll buy a take-away on the way home.*

The train was beginning to pull out of the station, and Joanna was contemplating what sort of take-away she fancied, when suddenly the door next to her opened, a briefcase skidded across her lap, and a man half-jumped, half-stumbled into the carriage, somehow pulling the door closed behind him. Unfortunately, Joanna's foot was on the spot where the man's right foot also landed heavily.

'Oh God,' he exclaimed to Joanna, 'I'm so sorry… have I hurt you?'

He retrieved his briefcase, which Joanna was holding out to him, and tried to regain his dignity. Joanna watched as the man re-arranged his jacket, sat down in the opposite corner with what sounded like a groan, and put his briefcase beside him.

'I do apologise,' he said to Joanna with a rather disarming smile. 'Why is it that trains decide to be on time when I'm running late?'

He then noticed the damage he had inflicted on Joanna's foot, tights and shoe. There appeared to be a mixture of mud and blood on her foot, her tights were clearly irreparable, and her shoe was also splattered with dirt.

'Oh hell,' he said, 'did I do all that? I'm so sorry.'

Notwithstanding the sharp pain in her foot, Joanna thought to herself, *I don't remember ever having three apologies from a man in as many minutes before! This guy's a bit different!*

'Not to worry,' she replied, 'no lasting damage, I don't suppose.'

'Well, at least let me give you some money for a new pair of tights,' he offered.

But Joanna assured him that there was no need for this. It had, after all, been an accident.

Why am I being so nice to this guy? she silently asked herself. *He's a clumsy idiot who barges into the carriage of a moving train, trampling people underfoot, and all because he can't get his act together and reach the station on time.* Amid her musings, Joanna looked up and then knew perfectly well why she was reacting like this.

The stranger sitting opposite her was forty-ish. He was slim, smartly dressed, but "not conventionally good-looking" in Joanna's opinion, as she later told Sophie. But there was something about his manner and his engaging smile.

So, enjoy the moment, she advised herself.

Just then a mobile phone rang further down the carriage, and a loud, one-sided conversation ensued.

'We're about five minutes from the station, so I'll see you in the usual place,' bellowed a male voice. 'We need to stop at the off-licence on the way home, as Jeff's coming round this evening to watch the match.' A pause. 'Yes, I know you don't like him, but it's all arranged now. See you in a few minutes.'

Joanna and the stranger looked at each other and smiled.

'Don't you like mobiles either?' he asked.

'It's more the people who use them like megaphones that I can't stand!' replied Joanna, laughing. 'They're very useful in their place, but I prefer my conversations to be a bit more private than that. I can just imagine the argument in that chap's car on the way to the off-licence. Perhaps he'll have to ring Jeff and cancel the arrangement!'

The stranger laughed too.

'That's my station as well, but sadly I'll never hear the end of their saga!' said Joanna.

'Well, at least they gave us something to laugh about. And I really do apologise for the way we met,' he replied.

A fourth apology, thought Joanna, *must be my lucky day!*

They smiled at each other as Joanna picked up her bag and got out of the train.

The stranger continued on his journey.

* * *

'It was just a nice little interlude at the end of a long day,' Joanna told Sophie on Saturday, 'a sort of cameo moment.'

'Leaving you with a distinctly bruised foot, ruined tights

and a scuffed pair of shoes,' laughed Sophie. 'Not to mention a disturbance in the hormones department!'

And Joanna was unable to deny this convincingly. It was a long time since Joanna had felt so attracted to a man, and she was fairly certain that the feeling had been reciprocated. That had boosted her self-confidence, although it offended her principles to acknowledge this. She looked back on the chance meeting with an element of satisfaction… but also with a twinge of regret that it was over so quickly.

Eleven

Joanna was walking slowly out of the gym, heading for her car. She was trying to remember the mental list she'd made of things she needed from the supermarket. She had left Sophie in the café, waiting for her daughter, Leonie, to arrive, as they were planning to go clothes shopping. Joanna couldn't imagine why either Sophie or Leonie wanted any more clothes, but she supposed that just highlighted their different priorities.

Joanna felt irritated, as she could only remember four things on her list, and she felt sure there were five.

Why didn't I make the list on my phone? she asked herself crossly.

She had nearly reached her car when she heard a familiar voice calling her name. Joanna instinctively froze.

What the hell does he want? Why won't he leave me alone? were her immediate thoughts.

Within seconds, Steve was standing by her side, smiling at her. Joanna tried to construct a neutral look on her face. Gradually she began to think more clearly, as the initial shock of Steve's presence receded.

Be civil, she advised herself, *don't give anything away, and don't be provoked. Remember what he did to your face.*

'Hi Jo,' said Steve, still smiling, 'great to see you, how was the workout today?'

'I'm sorry,' replied Joanna in a coldly civil tone, 'I'm in a bit of a rush… haven't got time to stand and chat, I'm afraid.'

She started walking towards her car again. Steve walked by her side, too close for Joanna's comfort.

'Well, I'm pleased you've got a busy life, you were always much happier when you had things to do. But perhaps you could find a slot in your hectic schedule to go somewhere with me?' he asked.

Joanna was astounded.

How dare Steve engineer a meeting in the carpark and then suggest what sounded like a date? Had he forgotten his assault on her? she silently seethed, trying to appear calm outwardly. *Why couldn't he just let go and lead his own life… without her?*

Before she could respond, Steve explained what he had in mind. He was smiling self-confidently at her, still invading her personal space.

'You remember our friends, Paul and Cilla, don't you? Well, they've offered me the use of their Cotswolds cottage for a weekend, and I thought you might like to go there with me. No dates have been fixed yet, as I told them I wanted to talk to you first. No strings, just a friendly weekend away… like old times,' he said.

Joanna could hardly believe what she was hearing.

Was Steve seriously suggesting a weekend away with him in a remote country cottage after all that had happened? Had he given Paul and Cilla the impression that a reconciliation was on the cards? And what the hell did "no strings" mean?

Her facial expression betrayed nothing, but her mind was buzzing.

How can I turn him down in such a way that he'll realise it's final but won't provoke him into anger? He's still trying to exert control over me, she thought.

'That's kind of Paul and Cilla,' she eventually said, indifferently, 'but I shall have to refuse the invitation. My life is pretty full nowadays and, as you said, that makes me happy. I really must go now.'

To Joanna's astonishment, Steve leaned towards her, as if to kiss her. She quickly ducked to one side and rummaged around in her bag for her car keys. Luckily, they were easily found, and she unlocked the driver's door.

'I'll give you some time to think it over,' said Steve, still with a fixed smile, 'in case you change your mind. There's no rush. I'll get back to you,' and with that he walked off.

Joanna was fuming but, she admitted to herself, a bit scared too.

Steve knew where she lived… he had proved that. He knew her routine of meeting Sophie at the gym. Did he know her mobile number? She wasn't sure. How friendly was he with Sophie's husband, Marcus, and was he a source of information about her? She thought she was so careful about what she told Sophie. But she had mentioned the incident with the stranger in the train, so had that been relayed to Steve, and possibly engendered some warped sense of jealousy or anger? She shuddered at the thought.

Joanna was trembling as she drove out of the carpark. By now she'd forgotten everything on her short supermarket shopping list. She didn't want to drive straight home, though, fearing that Steve might be parked nearby and approach her again. So, she went by a circuitous route to the out-of-town retail park, constantly checking her rear-view mirror to be sure that Steve wasn't following her. She parked a long walk from the coffee shop, where she intended to take refuge, and wandered into one or two shops on the way there. She felt fairly certain that Steve hadn't followed her.

Once in the coffee shop, she ordered a prawn, sweetcorn and mayo toasted sandwich and a cappuccino, and settled herself at a table with a clear view of the door and any customers coming in. She needed to calm down and do some uninterrupted thinking.

Twelve

In the past Greg Mortimer had occasionally watched television documentaries about life behind bars, but nothing had prepared him for the reality of it.

He learned fast that there are few secrets, and so-called facts get distorted in the telling. News of his arrival on C-Wing was quick to spread. There was a "kiddy-fiddler choir master" in C6. And paedos are the scum of the earth. Within days Greg was "accidentally" knee'd hard in the groin by another prisoner whilst in the shower. He was doubled over in pain, when another knee collided with the side of his head, and Greg went sprawling on the slippery tiled floor. By the time he managed to get up, the shower cubicles were empty, and his soap, towel and clothes had disappeared. Greg feared that he would have to get used to humiliation and abuse. He would just have to live with the injustice of it all.

Before coming to prison Greg had lived alone in a quiet lane not far from the parish church. If at home during the day, he heard few sounds coming from outside, other than the occasional delivery van door banging or his neighbour's motorbike being revved up. So he could work there in peace.

In contrast, life on C-Wing was an unremitting assault on all his senses. Greg had difficulty adjusting to the relentless noise in prison. Doors and metal gates constantly clanged, shrill alarm bells rang, boots thundered along landings in response to trouble, radios blared, orders were blasted over the Wing's loudspeaker system, abuse was shouted. This was all alien to him, and so were the smells in the Wing. The stench of sweaty bodies, unconstrained farts, smouldering testosterone, all conspired to corrupt the air. Greg sometimes thought that the pervasive smell of disinfectant did little to improve matters.

He had always valued moments of quiet contemplation in his previous life, but prison allowed him none of these. Not even during the night, and so it quickly became clear to Greg that he would have to devise new self-preservation strategies. Somehow, he had to detach himself from his incomprehensible surroundings, whilst not worsening his situation. He feared making himself even more vulnerable, and he was determined to avoid that.

He had always been something of a loner, so the isolation in prison didn't concern him. He reconciled himself to the fact that former friends were unlikely to visit him and that he might receive few letters. Initially he had anticipated going to chapel services and perhaps talking with the visiting chaplains. But one service had been enough for him. His religious faith, once so important to him, had been sorely tested and found wanting. His faith in humanity and justice had also evaporated, and his wish to participate in organised religion in prison deserted him. Cynicism had taken root in Greg.

He sought out sources of intellectual stimulation, but most of the formal education courses on offer were fully subscribed and had waiting lists. He had access to library books and took full advantage of this, even though the choice of reading matter was limited.

Better than nothing, though, he thought.

He had always wanted to write stories for children, which he would also illustrate, as he had a talent for art. He ditched that idea, though, when he thought about the links people would make with his conviction. He had long had an interest in village church architecture, so perhaps he could research that more while in prison. He couldn't see any reason for that subject to be misconstrued. He resolved not to atrophy mentally during his sentence, but to use the time as constructively as circumstances allowed. Or that was his determination on good days, at least.

Greg hoped that the overt hostility to him, and what he represented in others' perceptions, would lessen, when they saw that it apparently provoked no response from him. He accepted that this was a risky strategy on his part, as it might antagonise his aggressors more, but Greg considered this his best option for now. He gradually had fewer bruises and less abusive graffiti daubed on the inside of his cell door, but he was careful not to become complacent and was constantly on his guard.

* * *

While Greg's day to day preoccupations were about personal survival in a hostile environment, at night he was still tortured by thoughts of his wrongful conviction.

He knew that many convicted prisoners maintain their innocence, and he felt sure that some *are* unjustly convicted, but that was no comfort to him. If he "played the game", instead of refusing to acknowledge his guilt, he would be allowed to attend sex offender rehabilitation courses and thereby be assessed as reducing his future risk to the public. It might accelerate his release, if he stopped insisting that the prosecution and court had got everything wrong. But Greg's well-developed sense of justice wouldn't allow this… he was innocent, whatever others might think.

Thoughts of an appeal continued to plague him too. He wished there was someone, other than his lawyer whom he didn't trust, with whom he could have an informed conversation about all this. But he could think of no one. Various professionals within the prison had conducted assessment interviews with him, measuring his perceived risk levels. Greg had consistently repeated his version of events and bewilderment at his conviction, but these were met with scepticism. Worn down by this, Greg eventually decided to accept his fate and abandon all ideas of an appeal. He needed some support if he was voluntarily to go through more court processes, and he had none. Hopefully, at some stage in the future, he would be able to put this whole nightmare behind him.

But one aspect of the charges against him and his subsequent trial continued to leave Greg non-plussed and hurt. And this was the core of the issue.

Why, oh why, he constantly asked himself, *had his young accuser concocted the web of lies which had led to his conviction? And why had she persisted in her allegations over so many months? And how had she lied so convincingly to the court?*

These questions tormented and saddened Greg when he was locked in his cell.

Thirteen

Joanna parked her car a couple of hundred yards away from her apartment block, in a side-street. It was two hours since her unexpected and unwelcome conversation with Steve in the gym carpark. After lying low in the coffee shop at the retail park, she had driven to the nearby country park and walked around the lake there. She was furious with Steve for even thinking of a weekend away with her. The bloody cheek of it! Had he forgotten his infidelity, his theft, his violence? Joanna certainly hadn't.

But how to get rid of him, once and for all? she asked herself time and again.

* * *

Joanna decided to email Zoe and discuss the situation with her. Contact between them was irregular nowadays, but they quickly tuned into each other. Joanna's only hesitation was her knowledge that Zoe regarded Steve as a total bastard, and always had, so there were doubts about her ability to view Joanna's situation dispassionately.

But maybe that would be helpful in itself, she concluded.

Joanna was hardly through her front door, relieved to be home without any further confrontations with Steve, when she spotted a postcard on the hall floor. There was no stamp on it, so it must have been hand-delivered. Joanna picked it up, and her heart sank. The picture was of a Cotswolds village, and on the reverse the message read simply, "Looking forward to our weekend". The message had been printed on a sticky label and positioned carefully on the back of the card. Joanna threw it on the floor. She was shaking.

What the hell is he playing at? she thought in panic.

The following day, Sunday, Joanna received an email from her sister, with apologies for the delay in replying. Delphine had been rushed to hospital yesterday with suspected appendicitis and been operated on. Thankfully all was now well, and Delphine would be home again later today.

Well, thought Joanna, *that puts my trivial problems into perspective, doesn't it? Zoe must have been terribly worried, so perhaps I should keep quiet about Steve. I'll just stick to everyday things and ask her advice once Delphine has recovered.*

So she and Zoe just exchanged news about their lives and Joanna didn't go into detail about her problems. She gave the impression that all was fine.

* * *

Joanna went to work on Monday morning, trying to put the traumas of the weekend behind her.

Steve has no place in my life nowadays, she told herself sternly, *and that's how it's going to stay.*

Tony Stoneman continued to allow Joanna to implement innovative systems in the library. She was initially sceptical about how much freedom Tony would actually give her, as he was generally risk-averse and had, in Joanna's view, a frustrating lack of imagination and vision. But she determined to make as many changes as possible, before he reined in her ideas.

Today, though, she was having a particularly fraught time. Nothing was going according to plan, and colleagues were constantly interrupting her, asking for advice. She decided that a quick coffee break was the only solution. She had just finished making a cup of coffee when Tony came into the kitchen, saying that someone was at the desk asking for her by name. Joanna was immediately filled with anger. Surely Steve wouldn't try and talk to her at work, would he?

With an air of exasperation, she marched out to the public area and up to the desk.

And there stood the man from the train.

Fourteen

Gerry Thorncroft and his wife, Penny, had chosen Snaysby for their retirement. A picturesque market town nestling amid sparsely populated hills and dales, at the confluence of two meandering rivers, it seemed to them the ideal place to relocate to. After nearly thirty years in the police, and reaching a high-ranking position, Gerry decided that life must have more to offer him and Penny. He'd had enough of funding cuts and having to instruct front-line staff to "do more with less". So, with Penny's full support, he put a successful career behind him, and they moved to a run-down farmstead at least a hundred miles from anyone they knew. For them it was an exciting step into the unknown.

They had been to view the buildings and land twice before putting in an (in their view) insultingly low offer. To their amazement, it was accepted. This was an executors' sale, and the property had been on the market for a couple of years, with little interest being shown in it. But now it all belonged to Gerry and Penny. It slowly dawned on them what a daunting task they had taken on… certainly a "heart over head" decision.

Much of Hotheby Farm's land was rented to local sheep-farmers, and agreements were drawn up for this to continue. So, Gerry and Penny turned their attention to the many dilapidated buildings they'd bought. They had initially planned to live in the main farmhouse, an imposing Victorian stone house with beautiful views over the surrounding hills and valleys. But it was half a mile away, up a hill, from the cluster of buildings around the former farmyard, which they intended to focus their efforts on first. So, they moved into what had originally been the farm manager's house, which was dated in its décor, but habitable as an interim measure.

* * *

One morning, a few days after they had moved in, there was a knock on the back door. A woman, perhaps in her mid-sixties and huddled in a large coat, was standing there, her gloved hands cradling a large casserole dish.

'I'm Mrs Thwaites,' she said, 'I live in one of the cottages over there. I saw you'd arrived, so I thought I'd bring you some dinner for later. I hope you like it. I'll just put it in the kitchen, 'cos the pot is rather hot.'

Before Penny could reply, Mrs Thwaites had walked past her, into the kitchen, and placed the casserole dish carefully on a mat on the table.

Penny was amused, but quickly thanked Mrs Thwaites for her thoughtfulness. She was about to offer her a cup of tea, but Mrs Thwaites was already out of the door and striding purposefully across the farmyard.

* * *

'Oh dammit,' said Gerry, 'I'd forgotten all about our sitting tenant! I meant to go and introduce myself when we first arrived. Mind you, she sounds like an ideal tenant, if the smell of that casserole is anything to go by!' He laughed, while Penny gave him an affectionate look.

There were three small, terraced cottages a short walk from the farmyard, only one of which was still rented out. Mrs Thwaites lived in the furthest one, and Gerry was relieved to note that it looked well-maintained. She deserved that.

To make amends for not having visited her sooner, Gerry returned the casserole dish the following morning. Mrs Thwaites hesitantly invited her new landlord into her home. It was old-fashioned, but immaculate.

'I'm really grateful that I can stay here,' she began, 'me and my Bert were always so happy in this house, until he died, God rest his soul. He looked after the cows and pigs, when the farm was thriving, but gradually they all got sold off, and now the farm is in ruins. My Bert would've been so sad about that… he always worked so hard. So I'm pleased that you and Mrs Thorncroft have come. But there's so much work needs doing…' and she stopped, thinking that she shouldn't be saying so much.

Gerry smiled.

'You're certainly right about that, Mrs Thwaites,' he replied, 'but Rome wasn't built in a day, as they say, so we'll be tackling things one at a time.'

Gerry suddenly had a guilty thought.

'I'm so sorry, Mrs Thwaites, I haven't thanked you for that delicious casserole, which Penny and I enjoyed so much. It was very kind of you. You obviously guessed that we're in a bit of a muddle at the moment, and your lovely cooking was just what the doctor ordered!'

Mrs Thwaites beamed. She'd wondered whether it was the right thing to do, taking a meal over for her new landlord, but it clearly had been, and her cooking had been appreciated.

Taking courage from this, she tentatively asked, 'Will you and Mrs Thorncroft be living in the house here, or up at the big house, on the hill? I hope it's not forward of me to ask. It's just that I used to have a job up at Hotheby Farmhouse, the big house… I used to be in charge of the kitchens and cooking there.'

'Ah,' said Gerry with a smile, 'that explains the excellent cooking.'

Mrs Thwaites beamed with pleasure again.

'So, I just wondered, if you're moving up there, if there might be a small job for me again?'

Gerry tried to hide his surprise. He hadn't anticipated being asked for a job, however small. But he liked Mrs Thwaites and guessed that she was probably lonely since Bert had died, whenever that was, and it was certainly an isolated little house that she lived in.

'Let me talk to my wife about that,' he said. 'We haven't entirely decided what we're going to do yet. For the time being, we'll probably try and do up the house here first and start finding out what's in all our packing cases!'

Mrs Thwaites looked rather crestfallen, but she nodded. Gerry felt guilty for a second time.

Fifteen

Penny Thorncroft flopped into a threadbare old armchair in front of their kitchen range. She felt exhausted. They had been in their new home for over a week now, but Penny felt there was little to show for their many hours' hard work.

What have we taken on? she asked herself. *Thank heavens for Mrs Thwaites, though,* she added with a smile.

Gerry and Penny had decided to ask Mrs Thwaites if she would like to help them out three mornings a week, mainly in the kitchen and preparing meals. She agreed immediately. Her housekeeping skills quickly became evident, and she didn't seem to mind what jobs needed to be done. So, within days, the kitchen was well-organised and spotlessly clean. And she always cooked enough food for some portions to be put, clearly labelled, into the freezer for another time.

The farm manager's house, or Ivy House, as it was officially called, had clearly been well-maintained in the past, but it had been standing empty for at least two years, with some of the old furniture still in place. The rooms were initially musty-smelling, and damp had infiltrated some of the walls, but thankfully the early spring weather was mild and the windows could be wide open most days. The evenings and nights were cold, though, and Penny began to wonder what the winter would be like.

But this is our mid-life adventure! she reminded herself.

* * *

One morning, Gerry suggested to Mrs Thwaites that she should go with them up to the big house, Hotheby Farmhouse, and give him and Penny a guided tour.

It was an impressive building, with tall sash windows either side of a substantial brick porch with a slate roof.

It's a bit like a child's drawing of a house, thought Penny.

The first floor had matching windows, with an extra window between them above the porch. But the façade belied how far back the building stretched. It was a very large house. And over to the left, beyond a magnificent old yew tree, stood an enormous wood-clad black barn, partially hidden by tall trees.

'I haven't been in through the front door before,' confessed Mrs Thwaites. 'I always had my key to the side entrance.' Gerry smiled.

Unlike Ivy House, everything in Hotheby Farmhouse had been removed. There were no remnants of furniture, no curtains, no floor coverings. Their footsteps echoed as they walked around. Mrs Thwaites, usually a chatty person, seemed lost in her memories as she took Gerry and Penny from room to room.

'Of course, I only came into the upstairs rooms if my master was away from home,' said Mrs Thwaites. 'Most of my time was spent downstairs.'

Gerry and Penny exchanged amused glances. Penny had visions of a younger Mrs Thwaites in a calf-length black dress, black stockings, a starched white apron and a prim white cap on her head. She stifled a chuckle. Mrs Thwaites' service at this house had clearly been important to her, and a happy time too.

I bet she had to work hard, though, thought Penny.

* * *

'Well,' said Gerry, after the tour, 'thank you, Mrs Thwaites, that's been quite an eye-opener. It's a beautiful old house.'

'So, sir, d'you think you'll be moving up here?' asked Mrs Thwaites.

'Whoa, Mrs Thwaites, don't let's rush things! We've got plenty to keep you and us busy at Ivy House for now!'

Mrs Thwaites looked embarrassed.

'Yes,' said Penny quickly, seeing Mrs Thwaites' discomfort, 'I've been thinking. Would you mind helping me sort out a case of curtains and bedlinen which we haven't opened yet? We may want to use some of them at Ivy House, but they'll need to be washed and ironed first.'

Mrs Thwaites nodded enthusiastically. 'That sounds like tomorrow morning's job then. Let's hope it's fine weather,' she said.

She just wants to feel useful, thought Penny, with a kindly glance.

* * *

That evening, after enjoying one of Mrs Thwaites' delicious lamb and potato pies, Gerry and Penny were relaxing contentedly in the kitchen's armchairs.

'What did you think about Hotheby Farmhouse then?' asked Gerry.

'Apart from its feudal approach to its staff, you mean?' said Penny with a giggle.

'Hmm…' replied Gerry, 'I hope she won't start curtseying, as well as calling me "sir"! I thought those days were behind me!'

They both laughed. Gerry got up and poured another cup of coffee for each of them.

'Seriously, Penny, would you want to do that place up and live there? With or without our faithful retainer?' he asked.

Penny was quiet for a few moments.

'I don't want to make any decisions about that, or even think about it for the time being. I just feel that we're very lucky even to have a choice like that. We're both much more relaxed than we were a year ago, we're both healthy, and we're living in fantastic surroundings, so can't we just be happy with that for now?' she asked.

'Of course,' replied Gerry. 'Let's go into Snaysby at the weekend and find a nice pub overlooking one of the rivers, and toast our good fortune.'

'Hmm… good idea,' agreed Penny.

Sixteen

Joanna couldn't hide her surprise.

'Hello again,' said the man, with that disarming smile of his. 'I've brought you some tights, to make amends for my idiocy. I hope I've guessed the right colour!'

Joanna's colleague, Cheryl, was also working at the front desk, and she looked across at Joanna with an amused expression. *Sounds interesting,* she thought, eager to overhear more.

Joanna was momentarily speechless, but she quickly collected her thoughts.

'You really didn't need to… I'd forgotten all about it,' she said, not entirely truthfully. 'But how on earth did you find me?'

Cheryl looked up again, even more intrigued.

'Well,' he replied, 'that's a bit of a saga actually, so how about hearing it over lunch? I noticed a nice-looking Italian restaurant just down the road, so how about it? I suppose they do let you have a lunch-break, do they? The chap I spoke to seemed awfully suspicious of me, so perhaps he won't let you go off with a stranger! I gather he's the boss, is he?'

Joanna laughed.

Yes, no doubt Tony had been curious about her visitor, she thought.

'Well,' she said, 'I think the answer to all your questions is "yes"! And you're probably on the library's CCTV, so they'll send out a search party if I don't return. How about meeting at the restaurant at 12.30ish?'

'Sounds good to me,' replied the man, 'and I'll get the tights gift-wrapped in the meantime!'

He laughed as he turned to leave.

'You sly old thing,' said Cheryl, giving Joanna a teasing wink. 'A bit of your murky past coming out, is it?'

If you only knew... thought Joanna, wagging her finger at Cheryl and smiling enigmatically.

* * *

Joanna's mind was in turmoil. She had long since consigned her meeting with this man to the "pity, but it wasn't to be" compartment of her memory. When she had occasionally fantasised about "different endings", they had certainly not involved his coming into the library and talking to Tony! And how had he found out her name? And her place of work? That actually felt a bit unnerving. Did he know someone who knew her? *Please,* she prayed silently, *don't let it be bloody Steve, or someone else at Blakesford Golf Club!* And how she wished that she had chosen a more stylish outfit to wear to work this morning. And did she dare ask Tony for an extended lunch-break, without having to explain too much?

What a roller-coaster of a morning, she thought.

* * *

It began to rain as Joanna walked to the restaurant, feeling a mixture of excitement and apprehension.

Perhaps he will have changed his mind, she told herself. *Perhaps his memory of me wasn't matched by the reality of the person he encountered in the library. Perhaps he won't be there...*

But he was. The man was perched on a bar-stool, watching the door, and he got up to meet Joanna as she came in.

'We've got that table in the corner, by the tall plants,' he told Joanna and ushered her towards it. He took her damp coat and hung it up. 'What would you like to drink while we look at the menu?'

'Oh, red wine, please,' she replied, 'house red will be fine.'

The wine and meals were ordered, whilst Joanna was thinking, *but I have no idea who you are. This is surreal!*

Trying to sound casual, Joanna asked, 'So what's the saga about finding out who I am and where I work? And am I allowed to know *your* name?' She smiled, and her eyes were sparkling.

The man looked at her sheepishly and laughed.

'Sorry,' he said, 'I'm Mike.'

He made as if to shake hands with her, but thought better of it.

'The saga,' he began, 'well, finding out your name was hardly rocket science. You were wearing a name badge on your jacket!'

Joanna remembered that she'd left the conference in a hurry, in order to catch the train, and had forgotten all about the obligatory name badge.

'But finding out where you work was a bit more problematic,' he continued. 'There was a journal sticking out of your bag with only part of the title visible, but it seemed to be something to do with the book trade. I knew which station you'd got out at, and I guessed that you probably worked in Blakesford. So I came here a couple of times and tried all the likely places, the bookshops, the bookbinding place, the publishers near the football ground, and various others. I tried the college library, and they suggested the most obvious place of all, which was the central library. This morning was the first opportunity I've had of going there, and of course you know the rest. So, it's not really mysterious at all, it just required persistence! And I'm pleased I persevered.'

Joanna was wondering how to respond to all this, when their meals arrived.

* * *

Sitting at her computer later that afternoon, feeling distinctly mellowed by the wine, and trying to conceal this from Tony, Joanna reflected on how a day on which everything seemed destined to go wrong had taken a dramatic turn for the better. Lunch with Mike had not only been completely unexpected, but it had also stirred feelings in her, which she had not experienced for a long while. Sophie had been right! The incident in the train had had a greater impact on her than she would admit to herself, or Sophie. And the attraction must have been mutual, or why would he have gone to all those lengths to seek her out? Not just to give her some new tights! And they had arranged to meet for lunch again the following week. There had been no exchange of phone numbers.

Presumably, thought Joanna contentedly, *we just have confidence that we'll both be there.*

Seventeen

Greg Mortimer was working in the prison library, sorting out books requested by other prisoners. He was by now one of the small group of trusted inmates, so he applied for a job in the library when another man was released. He found it far more interesting than being in one of the workshops, and time seemed to pass more quickly.

Most days he was working with another prisoner, Kieran Mulholland. Kieran was a Lifer, and he was not expecting to be released for many years. His approach to his sentence, though, was to knuckle down and get on with it. He wasn't going to waste his energy kicking against the rules and being carted off to the Segregation Unit. He was more interested in completing his Open University degree in sociology, no matter how much sneering he had to endure from some officers.

Greg and Kieran didn't talk to each other about why they were in prison. But their cells were on the same Wing, and it was general knowledge that Greg was a "nonce". Kieran had heard that Greg had received rough treatment from other inmates.

One morning, when there were no prison officers within earshot, Kieran gave Greg a whispered warning.

'Watch your back when Officer Raynaud is around… he hates people like you. He's a conniving sod, and he'll get at you any way he can. Be very careful.'

Greg looked at Kieran and there was no doubt that he was serious.

Over the past few weeks Greg had noticed Officer Raynaud's contemptuous and provocative manner towards him, but until now he hadn't taken it personally.

There are just some officers who enjoy goading inmates, he'd thought, *but I'll heed Kieran's warning from now on. But Raynaud's the one who holds all the power.*

* * *

Greg's resolve was soon put to the test. The library door opened, and Officer Raynaud shouted, 'Mortimer, you're to go to Legal Visits. You've got a visitor. I'm escorting you there. Now.'

Greg's initial reaction was confusion. He hadn't put in an application for a lawyer to visit him, and, as far as he knew, there were no residual legal matters arising from his conviction.

'Are you sure it's me they've come to see?' he asked Officer Raynaud, immediately regretting that he might be seen to be questioning the officer's order.

'*Now*, Mortimer, get a move on. He's waiting,' was the aggressive reply.

* * *

Greg looked through the interview room window and saw two people, neither of whom he recognised. They were sitting behind a table, with a vacant chair opposite them. Officer Raynaud waited outside the interview room.

'Right,' began the man, gesturing to Greg to sit down, 'I'm DS Clive Meadows, and this is DC Sharon Page.'

Greg's confusion increased. *What the hell do the police want with me?* His anxiety levels rose.

'I'll come straight to the point,' continued DS Meadows. 'New allegations of sexual abuse have been made against you, and we are investigating them. They are historical… and serious.'

* * *

By the time the two police officers had finished outlining the allegations, Greg was slumped in his chair, in sheer disbelief. None of what they'd said made any sense to him. They knew that he had been a peripatetic music teacher at a school many years ago, but that was a matter of public record. There had never been any problems while he was there, so why would these incomprehensible allegations surface now? None of it rang true to him.

Greg was dumbfounded, but certain that he now needed a good lawyer. He wanted one who would take his denial of any wrong-doing seriously and represent him effectively. Deep down he still felt grinding anger towards the legal team who had not fought harder to prevent his current wrongful conviction, but he constantly tried to suppress this. The prospect of another trial filled Greg with terror.

Who is this person, now an adult, who must feel so vindictive towards him? he asked himself. *What would she have to gain by subjecting him to another humiliating court process? What was her connection with him, if any?*

While being escorted back to the library by Officer Raynaud, Greg tried to appear unconcerned. He was determined not to betray any emotion or give any clues about the interview to his escort. He'd learned the hard way, too many times, that it was unwise to show vulnerability in prison, to anyone. He could think of no one to discuss this evolving problem with. He would have to face it alone.

Earlier that day, Greg had seen light at the end of his current tunnel. There was a glimmer of hope, and he'd started planning for life post-release. He was fully aware that restrictions would be imposed on him as a convicted sex offender, and he tried to come to terms with that. Any contact with children would probably be out of the question. Teaching music had always been his passion, but he doubted if anyone would employ him now, even to teach adults. He'd been determined to make the most of his future, though.

But now, a few hours later, his plans had disintegrated. His world was again spinning out of control and the future looked bleak.

What had DS Meadows said? They would contact him again with the decision about whether or not he was to be charged. But how long might that take? he wondered.

Greg was in limbo again… and it scared him.

Eighteen

'Are you absolutely sure you know what you're doing?' asked Sophie, sounding concerned. 'You don't seem to know much about him. It all sounds very strange to me, him seeking you out for several weeks.'

Joanna smiled submissively. She'd pondered long and hard before mentioning the lunch with Mike. She had lingering concerns about whether information about her was passed from Sophie to Marcus to Steve. But Joanna refused to be stifled by this.

'I think it's quite flattering,' replied Joanna with a confident laugh. 'Nothing like this has happened to me for a long time, so I plan to enjoy it while it lasts!'

Sophie was quiet for a few moments and then asked, with a hint of hesitation, 'What do you know about his, well, er, personal circumstances?'

'Do you mean, is he married?' retorted Joanna, with an amused look on her face. 'Come on, Sophie, call a spade a spade!'

'Well, yes, has he got a partner, or whatever?' continued Sophie, appearing a tad uncomfortable.

'Well, to be honest, Soph, odd as it may seem, we didn't even mention current relationships, or past ones for that matter. So I have no idea about his marital status, and I'm not really bothered about it. Any issues there are between him and his conscience, as far as I'm concerned. We talked about a whole range of things, but the question of husbands and wives didn't crop up. Lighten up, Sophie, this was just a casual lunch, a few hundred yards from my workplace. It wasn't exactly clandestine!'

'I think that depends on one's perspective,' replied Sophie, sounding rather too straight-laced for Joanna's liking. 'Had you said that this man had quite coincidentally come into the library and recognised you, and you'd had a little joke about the incident in the train, that might be seen as casual, but the whole scenario sounds much too calculated to me. I just want you to be careful, that's all. I don't want to see you get hurt in any way. It's not very long since...' and her voice trailed off.

But Joanna didn't want to hear any parallels between her current situation and Steve's pre-divorce activities.

'Thanks, Sophie,' she cut in, 'I do appreciate what you're saying. And if everything goes haywire, you can remind me of your counsel of caution. At the moment, though, it's new and exciting, and I want to enjoy being wined and dined, even if it's only at lunchtimes! Don't worry, I'll be careful what I do.'

Sophie nodded indulgently, clearly not convinced.

* * *

After their second lunch in the Italian restaurant, Joanna and Mike agreed to meet at the same time the following week, but at a different restaurant.

Hmm... she thought, *feels like progress, but why always at lunchtime? Does Mike work around here somewhere?*

Joanna had mentioned a restaurant, which she'd never been to with Steve, that specialised in fish dishes and had a good reputation in the town. Again, no contact numbers were offered or exchanged.

On the morning they were due to meet, though, Tony took a call at the front desk, while Joanna was busy elsewhere. He told Joanna that Mike was "unable to keep their appointment today" and sent his apologies. Tony hadn't thought to ask for Mike's number, perhaps assuming that Joanna would know it.

During the afternoon, having eaten a take-away egg and salad baguette instead of a tasty fish meal, Joanna mulled over Sophie's reservations about the Mike situation. Did his cancellation of today's lunch simply reinforce them? She could almost picture Sophie quietly congratulating herself. It was true that Joanna knew very little about Mike. He was certainly good company and attentive when they met for lunch, but, with hindsight, she realised that he maintained the focus of conversation on her and gave few clues about himself. He was clearly adept at this, as it hadn't been obvious to Joanna at the time. Or did she just weakly succumb to flattery? Joanna was horrified at this thought.

How could I be that naïve? she asked herself.

* * *

Over the next few evenings, a glass of wine in hand and looking out across the rooftops glistening in the rain and moonlight, Joanna reproached herself for investing more feelings in her embryonic friendship with Mike than reality warranted. She had probably been nothing more to him than a temporary, amusing diversion. Perhaps his need for that had now passed, hence the cancellation of lunch and no further contact. She didn't know his surname, where he lived, what work he did, nor his phone number. And she certainly wasn't going looking for him.

So, Joanna was beginning to feel rather foolish, and she wished she hadn't told Sophie anything about it. Perhaps it would be better not to go to the gym on Saturday?

Don't be so bloody stupid, she told herself angrily, *don't let him interfere with your life like that! It was good while it lasted, and no harm has been done. Except a bit of hurt pride!*

* * *

After two weeks of silence from Mike, Joanna convinced herself that she'd regained her equanimity and finally banished the fantasies which she'd indulged in. It had been embarrassing when she acknowledged to Sophie that her advice to be cautious was justified.

'It was very sound advice,' Joanna conceded. 'There was something awfully attractive about him, though, and I enjoyed his attentions.'

'But how honourable were his *in*tentions?' asked Sophie, apparently seriously.

'Oh, come on, Soph,' replied Joanna, chortling, 'don't be such a prude! Anyway, that's irrelevant now, as we'll never know. I might have enjoyed finding out, though!'

Sophie put on her "you really do shock me at times" expression, much to Joanna's amusement.

* * *

At work a few days later, Tony bumped into Joanna as she was emerging from a long and tedious meeting.

'Someone rang you earlier, but he didn't leave his name or a message,' he told her.

'Thanks,' she replied casually.

No one ever rings me here, except Mike, she thought, *unless it's a dire emergency, and they're few and far between. It must have been him. Who else could it have been?*

An image of Steve flashed through her mind and a reminder

of the Cotswolds cottage, about which she had thankfully heard nothing more.

But, unless the man rang again, there was no way for Joanna to find out.

* * *

After leaving the library that evening, Joanna lingered in the nearby coffee shop, and spent several minutes looking through the magazine stand outside the station, before telling herself to stop being an idiot. If Mike intended to meet her, he wouldn't be loitering in the shadows, waiting for her to emerge. He would be standing in full view, and he wasn't.

Shortly after Joanna arrived home, Sophie rang her. This was unusual, and it took Sophie a few minutes to get to the point. Joanna guessed, more or less, what was coming.

'Marcus and I are going to a private viewing of the new art exhibition on Thursday evening, so I wondered if you'd like to join us. Unfortunately, the friends we'd invited have had to pull out. But I don't want you to think that you're second best,' she hurriedly added. 'I thought you might enjoy it, you know, champagne and nibbles, and meeting one or two of the artists. It would be so nice if you could join us.'

'That's really sweet of you, Sophie, but I actually have a theatre ticket for Thursday,' Joanna lied, fervently hoping that there would still be a ticket available for that evening, 'so I'll have to turn down your kind offer. Is there someone else you could invite?'

Sophie's response didn't surprise Joanna.

'Well, we had thought of inviting Sean too,' she said, 'but perhaps I'll have a re-think.'

Joanna knew that Sophie was full of kind intentions. She'd tried on previous occasions to introduce their friend, Sean, to her.

But Joanna had no desire for Sophie to choose new friends for her, particularly not one who was still grieving for his late wife, and who belonged to the same golf club as Steve.

Joanna ended their call, with apologies and thanks… and relief.

Then, with fingers firmly crossed, she rang the theatre.

Nineteen

On Saturday morning, Joanna and Sophie were leaving the gym together, chatting. The carpark seemed remarkably empty. When she'd arrived, only ninety minutes ago, Joanna had had great difficulty finding a space, and now her car was almost alone on the far side. Sophie was rushing off, as she had to collect Leonie from the station, so Joanna sauntered over to her car.

She became aware of footsteps behind her and turned around. There was Steve, more scruffily dressed than usual. Joanna thought he must have forgotten to shave, too.

'Hi, Jo,' he said, catching up with her. 'Have you decided about the Cotswolds yet?'

He was standing too close for Joanna's comfort, and his breath smelt unpleasant. There was no one else in this section of the carpark, and Joanna began to feel uneasy. She just wanted to get into her car and drive off, but there was something bizarre about Steve's manner, which made her wary of opening the car.

'Steve,' she said, in as forceful a tone as she could muster, 'we're over, divorced, leading separate lives. Get it into your head, for heavens' sake, that I have no desire to meet up with you, anywhere, ever, and certainly not to go for a cosy weekend away. So, stop hassling me. I want nothing to do with you.'

'But I still love you, Jo,' he said, in a "little boy" voice, 'I miss you. Can't you understand that?'

Steve tried to put his arm around her shoulders. Jo was furious.

'Get away from me, and get real,' she snarled, glaring at Steve. 'What are you really after?'

She immediately regretted asking that. She'd given him an opening, and, sure enough, he took advantage of it.

'Well, could you lend me some money?' There was now a steely edge to his voice. The "pathetic" approach hadn't worked, so now he would play "tough".

'Don't you remember I gave you £500?' he said, sounding threatening. 'Well, now you can give it back to me. I've got problems.'

Joanna's fury was increasing by the second.

'Just to remind you,' she retorted, a venomous look on her face, 'I didn't take that bloody £500, and you know it! I have no intention of lending you anything. Go and ask your parents, or your sister, or your friends. You'll get absolutely nothing from me.'

Steve's face was becoming ever redder. He pinned Joanna's back against the car, the door handle digging into her, and punched her hard in the solar plexus. He immediately turned on his heel and ran. Joanna crumpled onto her haunches, leaning against the driver's door, clutching her stomach. She struggled for breath.

Seemingly out of nowhere, a car pulled up beside her, and a woman in her late twenties, with collar-length auburn hair, wound down her window and called out to Joanna.

'Are you OK?' she asked. 'I saw you collapse and thought I'd better come over. Has that chap gone into the gym to get help?'

Not much chance of that, thought Joanna.

'That's really kind of you… thanks,' she replied. 'I probably just overdid it in the gym. I'll be fine in a minute. But thanks for stopping.' Joanna tried to smile at her.

'Well, if you're sure,' said the woman, 'but, to be honest with you, I saw what happened. I saw him thump you hard in the stomach. Do you want my phone number, in case you decide you want a witness? I was a victim of violence once too, so I'd willingly help you.'

Joanna was touched by the woman's offer. She doubted if that happened very often. But she declined with a wan smile and a shake of the head.

'Well,' said the woman, 'I'm an officer at the local nick. I shan't forget what I saw, I remember details. And I've got your car reg, just in case.'

She gave Joanna a sympathetic look, and, as she drove off, called out 'My name's Jade Henton...', but Joanna could scarcely hear her above the sound of the engine.

She struggled to her feet, picked up her bag, took some painful deep breaths, got into her car and locked the doors.

What the hell will Steve do next? she wondered.

She was shaking.

* * *

Throughout the rest of the day Joanna felt queasy. She hadn't initially realised how viciously Steve had punched her. But she'd somehow managed to drive home.

She lay curled up on her bed, her arms around her stomach. She must have fallen asleep, as the room was beginning to darken when she felt like getting up. She went into the kitchen. She didn't fancy eating anything, but she thought she probably ought to have a drink of water at least. She spotted a tub of mushroom soup in the fridge and decided to heat that up.

Gradually her pains eased. She went to bed early and lay in the dark listening to the radio. Sometime after midnight, she was startled by a noise. She turned off the radio and lay motionless, listening. Was someone on the landing outside her front door? She tried to work out what the muffled noise was. Then there was a dull thud, and she recognised it as the sound of her letterbox. Something had been put through her door.

But it's after midnight, she told herself, *no one can be delivering things at this hour!*

Joanna struggled out of bed and cautiously peered into the hall. The streetlights cast an eerie sliver of light through the narrow glass panel in the front door. There was something rectangular lying on the floor. She picked it up and saw that it was a postcard.

Not another of his ridiculous games, she groaned despairingly.

But this postcard had a more sinister message on it. The picture was a collage of miniature £ and $ signs. On the reverse there was a printed sticker, which simply stated "BITCH" in large, bold letters.

Joanna crept into her lounge and looked carefully at the street outside, moving the curtains as little as possible. She could see no movement, and she heard no cars.

I think I'll talk to Jane Denton after all, she decided.

Twenty

The phone kept ringing and ringing.

'Oh, come on,' muttered Joanna, 'before I change my mind.'

Eventually a voice said, 'HM Prison Burntley, how can I help you?'

'I'd like to speak to Officer Jane Denton, please,' replied Joanna.

There was a long silence.

Then the voice said, 'Did you say Jane Denton? I can't find anyone on the staff list of that name. I'll just have a word with my colleague, hold on…'

The voice returned. 'No, she doesn't work here. Could someone else help you?'

Joanna was mystified. She felt sure that it was the right name and prison.

'So, is this the only prison around here?' she asked. 'Perhaps I got the name wrong.'

'Yes, the only one,' was the reply, 'but if you're trying to locate a specific prisoner, I can give you another number to try.'

'No, no,' said Joanna, 'but thanks for your help.'

She hung up, confused.

* * *

Joanna returned to the front desk in the library. She'd already answered about six calls and was beginning to curse their assistant whose partner had been rushed into hospital the previous evening.

But this call was a pleasant surprise.

'Well, well,' said the caller, 'where's the dullard today?'

'Mike!' exclaimed Joanna. She quickly regained her composure and continued, 'This is a nice surprise!'

'Well, hopefully I've got another one for you too,' said Mike. 'We've finished our work here a couple of days ahead of schedule, so I shall be home tomorrow. How about dinner on Friday evening?'

Joanna could hardly contain herself. No, this was not an offer of lunch, this was dinner… and this was progress! As his question had been followed by a long silence, Mike suggested that he come and pick her up just before eight o'clock.

'I've done my homework,' he laughed. 'I know where you live! So, does that all sound OK to you?'

'Absolutely fine,' she confirmed.

'Great,' said Mike, 'see you on Friday, then,' and he ended the call.

Joanna quickly decided to check what number he had called from, but it was "withheld".

What else would I expect? she asked herself, with a sigh.

* * *

That evening Joanna rang Sophie to tell her about the dinner date with Mike on Friday. This was unusual for Joanna, but she hoped that Sophie would be pleased for her.

'He hasn't been exactly reliable in the past, has he? Are you sure he'll turn up?' asked Sophie. 'And you really must ask him how he got your address. I'm a bit concerned about that.'

Not for the first time Joanna immediately regretted telling Sophie about something exciting in her life. She was an expert at putting a damper on Joanna's happiness.

Couldn't she, just once, be pleased for me? she asked herself sadly.

* * *

Notwithstanding Sophie's doubts, Friday evening arrived, and so did Mike. The intercom buzzer sounded just before eight. Joanna grabbed her jacket and went downstairs to meet him. Prior to his arrival, Joanna's apartment had been the scene of frenzied activity, with items of clothing being tried on and rejected, some being deemed too formal, others too casual. She threw the rejects into the bottom of her wardrobe, out of sight.

Mike greeted her with a brief kiss on the cheek and ushered her to his car.

'Sorry,' he said, 'I go in for functional rather than flashy cars.'

Still apologising! she thought.

Joanna felt pleased, though, as she wasn't in favour of ostentation, *like Sophie!*

'I've booked a table in a nice-looking gastropub in a village not far from here. I haven't been there before, but it's had good reviews. I hope you'll like it, but I haven't checked the wine list!' Mike looked across and smiled.

'Sounds perfect,' replied Joanna.

As they were driving along Joanna had a sudden thought. Sophie had made her promise to text her and say where they were going and what sort of car Mike drove. 'You can never be too careful,' she'd said, raising Joanna's anxiety levels.

But the phone was lying on the window-sill in Joanna's kitchen, plugged into the charger and forgotten until now.

Oh well, she thought, *let's hope nothing untoward happens, and I can tell Sophie all about it in the morning!*

* * *

While waiting for their main courses, Joanna decided to broach the subject of Mike knowing her address. He laughed softly, perhaps a little embarrassed.

'Hmm...' he began hesitantly, 'I thought afterwards that I shouldn't have said that. I really didn't want to worry you, but perhaps I did. I'm sorry.'

This man could make apologising into an art-form, if he really tried! thought Joanna silently.

'Yes, but *how* did you find it out?' she asked again, rather more straightforwardly. 'It's just that if *you* can, so can anyone else!'

'Well,' said Mike, putting his hand on hers across the table, 'would it put your mind at ease if I tell you that I have certainly *not* been stalking you? I can honestly say that I haven't been in the vicinity of your home before this evening, well, not knowingly, anyway. But it really isn't difficult to find out quite a lot of personal information about people without their knowledge. And I don't mean by rummaging through their garbage! I do confess, though, that I deliberately tried to find out where you live. I assure you, though, that I will never turn up there uninvited, and I will never give your address to anyone else. I just hoped that I could pick you up there sometimes, like this evening, rather than only meeting at lunchtimes.'

So why didn't you just ask me? she wanted to ask, but somehow the moment didn't feel right. *Perhaps one day you'll tell me.*

So, Joanna's question remained unanswered.

Twenty-One

Joanna set off for the gym next morning, wondering how much she should tell Sophie about her date with Mike the previous evening. She was feeling upbeat, particularly as Mike had suggested lunch again on Wednesday. But Sophie had an uncanny knack of pouring cold water on Joanna's pleasures. She didn't think it was deliberate, but just a reflection of Sophie's more cautious, and perhaps old-fashioned, outlook on life.

Well, thought Joanna, *she isn't going to deflate my bubble today!*

After a strenuous workout, they were sitting in the café, with Sophie drinking an espresso, while Joanna indulged in a latte and a generous slice of carrot cake.

'So, did Mike turn up? You didn't phone me…' began Sophie.

'I'm very sorry,' replied Joanna. 'I stupidly left my phone at home. But anyway, yes, he did turn up, and we had a lovely evening. He was a perfect gentleman, and we're lunching again on Wednesday.' Joanna couldn't help smiling at the thought.

'So,' said Sophie, 'tell me all about him. What work does he do? Where does he live? Is he married, or in a relationship? And…'

'Hang on, Sophie, don't give me the third degree!' protested Joanna, laughing. But she actually felt a tad uncomfortable, as she still wasn't able to answer Sophie's first two questions. As usual, Mike had shown a practised facility for evading issues, whilst appearing not to. But at least Joanna could satisfy her friend's curiosity on the third point.

'He told me that he's been married in the past, but that he currently has no wife or partner in the wings waiting to confront me about secret meetings with him. He'd been concerned that I might think he couldn't get away in the evenings, hence our lunches, but he assured me that he lives alone. And I told him my situation. So, Sophie, it's all above board, with nothing to worry about.'

'But what about his work?' persisted Sophie.

'Well, it involves a lot of unsocial hours, and he has to travel all over the place,' said Joanna, fearing that the vagueness of her answer wouldn't be enough for Sophie.

'But you and Marcus really should try the super gastropub we went to,' continued Joanna, trying to steer Sophie onto safer subjects. 'They had a huge range of dishes, including vegetarian and vegan, so Leonie might enjoy it too. Have a look at their website,' she suggested.

* * *

As Joanna left the gym she looked around, silently praying that Steve wouldn't be in the carpark today. Relieved that there was no sign of him, she walked, head held high, over to her car. If he was watching her, she wanted to present a picture of self-confidence.

She hadn't mentioned to Sophie what had happened in the carpark last Saturday. She still had concerns about whether gossip was relayed to Marcus. So, she'd been circumspect, too, about how much she'd disclosed about Mike. This relationship felt special to Joanna, and the last thing she wanted was for Steve to try and disrupt it.

* * *

Driving home, Joanna thought about Jane Denton. At the time, Joanna had taken their brief encounter at face value and been grateful for Jane's solicitude. But with hindsight, and in the light of her abortive phone call to the prison, Joanna wondered what it was all about. She was convinced that she'd remembered Jane's name correctly. But perhaps that wasn't really her name.

Come on, she remonstrated with herself, *you'd just had an almighty thump in the abdomen, you were winded and felt sick. And someone took pity on you. Is it really any surprise if you got the woman's name wrong? Stop trying to see mysteries where there aren't any!*

She parked her car in a road parallel to hers, annoyed at her paranoia, and walked back to the flat, fervently hoping that there wouldn't be any more threatening postcards on her hall floor.

Much to her relief, there weren't.

Twenty-Two

'Whew,' said Penny Thorncroft, smiling at her husband, 'what an exhausting week!'

Gerry leaned across the table and re-filled her wine glass, nodding in agreement.

'But think of all the progress we've made,' he said. 'Workmen coming in to fit a new bathroom next week, you've done wonders painting our bedroom, all the kitchen appliances are plumbed in and working. It's amazing! And, of course, we've acquired you, Carruthers!' The dog opened one eye, looked at Gerry and returned to his dreams.

This was Carruthers' first full day in his new home, and he was lying contentedly on the hearth rug, blending in with the shaggy brown and cream pile. Carruthers was a dog of unknown parentage and history. He was a mature dog, in age at least, and Gerry and Penny had both fallen for him at the dog rescue centre. The feelings were obviously reciprocated, and after only two visits to the centre, it was agreed that the Thorncrofts would be Carruthers' new owners. Mrs Thwaites had been warned that she was about to have a competitor as far as ruling over Ivy House's kitchen was concerned!

Mrs Thwaites was proving to be a real asset. She went by bus to Snaysby market every Wednesday morning to buy fresh fruit and vegetables for Ivy House. She didn't seem to mind what chores were needed. But she had firm ideas about how someone in her position should behave towards her employers. It would be improper to address them by their first names, and she would be called Mrs Thwaites. She had a key to Ivy House's back door, but always knocked before entering, and she wouldn't even think of using the front door. She always ensured that the kitchen was spotless before going home.

Gerry and Penny chuckled about Mrs Thwaites and her strict boundaries, but they were fond of her, too.

'She's definitely a one-off,' said Penny, 'but we're very fortunate to have her.' Gerry smiled in agreement.

'There even seems to be a correct number of biscuits to put on a plate when she makes coffee for us,' he said. 'Have you noticed it's always the same?'

* * *

As time went by, and Ivy House became a bright, comfortable home, Gerry and Penny gave more thought to their plans for all the land and for Hotheby Farmhouse. They were getting to know some of the local people by now, too, although there were no houses near to Ivy House, apart from Mrs Thwaites' home and the two empty cottages. One of these apparently used to be let to holidaymakers, whilst the middle one was for another farmworker, like Bert Thwaites.

The cottages had been vacant for several years, but they were basically in good condition. Penny warmed to the idea of sprucing them up and renting them out during the summer months.

'We're surrounded by lovely countryside, good walking country, and there are lots of leisure facilities for families in Snaysby, like boat trips, not to mention excellent pubs and restaurants,' she said to Gerry one evening.

'You seem to have compiled the brochure already!' laughed Gerry. 'But there's also Mrs Thwaites to consider. How will she take to kids running around near her home, car doors slamming, and all the rest? She's used to peace and quiet.'

'I suspect she'll be pleased to have people around,' replied Penny, 'but of course we must consult her.'

* * *

Mrs Thwaites had been concerned, she told Penny, how much longer she would be needed at Ivy House, now that the renovations were going ahead apace. She'd been worried, she confided, that the Thorncrofts would soon manage very well without her.

But Penny was quick to reassure her that other plans were being made, and they wanted Mrs Thwaites to have an important role in them.

Much to Penny's relief, Mrs Thwaites liked the idea of the two vacant cottages being rented out to holidaymakers, for a week or two at a time. She didn't think that the comings and goings would disturb her, and in fact, it would be nice to see children running about, enjoying themselves. And Mrs Thwaites offered to clean the cottages between lets, making sure they were ready for the next people.

Mrs Thwaites didn't usually show much emotion, but the following day she talked enthusiastically to Penny about a suggestion she had.

'I hope it's alright to say this,' she began, initially tentatively, 'but I've been thinking about the cottages.'

Penny smiled encouragingly.

'Well, my Bert's brother has got a son, Sam, who lives in Snaysby, and he's been out of work for a few months. I think it's hard for him to make ends meet, so I wondered if he could help do up the cottages, and perhaps he could keep the gardens nice and tidy too? He's a good odd-job man. I don't mean to be forward in asking you, I just thought it might help everybody…'. Mrs Thwaites' voice trailed off, as she lost confidence in what she was saying.

Penny recognised this trait in Mrs Thwaites and tried to reassure her.

'Well, Mrs Thwaites,' she said, 'that sounds like a useful idea, so I'll talk to my husband about it. We haven't sorted out the details yet, but I'll certainly mention Sam to him.'

Mrs Thwaites looked relieved.

* * *

Gerry and Penny sat in The Cross Keys pub in Little Cragworth a few evenings later, each with a glass of cider. Carruthers was lying contentedly at their feet.

It was decision time. They'd talked and talked about the future of Hotheby Farmhouse and whether they really wanted the hassle of renovating it. And then there was the huge barn to consider too, which could be transformed into a sensational home, given sufficient resources. But was that what Gerry and Penny wanted to spend their time and energy doing?

A couple of hours later, they had reached their decision. They agreed that this was the final decision, and there would be no changing of minds after today.

Ivy House and its adjacent farmland would remain their home, and Mrs Thwaites would be their tenant for as long as she wished. The other two cottages would become holiday-lets. If that developed into a successful business venture, then they might expand into renting out luxury holiday caravans too.

But Hotheby Farmhouse, complete with its stunning views and potential barn conversion, would be sold. Gerry and Penny both felt a twinge of regret about this. They could have had a very

81

grand home, but comfort and leisure were more important than grandeur, they decided.

'Who on earth will want to buy an enormous place like that?' asked Penny.

'Well, we did,' replied Gerry with a laugh, 'and I don't doubt that someone else will see its potential too! Perhaps we'll see Mrs Thwaites in her starched white apron and cap yet!'

Twenty-Three

'Miss Wilkinson, could I have a quick word, please?'

Mrs Lassiter had just come into the staffroom and beckoned to Marie. They walked together to the head's office, while Marie wondered what this could be about.

'The office took a phone call this afternoon from a rather pushy caller, I gather, who wanted to speak with you,' began Mrs Lassiter. 'She was insistent that she spoke to you in person and wouldn't give any indication of what she wanted. She just left her name and number, and she wants you to call her back. Sally, who took the call, thought she recognised the name… you know how Sally remembers everything that happens here… so she looked through her records, and sure enough, she was right. It was Lucy Flynn, and she's the reporter who was hanging around the school gates at the time of the concerns about Louise Purvis-Brown. I'm sure you recall all that, don't you?'

Marie nodded. In fact, she remembered the whole sequence of events very clearly.

'But I don't understand,' began Marie. 'That was all ages ago, and the man was sent to prison, so what does she want with me now?'

Mrs Lassiter could see that Marie was genuinely perplexed.

'Well,' she said, 'I advise you, Marie, to be very careful when contacting anyone from any form of the media. But if you do call her back, and if the substance of her enquiry is in any way connected with the school, then please inform me immediately. And if it's a purely social call, then please ask her to contact you privately and not through the school office. I'll give you the number she left, which of course is now in Sally's records too. But Marie, tread carefully.'

She left Mrs Lassiter's office unsure whether or not to return Lucy's call. Her interest, though, had undoubtedly been piqued.

* * *

By the following Saturday, Marie felt sufficiently prepared to contact Lucy Flynn. She was partly swayed by not wishing Lucy to ring the school again and further incur Mrs Lassiter's displeasure. But Marie was mainly driven by curiosity. She felt sure the call must be linked to the court case concerning Gregory Mortimer, at which she'd considered that justice had not been served. It was outside the court that Lucy Flynn had first approached her.

Marie gave a lot of thought to how much she would say to Lucy. She didn't know who Lucy worked for, or what her motives were in following up Louise's story. She would follow Mrs Lassiter's advice and tread cautiously.

* * *

Marie and Lucy agreed to meet in the café of a garden centre on the edge of town. It was late afternoon, and they hoped that most shoppers would be leaving by then.

They settled with a coffee in a secluded corner. Lucy confirmed that she wanted to discuss the Mortimer case. But Marie insisted on some ground-rules being agreed, before anything more was said. Their discussion was not to be electronically recorded, and Lucy must explain fully what she planned to use any information for. And if Lucy intended to quote Marie at all, then the wording was to be checked with her first.

Lucy agreed to all of Marie's conditions. Marie hoped that she could trust her.

'Before I went into journalism,' began Lucy, 'I studied criminology briefly. I developed an interest in miscarriages of justice, as much from a human-interest perspective as any other. I had concerns about how such events impacted on the lives of those wrongly convicted, and what, if anything, could be done about this. It all got terribly theoretical, so I decided to try my hand at investigative journalism and see if I could make a small difference in a more practical way.'

Lucy laughed.

'Saying all this,' she continued, 'it sounds horribly pompous and idealistic, and probably not what you'd expect a stereotypical hack to say, but that's the truth of the matter.'

She laughed again, with a hint of embarrassment.

'But presumably you sell your stories to the highest bidder, don't you, so how do you square that circle? You might actually be making matters far worse for the people you claim to champion,' said Marie, who'd been listening to Lucy with a degree of scepticism.

Lucy looked at Marie, somewhat abashed.

'Believe me, Marie, I've struggled with those sorts of issues for a long time. My obsession has cost me a partner, who couldn't put up with it, and one or two other friends,' said Lucy ruefully, 'but my inbuilt sense of justice won't let it go.'

* * *

An hour later Marie and Lucy were still in the café. They had talked about Gregory Mortimer's trial and the prosecution evidence. They agreed that the defence team had been deplorably weak in their submissions.

'But we don't actually *know* whether or not it was a miscarriage of justice, do we?' asked Marie. 'All we've got are the assessments of two amateurs! But you seem determined to pursue this for reasons that I still don't fully understand. And you haven't explained where I fit into your plans. You've kept very quiet about that.'

'Well,' replied Lucy, 'the only people who know the truth are those central to the whole story.'

'Hang on, Lucy,' objected Marie vehemently, 'this isn't just a story. We're talking about two people's lives, and one of them is a vulnerable teenager, while the other is probably a vulnerable prisoner. So where've all your high-minded principles suddenly gone?'

Lucy was taken aback. This conversation wasn't as easy as she had envisaged. But she acknowledged that Marie was right, and held up her hands, palms facing Marie.

'You're right, of course, sorry,' she said. 'OK, what I'm hoping for is an interview with either Louise or Mortimer. Now…' she hesitated, 'I think it's going to be virtually impossible to talk to Louise, certainly without her dad present, so that leaves Mortimer.'

'You're not expecting, are you, that *I* should go and talk to him in prison?' asked Marie, utter disbelief in her voice. 'You must be mad,' she continued, 'why would he talk to a complete stranger, even if he agreed to a visit, which is a big "if"? And anyway, why don't *you* arrange to see him yourself?'

'Several things,' answered Lucy, who seemed to have thought this objection through. 'Firstly, he might remember me from the Press seats at his trial. Secondly, I guess that it'll be more difficult for me, as a journalist, to get a visiting permit, than for you, and thirdly, he may be less circumspect when talking to you.'

Marie was dumbfounded. Lucy had all her arguments ready, but she wasn't going to be bullied or rushed.

'I need to give this a lot more thought before I agree to anything,' said Marie eventually. 'How about I ring you in a week or so?'

'That's fine,' replied Lucy, quietly pleased that Marie was not rejecting the whole idea immediately.

'There's just one final thing you should know, though,' added Lucy. 'My sources tell me that Gregory Mortimer is under investigation for more similar offences. So what do you make of that?'

Twenty-Four

Marie didn't know what to make of Lucy Flynn's parting words to her. It had seemed like a throwaway comment, but in reality, it was hugely significant, if true. It might put a different complexion on her previous thoughts about Gregory Mortimer's guilt or innocence.

But why should it? she asked herself, annoyed by the thought, *he's innocent of any new charges until proven guilty.*

Marie decided to find out as much as she could about Lucy Flynn. She had sounded plausible, when they were talking in the café, but Marie wasn't yet ready to cooperate fully with her, however worthy the cause might seem.

Lucy's asking a helluva lot of me, she thought.

But internet searches disclosed little information about Lucy. Marie found a few articles which she'd written, none of which seemed contentious in any way.

It's possible, though, thought Marie, *that she writes under other names too, but I've found nothing to confirm that.*

Marie decided to give it all more consideration before contacting Lucy.

* * *

One Saturday afternoon a few weeks later, Marie was driving to

HM Prison Falkenside. She'd had two more meetings with Lucy Flynn, and she'd agreed to visit Gregory Mortimer. It had been a long and complicated process locating him and arranging the visit.

Greg was initially mystified by a letter from a woman asking if she could come and talk to him. He occasionally received official letters, but this was handwritten and personal. He discreetly showed it to Kieran, whose first reaction was to laugh and congratulate Greg on having a fan somewhere out in the community! But he then advised Greg to "go for it" and let her visit. She'd said very little about herself in the letter, and the two men speculated on what she would be like.

Marie had received a Visiting Order by post and was now at the entrance to the prison's visitors' carpark. She'd also been sent clear instructions about what items were prohibited in the prison, and she was forewarned that visitors were subject to searches.

She sat in the car for a few minutes, watching other visitors arrive. Most came by the prison shuttle bus which collected them from the railway station two miles away. There were young women, some with excited children in tow, and Marie wondered how they coped with everything while their partners were in prison. The small children were pulling at their mothers' hands, eager to get inside.

Marie summoned up her courage and headed for the entrance, copying what other visitors did. Eventually she was in the noisy Visits Hall and was told where to sit. Greg Mortimer appeared after a short while and sat across the table from Marie.

* * *

After forty-five minutes, a shrill bell rang and all visits were ended. Prisoners left by one door and visitors by another, at the opposite end of the Visits Hall. A few minutes later, Marie was back in her car, feeling dazed. She wanted to process mentally all that had happened to her that afternoon, but she noticed that the carpark was emptying quickly, and she thought she should leave too.

Not many miles from HMP Falkenside, Marie spotted a fast-food café next to a petrol station, so she pulled in. She was hungry, not having had any lunch. There were no other customers in the café. She ordered egg, bacon and chips, and a bottle of sparkling water, and reached into her bag for her tablet. She wanted to make detailed notes of her visit, and later she would decide what to send to Lucy.

Greg had talked to Marie, in as quiet a voice as the environment allowed, about his bewilderment at Louise's allegations and how she had persisted with them during the court proceedings. He had scarcely known her, as she was just a member of his children's choir. Her step-mother had brought her to the initial audition, but neither parent came to support concerts or church services in which she sang. Then, out of nowhere, Greg had found himself at the centre of a police enquiry, and Marie knew the rest, he said.

Greg seemed so willing to talk about his case, that Marie was honest about how her visit had come about. She explained that she'd taught Louise some time ago, and that she'd sat through Greg's trial. She also told him how a journalist, Lucy Flynn, had been at the trial and had an interest in whether or not his conviction was just. It was Lucy who had persuaded Marie to visit him. Marie felt awkward about not having spelled all this out to Greg in her letter.

'Probably good that you didn't,' he'd said in response, 'as I'm told that all our letters are read before we get them, and I probably wouldn't have agreed to the visit.'

Marie continued to sit in the café, having finished her food, and noted down all she could remember of her conversation with Greg.

He came across as so ordinary, so genuine, and likeable actually, she thought. *I wouldn't mind visiting him again. Or has he pulled the wool completely over my eyes? Sex offenders can be skilled at manipulation, can't they? But is he a sex offender? That's the question.*

She looked out of the café window, having noticed that it was getting dark outside. Then there was a loud thunder clap and the heavens opened.

'Oh, sod it,' muttered Marie, 'I've left my brolly in the car.'

It appeared that the heavy rain had set in, so Marie decided to make a dash for the car, which was only yards from the café door, and resume her journey home.

First, though, she said to herself, *I'm going to send all these notes to one of my private email accounts… just a belts and braces precaution! I don't want to lose any of this!*

* * *

The windscreen wipers could hardly cope with the torrential rain, and visibility was poor. Marie turned the radio to her favourite music station, hoping that it would compensate for the miserable driving conditions.

There's only one stretch of road which might be difficult, she thought, *where the river is so close to the road. I'll take it extra slowly there.*

On the way to Falkenside she'd noticed how picturesque the landscape was in the sun, with an occasional heron standing motionless at the river's edge, poised for a catch. But now the atmosphere was more menacing, as the thunder and rain continued in the premature darkness. It was still a mile or two before Marie reached the road beside the river, so she hoped that the weather would start to improve.

Marie drove carefully, but she was preoccupied with thoughts of Greg and whether or not he was being honest in his claims of innocence. He didn't tell her that he was subject to a new investigation. *Maybe next time,* she thought. He'd implied that he would be willing to send her another Visiting Order, if she wanted him to, but nothing had been fixed.

Marie reached the stretch of road which ran alongside the river. The sky was gunmetal grey and the rain was beating relentlessly against the windscreen. Her car headlights seemed to reflect off the driving rain into her eyes.

Right, she told herself, *take it slowly… and concentrate.*

There were two lines which Marie could use to guide her. On the left was a solid white line marking the edge of the road, from which the grass verge sloped down to the river, with well-spaced willow trees on its bank. To Marie's right was an intermittent, broken white line indicating the middle of the narrow road. Gradually she felt more confident driving along with these guides, but she stayed as far away from the left as she dared. Luckily, there were no other cars about.

Suddenly she was momentarily blinded by white flashing headlights in her rear-view mirror.

My God, she thought, *he's in a bloody hurry!*

There were no blue lights to suggest that it was an emergency vehicle, but Marie slowed down to let the car pass her.

But the other driver didn't overtake Marie's car, he or she just slowed down too. The car was so close to the rear of Marie's car that she couldn't see its headlights. So she stamped on the accelerator, trying to put space between them. The car behind her speeded up too, its lights still on full beam.

Marie was terrified. Why would anyone play idiotic games like this, in such dreadful weather? There were no turnings off this road for a long way, as far as Marie could remember, so she would just have to keep driving, at a speed which she considered safe. She would leave room for the other car to overtake her.

For half a mile or so the two cars continued, with the second car keeping its distance. Marie began to relax a little, hoping that all the stupidity was over.

Suddenly the lights behind were flashing again and Marie could see the other car catching her up. Then she felt her car jolt forwards. She'd been shunted from behind. She was able to retain control of her steering, but she was trembling with fear.

Just keep going, she told herself, *you've got to get away from this maniac…*

A zigzag lightning flash lit up the sky, frightening Marie even more, and this was immediately followed by a deafening clap of thunder. She tried to steady her nerves, knowing that her only escape route was forwards. She tried to block out from her mind whatever the car behind was doing.

But then, her car was hit from the rear again, and this time there was undoubtedly serious intent. This was not a stupid game.

Marie's car swerved to the left, out of control, and slid down the sodden embankment into the fast-flowing, swollen waters of the river.

No one stopped to assist Marie.

Twenty-Five

'What do you mean?' asked Joanna, looking astonished. 'Are you saying that Steve's been thrown out?'

'I suppose I am,' replied Sophie. 'I thought you probably knew that he'd been asked to leave.'

'And why on earth would I know that? I want nothing to do with him, or that bloody golf club,' said Joanna, her face turning scarlet as she spoke.

Sophie was having difficulty hiding her embarrassment, and she shifted uneasily in her chair. She'd hesitated about mentioning what she'd heard from Marcus, but she'd assumed that Joanna would know about it anyway.

'I'm so sorry, Jo,' she said, 'this seems to be the second time I've landed a bombshell about Steve in your lap. I honestly thought that you must be aware of the scandal, especially as some of the pictures are of you.'

'WHAT?' screamed Joanna. 'What pictures? What the hell are you talking about?'

* * *

Sophie looked very flustered. Joanna fetched another coffee for them both. *No camomile tea for her at the moment!* thought Joanna.

'Right,' she said firmly. 'I need to hear the whole story and why I figure in it. Come on, Sophie, the whole thing.'

'Well, if you're sure...' began Sophie hesitantly. Joanna nodded decisively.

So Sophie gradually described the version of events which Marcus had told her, and which Sean had confirmed. Joanna's heart sank.

Why am I the last to know? she wondered, but she didn't interrupt Sophie.

It transpired that pictures had been circulating among golf club members on social media which had led the committee to demand Steve's immediate resignation. His conduct was deemed to bring the club into disrepute. And a couple of the pictures clearly showed Steve assaulting a woman, and a third was of her slumped on the ground beside a car. Sophie reluctantly admitted that the woman was, without doubt, Joanna.

As if to offer a crumb of comfort to her friend, Sophie added that there were pictures of an assault on another woman, too. But Joanna didn't feel comforted. Humiliation swept through her, quickly followed by anger. Without seeing the pictures, she immediately guessed who had taken them. There'd only been one occasion when Steve had hit her in public.

So who is this so-called Jane Denton, and what the hell was she doing taking photos on her phone when posing as a Good Samaritan? she asked herself. *It can't have been anyone else, can it?*

Joanna kept quiet about these thoughts. There was enough circulating around Blakesford Golf Club, without her adding fuel to the fire. She decided just to assure Sophie that she'd been right to tell her. Otherwise she reacted visibly as little as she could, but inwardly she was fuming.

Then another thought struck her.

My car is out there in the same carpark, and I'm leaving at about the same time as usual. Steve must be furious at having to resign, so will he think it's my fault somehow? Will he be out there lying in wait?

When she and Sophie left the gym, Joanna looked around furtively as she opened the foyer door, took a deep breath, and held her head up as she strode confidently over to the car.

* * *

Much to Joanna's relief, the drive home was uneventful. She'd quickly scanned the carpark before setting off, and there were no cars she recognised. On the way home she checked her rear-view mirror several times, hoping that she was not being followed, and all seemed well.

In the hallway of her apartment block she met one of the other residents, a woman in her thirties. Joanna didn't know her name, or which flat she lived in, but they occasionally chatted if they happened to meet.

'There was a man looking for you a bit earlier,' her neighbour said cheerfully to Joanna, 'he was upstairs knocking on your door. I asked if I could help, but he just said that he'd try again another time.'

Joanna thanked her nonchalantly, and the neighbour smiled and went on her way. Joanna felt sick.

That's all I need, she thought, *Steve turning up. Who the hell else could it have been?*

Twenty-Six

'That's exactly what we want,' said Gerry exultantly, when he put the phone down. Penny lay her book on the table next to her.

'So, what's the news?' she asked.

'As you probably gathered, that was the estate agent,' replied her husband, 'and there are already two parties interested in looking at Hotheby Farmhouse. That's what we need, two lots in competition with each other. Apparently, one is a private buyer, and the other is a consortium employing an agent. But, from what the chap said, they are both in a position to buy fairly quickly. But neither of them has viewed it yet.'

'Was anything said about the asking price?' said Penny. 'I honestly don't think it's realistic to be asking that much. It's more than we paid for the whole farmstead, not that long ago.'

'Perhaps it's a more saleable proposition, just one large house with manageable grounds and the barn,' replied Gerry. 'After all, it was on the market as a huge property for two years before we came along. And we paid a ridiculously knock-down price! I shan't complain if we achieve more than we paid!'

'But I just don't want us to be disappointed if it all sells for much less,' persisted Penny. 'I confess that I do still have occasional twinges of regret that we're selling the big house, but I know, it's a massive place and we don't need all that space. Perhaps a little bit of me would like to be the lady of the manor, though!'

Gerry laughed.

'It might've been fun,' he agreed.

* * *

Mrs Thwaites and her nephew, Sam, had ideas about how to renovate the two cottages. Gerry had to remind them gently that the budget for the work was not limitless. So gradually, realistic plans were made, and Sam started work. It soon became evident that he was prepared to put in long hours, like his aunt, and he, too, took pride in his work.

Carruthers ambled over to the cottages whenever Sam was there, knowing that he kept a few dog treats in his pocket. Sam was tolerant of Carruthers, who frequently got in the way. He'd like to have a dog himself, he told Gerry one day, but it wouldn't be fair on the animal to be left at home while he was working.

Sam was friends with many local tradespeople. He introduced Gerry to an electrician, a plumber and a plasterer, all of whom came and worked for a while on the cottages. So the holiday-lets took shape more quickly than Gerry and Penny had expected.

Penny and Mrs Thwaites went to Snaysby market and bought bedding, curtains and crockery for the cottages. Their tastes proved to be different, but amicable compromises were reached! Penny then insisted that they went to a little teashop near the market. Mrs Thwaites initially seemed hesitant about this, but Penny persuaded her that they both deserved a cup of tea and a cake.

Hopefully it'll be a treat that she can tell her friends about, thought Penny, *her mistress taking her to a teashop!* Penny smiled to herself.

* * *

Two weeks later the estate agent rang again, and Gerry spoke to him.

'Well,' he said to Penny, after finishing the call, 'that sounds like progress. Both potential buyers have been to look at the farmhouse now, and the consortium's agent has made an offer. Our chap advises that we hold out, though, as he describes it as a "cheeky" offer. But at least it's a start. There's been no news of the other buyer.'

'Wow,' said Penny, 'that's amazing… an offer already! I wonder what plans they've got for the farmhouse. I seem to recall that there are restrictions on what can be altered, both inside and out, but their architect will be aware of all that.'

'Yes, you're right,' confirmed Gerry, 'I remember that too. But hopefully we'll soon be able to watch it all as interested bystanders, and they can have the headaches! Let's hope they decide to go ahead.'

'I can't believe how quickly things have moved since we bought this place. It feels as though we've always been here. Do you ever regret leaving the police and moving up here?' asked Penny.

'No way,' replied Gerry, with a broad grin, 'best move of my life, except for marrying you, of course. So let's go to the pub in Little Cragworth for a meal this evening, to celebrate. But don't tell Mrs Thwaites!'

Twenty-Seven

Zak Lewis usually went out for a run in all weathers. But it had been teeming down with rain incessantly for the past forty-eight hours and all his usual routes were flooded or too slippery. There had been warnings on the radio about impassable roads, and the rivers in this area were dangerously high. So he'd waited for the rain to ease off.

Zak's favourite run was along the path beside the river, especially in the early morning. So he set off, wondering whether or not the path would still be under water. He'd never seen the river so high or fast-flowing. It seemed to be almost up to the edge of the road on the far side. But he knew the path well and thought it was safe enough.

It was about two miles to the weir, so Zak decided to run there and then back along the same path. It felt good to be stretching his legs again after two days without a run.

As he approached the weir, Zak stopped to do some exercises and to look at the flotsam gathered there following the torrential rain. There were large broken branches strewn across the water, an old bicycle, plastic bags and other rubbish. This was usually a picturesque area, and Zak was sad to see such a mess. Then he spotted a big piece of coloured metal in the water, just below the surface.

'Oh my God,' he said aloud, 'it looks like the roof of a car! I've never seen that here before.'

He leaned cautiously over the metal railings that edged the path, to get a better view. As the dirty waters swirled about in the wind, more of the car was briefly visible, before disappearing again beneath the water.

Zak looked around but no one else was in sight. He was feeling cold and wished he had a jacket with him. He peered over and took another look at the submerged vehicle. He was in two minds. He had his phone with him, so should he call the emergency services now? Or could it wait until he'd run home and put some warm clothes on?

He had no idea when the car had entered the water, so perhaps there was someone in it, who should be rescued. That thought decided him. He unclipped his phone from his belt and dialled 999. He was shivering, and his voice sounded unsteady. The police told him to stay at the scene until they arrived.

Zak jogged along the path a little way and then back again. He did more exercises to keep warm, hoping that the police would come soon.

They'll have a blanket in their car, won't they? he hoped.

* * *

Zak sat in the relative warmth of the police car, huddled in a metallic blanket, while a police officer took details from him. Her colleague was surveying the scene and talking to the crew of a fire engine which had also arrived.

'Sarge,' came a shout, 'we've got a body.'

Zak felt sick.

What an horrendous way to die, he thought.

The police officer asked Zak if someone could come and collect him. She considered that he was too shaken up to attempt to run home again along the treacherous path. So Zak phoned his partner, and within ten minutes she'd arrived and they were driving home with the car heater on maximum. He said nothing during the journey.

* * *

Meanwhile, in Hadley St Giles, Mrs Lassiter was at the end of her tether. Celine Martin had phoned earlier to say that she was at the hospital with her young son, who'd been knocked off his bicycle and was in a bad way. She promised to be back at school tomorrow, when she'd made suitable arrangements for her son's care.

Mrs Lassiter quickly made adjustments to Celine's timetable, but it meant that she herself would have to cover most lessons.

There had, however, been no word from Marie Wilkinson, who hadn't come into school yet. This really concerned Mrs Lassiter as it was completely out of character for Marie. She was probably the most dependable member of staff, so her unexplained absence was worrying. Mrs Lassiter could recall only one previous occasion when Marie hadn't been able to work, and that was the day her mother had died. Marie had kept the Head informed of the situation then.

But Mrs Lassiter's top priority was to organise Marie's class and to ensure that they got on with their schoolwork. She rang two supply teachers, whom she'd called upon in the past, but neither was available. She was aware that Marie's class had some difficult and disruptive pupils in it, so a skilled teacher was needed.

Eventually she decided that the only solution was to improvise. She would supervise Celine's and Marie's classes together in the school hall, the only space large enough to accommodate them together. There were no tables in the hall, so the children would have to be either moving around or sitting on the floor. She drafted in two teaching assistants from other classes to help. It wasn't ideal, but Mrs Lassiter hoped that Marie might appear later, or that, at least, the syllabus would be disrupted for only one day.

I just hope that nothing has happened to Marie, she thought.

* * *

Lucy Flynn was keen to hear from Marie too. She'd been thinking about the visit to HMP Falkenside and her meeting with Gregory Mortimer. Lucy would have preferred to go and see him herself, but she felt certain that he would open up more to Marie.

It's possible he would've remembered me, she reminded herself.

Lucy had agreed to wait for Marie to contact her, and she was determined not to pressure Marie, as that might prove counter-productive. So Lucy persuaded herself to be patient.

Twenty-Eight

Joanna resolved not to open her front door to anyone. She still didn't know who'd been looking for her on Saturday. She thought it must have been Steve, but why?

Presumably he's angry about being ignominiously thrown out of the golf club, she surmised, *but why would he think that I had anything to do with posting those bloody pics? I don't want people viewing them, any more than he does!*

* * *

At work on Monday morning her colleague, Cheryl, took Joanna aside and quietly asked if she knew what was circulating on social media. Joanna's heart sank, but she shook her head and looked at Cheryl enquiringly.

'It's none of my business,' continued Cheryl, ensuring that no one else could hear her, 'but my boyfriend plays at Blakesford Golf Club with a friend of his. This friend showed Darren some photos, because the chap in them had been chucked out of the club. He was thumping a woman, and the club wouldn't tolerate his behaviour. Anyway, Darren showed the pics to me, and I saw that the man was assaulting you. I'm so sorry, Joanna, that must've been awful for you. But I thought you'd want to know that these pics are out there.'

Joanna felt like bursting into tears of exasperation. Not only had she been assaulted, twice, by the man she used to love, but now the whole world could witness it. She felt degraded. But she tried to put on a brave face and talk to Cheryl in an unemotional way.

'Thanks, Cheryl, but you're not the first to tell me about this. You're right, the incident was humiliating enough, but now it's all been compounded by these blasted pictures. The scandal factor has been ratcheted up a few notches, but I'm not sure who took them, or why. I admit I'm scared by it all,' said Joanna.

She immediately regretted saying this, as she didn't know who Cheryl's boyfriend was, and whether he was a friend of Steve. She didn't want any admission of fear being relayed back to Steve.

'So,' she asked casually, 'does Darren know Steve?'

'No,' replied Cheryl, 'he was disgusted by the chap's behaviour and is pleased he got thrown out. Can I just ask, though,' she hesitated, 'is he your husband? It's just that I noticed the same names…'

'He *was* my husband, and he doesn't seem to accept that it's all in the past now,' said Joanna dolefully. 'I know it's asking a lot, Cheryl, but would you mind keeping all this quiet, at least among library colleagues? It's bad enough hearing about it away from work, but I really don't want Tony, in particular, taking an interest.'

'Of course,' said Cheryl, 'my lips are sealed, but if ever you need a sympathetic ear, let me know.'

Joanna thanked her, and they both returned to their work.

At least Joanna had lunch with Mike on Wednesday to look forward to.

* * *

As they were finishing their meals, Mike leaned over and put his hand on Joanna's. She wasn't her usual cheerful self, and Mike understood why.

'Well, Jo,' he began, 'from all you've told me, I have the impression that you have two major decisions to make. I don't doubt, though, that lots of other issues will flow from them. Does that sound right to you?'

Joanna nodded. She hadn't intended to tell Mike so much about her problems, but she suddenly found that she needed to let go, and Mike was so easy to talk to.

'As I see it,' he continued, looking at her affectionately, 'your job is clearly getting you down. You're being stifled by that crass boss of yours. From what you say, he allows you an ounce of initiative now and again, and almost immediately feels threatened and backtracks. That's no good for anyone's morale. So perhaps some job-hunting is called for?'

Joanna tried to suppress a laugh. Mike had quickly homed in on the nub of her first dilemma, whereas she'd spent many hours churning it all ineffectually around in her mind.

'That's about the sum of it,' she said, 'so is this what you do professionally?'

Mike gave her an amused look.

'Not usually,' he answered, 'but I'll take that as a compliment! You've been thinking about it too much. It's time for action! So that leads us to dilemma two, which may be more difficult to resolve.'

Joanna hadn't talked about what had led to her divorce. That was water under the bridge, as far as she was concerned. But she had told Mike about the assault in the carpark, the woman who'd shown kindness (or so Joanna had thought), and how pictures had subsequently been posted on social media and the impact of that.

Mike seemed to be deep in thought.

'I'm no expert at analysing these things,' he began cautiously, 'but my first question would be, should the police be involved? There's apparently indisputable evidence of his assaulting you, so should you report it? Would that prevent him from doing it again to you… or another woman?'

'I didn't mention it,' confessed Joanna, 'but there are already pictures of him hitting someone else on social media too, so perhaps she'll report him.'

'Wouldn't it be better, though, if you made a conscious decision about whether you should report him, rather than let someone else do it, by default, so to speak?' suggested Mike.

'There's something else I haven't told you about, too,' said Joanna. 'The other day there was someone knocking on my front door apparently. He didn't leave a message with the neighbour who saw him, but just said that he'd return. I've no idea who it was, but I'm scared it was Steve.'

'Hmm…' said Mike, 'we need to discuss this more, if you think it helps? So, are you free on Friday evening? After that I'll be away for a while working, but perhaps we could make some headway over a meal on Friday? Shall I pick you up at 7.30?'

'That would be great,' replied Joanna, 'and thank you for taking my difficulties so seriously.'

'You're worth it,' said Mike and went to fetch Joanna's coat.

Twenty-Nine

There was a knock on Joanna's front door. It was 7.15 on Friday evening, and she was getting ready for her dinner with Mike.

Oh hell, she thought, panicking, *he's early… and he's never come up here before… he always waits in the foyer.*

She looked through the spy-hole and saw a man standing in the hall outside. She didn't recognise him, so decided to open the door with the chain on.

'Good evening, Mrs Hearnden,' said the man, with a slight smile. 'I'm DC Don Jackson from Blakesford police.' He held up his identity badge and showed it to Joanna through the partial opening of the door. 'Could I come in for a word, please?'

'Well…' stuttered Joanna, 'I'm expecting a friend at any moment, and we're going out.'

'This shouldn't take long,' continued DC Jackson. 'I'm just making some enquiries.'

Joanna felt obliged to let him into her apartment, at the same time wondering what this was all about. She hoped that Mike would arrive soon.

Once inside, DC Jackson explained that a young woman had reported that she was the victim of a violent assault by a male. During their investigations, she had shown the police some photos which had been posted on social media, and which, she told them, depicted the same man assaulting her, Mrs Hearnden. So the police were following this up. They knew the identity of the alleged perpetrator.

The intercom buzzer sounded, startling Joanna, even though she was expecting Mike.

'Perhaps you'd better answer that,' prompted DC Jackson, when Joanna seemed rooted to the spot. 'Or shall I do it?'

Joanna quickly responded and suggested to a surprised Mike that he should come up to the apartment, adding, 'I've got an unexpected visitor from the police, but I'd like you to be here too.'

* * *

'I was mightily relieved when you arrived,' admitted Joanna, when she and Mike were sitting in the gastropub. 'So many strange things have happened recently, I was beginning to wonder if he was genuinely from the police. I wasn't going to tell him anything without having someone else with me, so thank you for being that someone.'

Mike had actually said little to the police officer, but just being a supportive presence was enough for Joanna. He was listening very carefully, though, as he always seemed to.

'Well,' he eventually began, 'I have the impression that we have new items to add to our list of topics to discuss.'

Joanna agreed.

'But do you really want to get dragged into all my problems? I'll bet that you never anticipated any of this when you stumbled over a woman in a train!'

'Too true,' laughed Mike, 'but do I look as though I'm suffering?' He paused, 'I think I can cope!'

Their meals arrived, and the conversation lapsed for a few minutes.

'Right,' said Mike, 'let's get down to business. As I told you, I'll be working away for a while, possibly three or four weeks, so we need to get you on the right track this evening.'

Joanna suddenly felt despondent. She wouldn't be seeing Mike for several weeks, and she was certain that he wouldn't give her his contact details or tell her where he was going.

Oh well, if that's the price I have to pay, I'll just put up with it, she decided, *but I'll make the most of his help now.*

'On Wednesday,' continued Mike, 'we talked about whether a change of job would be a good idea. You're clearly undervalued at the library, and you say that there's no sign of your boss moving on now. You can do your job standing on your head, and it seems to me that you're wasted there. So, do you want to continue working in a library somewhere, like a university, or a specialist library, or would you consider branching out and doing something different? But changing your job might also involve moving elsewhere, so how would you feel about that?'

'How do you think so analytically about my life, when I can't?' asked Joanna.

'Possibly because I don't know what emotions are attached to any of my suggestions. It's always easier to look at things from the outside,' he replied.

They returned to their meals, and Joanna could feel the wine relaxing her, as well as Mike's company.

'The other issue we were going to discuss was whether or not you should report your ex-husband's assault to the police,' continued Mike, 'but that's been taken out of your hands to some extent, hasn't it? They've got evidence, and a similar allegation from someone else. I have to admire the way you handled his questions though, Jo, giving yourself more time to decide whether you want to press charges. I can understand your fear of what might happen if he's prosecuted, but equally, the repercussions for you if he isn't. It's one hell of a dilemma for you.'

Mike leaned across and briefly held Joanna's hand.

They spent the next half-hour discussing how Joanna could tackle the issues facing her, and then Mike called a halt.

'Right,' he said decisively, 'that's enough for now. You've got your plans, and plenty to mull over, so now we'll talk about other things. Are you going to the theatre next week?'

As usual, Mike kept Joanna as the focus of the conversation. They were about to leave the pub, when Joanna heard her name being called. Coming towards them were Sophie, Marcus and Leonie.

'Hello, Joanna,' said Sophie, 'after your recommendation last week we thought we'd try out the pub this evening. You were right, they produced a lovely vegetarian meal for Leonie, and some beautiful fish dishes for Marcus and me.'

Joanna thought she should introduce Mike, fully aware of what tomorrow's main topic of questioning at the gym would be!

It'll be interesting to hear what Sophie says, she smiled to herself.

Thirty

By the end of the school day, Mrs Lassiter was feeling exhausted. Thankfully the improvised day had worked out well, with the children from Celine Martin's and Marie Wilkinson's classes cooperating surprisingly well with each other, and with her. But Mrs Lassiter had to make plans for the following day. Celine had phoned in to say that her mother would look after her son tomorrow, so she would definitely return to school. Sally, the school's office manager, had telephoned Marie's home and mobile several times during the day, leaving messages, but there was no response. Mrs Lassiter asked Sally to arrange for a supply teacher to be on stand-by, in case there was no contact from Marie.

The headteacher had an uneasy feeling about Marie's absence. It was so unlike her not to turn up, without a word. But she knew little about Marie's private life, although she was fairly certain that she lived alone. So she decided to call at Marie's home, when she'd finished her day's work, and find out if she needed help in any way. She was fond of Marie.

***

She looked up at Marie's small end-of-terrace house, on the outskirts of the next village. The front garden was neatly tended.

Mrs Lassiter looked around, but she couldn't see Marie's car, and although dusk was beginning to fall, there were no lights on in the house. She knocked on the front door and waited. There were no sounds from inside the house, and there was no answer to her knock.

A young woman came out of the adjoining house, going to put her rubbish in the bin.

'Can I help you at all?' she asked Mrs Lassiter. 'I don't think Marie's home from school yet, but I don't suppose she'll be long. Come to think of it, I didn't see her at all over the weekend, so perhaps she's been away.'

Mrs Lassiter thanked the woman and said, 'Don't worry, I'll ring Marie later.'

She drove home, increasingly concerned about Marie's absence.

* * *

Lucy Flynn was scrolling down the local news stories on her phone. There were none that immediately sparked her interest, nor any that she needed to follow up.

She'd expected to hear something from Marie Wilkinson by now, but she hadn't. She began to wonder whether Marie had actually gone to the prison at all. She had seemed well-disposed to the idea, if not exactly enthusiastic, and they had come to an agreement.

Have I misjudged her? Lucy asked herself. *Well, if she's opting out, I'll just have to see if I can interview the man myself. I'll give her until tomorrow evening, and then I'll ring her and see where things stand. There's a good story in all this, and I want to be the one to tell it!*

Thirty-One

Greg Mortimer was working alone in the prison library when Officer Raynaud came in. He was immediately on his guard, anticipating abuse from Raynaud, as usually happened if the two of them were alone. Kieran had been right in his warnings to Greg.

'Where did you manage to find yourself a tart like that then?' sneered Raynaud. 'She turned a few heads in the Visits Hall, I'm told. Got young children, has she? Can't wait to get your hands in their knickers, I'll bet.' There was hatred in Raynaud's eyes, as he spat at Greg's face. 'You're filthy scum, you nonces,' he continued, but then the library door opened, and Kieran came in, with an armful of books. Raynaud stepped backwards and folded his arms across his chest.

Kieran could sense that Raynaud had been goading Greg.

He turned to Greg and said, 'Give me a hand with these will you, Mortimer?', and Greg took some of the books from Kieran and put them on a table. That at least put some space between Greg and Raynaud.

Suddenly an alarm bell rang, and Raynaud had to run off in answer to it.

'He been giving you a hard time?' asked Kieran.

'He always does, if no one else is within earshot,' replied Greg.

'It's sad that he's so full of venom, especially in this job. Why does he work here, if he can't stand some of us?'

'Where else would he have the same level of power over people?' said Kieran. 'He just revels in that power, but he's a coward too. Try to ignore him, and don't waste your sympathy on him.'

* * *

Two days later Greg was sitting in an interview room again, opposite DS Clive Meadows and DC Sharon Page. Greg had hoped that they would tell him there was no corroborating evidence in respect of the historical allegations. But those hopes were quickly dashed by DS Meadows stating that the investigation was still ongoing. They were here today about a different matter.

Greg's spirits sank. *Not yet more allegations,* he thought despairingly.

'We understand that you had a visit last weekend from a Marie Wilkinson. Is that correct?' asked DS Meadows.

Greg confirmed that he had.

'And have you heard anything from her since the visit?' asked DC Page.

'No,' replied Greg, 'but why is this of interest to you?'

He was confused.

'Well,' explained DS Meadows, 'we have reason to believe that you may have been one of the last people to speak to her.'

Greg was in shock. Were they conveying to him that she was dead? It sounded like that.

When Greg said nothing in response, DS Meadows quietly told him that Marie may have died in a traffic accident on her way home from the prison.

'Oh, my God,' exclaimed Greg, 'are you sure it's her? That was the only time I met her, but she seemed so nice, and much too young to die.'

His face had drained of its colour.

'We're trying to piece together what happened to her, so could you tell us why she was visiting you, and what her mood was like when she left?' asked DC Page. 'Was anything in particular troubling her, do you know?'

Greg explained how the visit had come about, and how he had spoken with her about his conviction, and his denial of any wrong-doing.

'It was just an ordinary, adult conversation about things which were of interest to both of us,' said Greg. 'She was pleasant to talk to, and I didn't pick up that anything was troubling her. But we'd never met before, and now we never will again.'

There was a sad expression on Greg's face.

'Did she say anything about her journey to the prison, or her route home?' asked DS Meadows.

'Not a word,' replied Greg. 'We didn't touch on that subject at all, as far as I remember.'

Greg wanted to know more about the accident. He asked if Marie had been killed outright, and if anyone else had been hurt. DS Meadows hadn't got all the details yet, he said, but he could inform Greg that Marie's car had somehow entered a fast-flowing river and was found submerged. He had nothing to suggest that anyone else was involved.

'Oh, the poor woman,' said Greg, very softly, 'what a dreadful end to her life.'

* * *

'I think he was open and honest with us, and genuinely upset by the news, Sarge,' said Sharon. 'What did you think?'

They were driving back to the police station.

'I go along with that,' replied her boss, 'but I'd like to find out more about this Lucy Flynn. Why did Marie Wilkinson go and see Mortimer, rather than her, if she's the one lobbying on behalf of victims of injustice?'

'I'll get onto it as soon as we get back,' volunteered Sharon.

'And we need to talk to the forensics team again. Is there any reason to think it may not have been an accident?' said Clive, slowing down, before he pulled out to overtake a bicycle.

'What about checking when the torrential rain started in the area and any info about the river, and visibility, road surfaces, and so on,' added Sharon, 'and how all that ties in with when the car went into the river... or should we leave all that to the forensics team?'

Clive laughed. Sharon was the most enthusiastic DC he'd ever worked with. She would look at every angle of a case, and she revelled in complex work, but she sometimes lacked clarity about boundaries. She learned quickly, though.

'Sounds like your task list is lengthening, Sharon,' he said. 'I think we should make a detour now and take another look at the scene of the accident, don't you?'

Thirty-Two

Gerry Thorncroft had been to Snaysby this morning. Sam Thwaites had recommended a company where Gerry could hire a rotavator and buy some new gardening tools. He and Penny had decided to tackle the jungle of a back garden at Ivy House, which had been neglected for the past two years and would soon be completely out of hand. He loaded everything into his truck and then decided to call in at the estate agents, to find out what progress there was towards the sale of Hotheby Farmhouse.

Gerry arrived home feeling pleased with life. He went straight round to the back garden where Penny was busily measuring the areas in which they would grow vegetables, and where she hoped a new greenhouse would eventually be sited. For some weeks she'd been noting when the sun shone on particular patches and which remained largely shaded. She was marking out her ideas with heavy-duty twine secured on small metal posts.

She stood up, clutching her aching back, when she heard Gerry.

'Did you manage to get everything?' she asked.

'Not only that,' replied Gerry, grinning broadly, 'I've got other news too. I went into the estate agents for an update on the sale, and guess what, the potential purchasers' agent is viewing the farmhouse with a surveyor this afternoon, to see what's feasible in terms of alterations. So they're certainly serious buyers, by the sound of it, whoever "they" are. And they seem to want to proceed with everything quite quickly, which is great for us.'

'But we've still no idea who this so-called consortium consists of? Or what their plans are?' asked Penny, feeling bewildered.

'Not a clue,' replied Gerry, 'but whatever they're planning, the house is far enough from here not to impact on our lives, don't you think? We can't control what happens once we've sold it,' said Gerry, trying to sound reassuring.

'It just seems a bit cloak and dagger-ish,' said Penny, 'but perhaps I read too many novels!'

Gerry decided to change the subject and suggested they make some coffee and then unload the truck.

'We've only hired the rotavator for forty-eight hours,' he said cheerfully, 'so there'll be no slacking!'

Thirty-Three

'Right,' said DCI Couzens, opening the morning briefing, 'what have we got so far on the car in the river? Clive?'

DS Meadows looked up from his notes and reported, 'The identity of the body has been confirmed as that of Marie Bernadette Wilkinson, aged thirty-eight years, divorced, no children, and a teacher at Hadley St Giles' school. Next of kin is a sister, Rosie Bancroft, living in Edinburgh with her husband and two children. She's been visited by our colleagues in Scotland and is described as being devastated by her sister's death. The husband's been interviewed too.'

Clive paused.

'What do we know about Wilkinson's state of mind prior to the incident?' asked DCI Couzens.

'That needs to be followed up, sir,' replied Clive.

'Right,' said DCI Couzens decisively, 'house-to-house in her immediate neighbourhood. Who are her close friends, etc.. The headteacher needs to be interviewed too. Any causes of concern in her job? And we need more intelligence on Wilkinson's former husband… are they in contact? are there any issues? And we must not ignore the runner, Zak Lewis, who first reported the car. Are we convinced that was his only involvement?'

These tasks were delegated to PC Hughes and PC Cornell.

'I also want every electronic device found in the car and at Wilkinson's home to be scrutinised thoroughly, as quickly as possible,' he added, looking at DC Kristiansen, one of the tech team.

'And I'll get forensics to fast-track work on the car. Their team's overloaded, but this needs to be high priority,' he said.

'And finally, for the moment,' the DCI concluded, 'Clive, I want you and DC Page to investigate Wilkinson's movements prior to the accident, and why she was on that stretch of road at the time of the storm. We know there's a link to the prisoner, Gregory Mortimer, and that you've interviewed him, but we need to know more about that relationship. And we all convene again, ten o'clock tomorrow morning. Any questions?'

After a momentary pause, the DCI left the meeting.

* * *

It was late afternoon, and Clive asked Sharon to summarise the day's progress.

'Well, Sarge,' she began, standing erect and holding her notebook in her left hand, 'first of all, I've done some digging around on the journalist, Lucy Flynn, as you asked.'

'Sharon,' cut in Clive, 'do sit down and relax a bit. You don't need to be on ceremony whilst giving me feedback, I know it'll be useful!'

Sharon smiled and sat down opposite him.

'Sorry, Sarge, it's just that my last boss insisted on formality at all times, and it's a difficult habit to break,' she explained, 'but I'll try!'

'Right,' said Clive, 'give me the low-down on Lucy Flynn.'

'Well,' she began again, 'she's some sort of freelance reporter. She's written for several women's magazines on a range of topics, but nothing controversial or relevant to us, as far as I could see.

But Mortimer was right when he told us that she's interested in victims of injustice. She's had her fingers in a few cases like that, and not only criminal cases. I found a lengthy piece she'd written about a transgender teenager and how the youngster was being disadvantaged within the school system. I would guess that Lucy could be quite a formidable opponent once she decides to fight a cause.'

'And you think that she's now interested in Mortimer's case for some reason? He hasn't been whipping up support for himself in the community, claiming to have been wrongly convicted, has he? And Lucy's jumped on the bandwagon?' asked Clive.

'That's not my reading of Mortimer at all,' replied Sharon. 'On the contrary, I have the impression that he keeps his head down. He's decided to serve his time and get out at the first possible opportunity. As he mentioned, it was Lucy Flynn's initiative to delve into his case, not his. But why she is focusing on *his* case particularly is beyond me at the moment. Or perhaps she's following up other so-called wrongful convictions, too.'

Clive got up from his chair and walked over to the window, thinking through what Sharon had told him. It was a gloomy day, with leaden skies, which prompted reminders of Marie Wilkinson's untimely death.

'Right, Sharon,' he said, turning to face her, 'we need a wallchart with the key points that we mustn't lose sight of. So firstly, Lucy Flynn, we need to talk to her. Then there's Mortimer. What's the underlying link with Flynn? Then there's his ongoing investigation? He must be due for release fairly soon, so what are his plans? And ...'

Twenty minutes later they had a complex chart showing known links between people and a list of priority tasks.

Clive took an opened packet of chocolate biscuits out his of desk drawer and offered them to Sharon. She hadn't had time for lunch today, so she gratefully accepted one.

'Well,' said Clive, 'that's a useful start, but I've also been speaking with the forensics team today. As usual at this stage, there were lots of caveats about how these are preliminary findings and so on, and how the weather conditions at the time of the accident may have compromised some potential evidence, but, apart from all that, there may be some helpful info too.'

Clive took another biscuit, and Sharon waited for him to continue.

'Perhaps you should do a second wallchart with forensics info on it, please, Sharon. So, the identity of the body in the car has been confirmed as Marie Wilkinson, a teacher, aged thirty-eight years, divorced, living alone. It's been established that she was alive when the car entered the water, during her journey home from HMP Falkenside, and she drowned inside the car. She was the driver and was alone. Personal items have been retrieved from the car, but we don't know how much damage will have been done to her phone, and so on, by being in the water for forty-eight hours, so we'll have to wait for those results. And, of course, the car itself is being forensically examined, too.'

Sharon's hand shook a little as she noted down the manner of Marie's death. Clive noticed but didn't comment. He was developing great respect for his new DC and didn't want to embarrass her for being sensitive.

'There were also some interesting interim findings about where the car actually went into the river. We know that there was torrential rain that evening, and the river was unusually high and fast. Well, it seems that the car was swept nearly a quarter of a mile down the river by the force of the current, before it came to rest submerged at the weir. So, there are two distinct sites to examine. Firstly, the point at which Marie's car came off the road and slid down the embankment, getting no grip on the sodden mud, and secondly the area where it was found at the weir. But my main question is, *why* did her car come off the road? Given the conditions, she surely would've been driving very cautiously, wouldn't she?'

'So are you suggesting, Sarge, that her car was pushed off the road? That it may have been a deliberate act?' asked Sharon hesitantly, aghast at the thought.

'We have to keep open minds, Sharon. It occurs to me, though, from our look at the area, that there was a petrol station only a mile or two before the particularly treacherous stretch of road where the car went into the river. With a bit of luck, they may have some CCTV footage, and with an even bigger chunk of luck there may be something useful on it! We should pay them a visit. No time like the present. Come on, Sharon.'

She had been planning to meet up with a friend in an hour or so, but, in her life, work had to come first. She made a quick apologetic phone call.

Thirty-Four

In the weeks before Greg Mortimer's release, he was interviewed by various professionals, people with whom he'd previously had little or no contact. One of these was the chaplain, whom he hadn't seen since his first days in Falkenside. It all felt rather meaningless to him, but Greg accepted that the required formalities had to be completed, and forms filled in, before he would be released.

He'd received a letter two weeks ago from Charlie Johnson, who was to be his supervisor in the community. The letter was full of apologies that no visits or personal introductions had been possible due to budget constraints. But accommodation had been found for Greg in Mulchester, where Charlie was based. An accredited volunteer driver, Bill Jones, would meet Greg outside Falkenside on his release date. Once in Mulchester, Charlie would go through the conditions attached to Greg's supervision.

The letter had struck Greg as impersonal. And he'd never heard of Mulchester. But at least he had somewhere to live, for the time being.

Greg seemed quieter as his release approached, and Kieran wondered what was bothering him. Greg hadn't said much about his release to Kieran, as he realised that his friend still had many years of incarceration ahead of him. But Kieran was philosophical about that.

'You should be pleased,' said Kieran, 'you've done the worst part of your sentence. At least the rest of it will be outside prison walls.'

'It's all the restrictions, though,' replied Greg, 'where I have to live, who I can and can't be friendly with, what sort of work I can do, all those sorts of things. And I'm sure there'll be people like Raynaud out there. I remember hearing about cases of vigilantism, gangs attacking houses they think a paedophile lives in. And the fact that I deny what I was convicted of will probably just makes matters worse for me.'

'I may have it easy in here compared with you, but, believe me, I'd give anything for my freedom,' confided Kieran.

* * *

On the morning of his release, at just after eight o'clock, Greg took his first steps of freedom, wearing the same clothes he had worn to court all that time ago, and carrying the same canvas holdall.

He looked around apprehensively. He knew that the more recent allegations against him were still being investigated, and he half-expected to be arrested again, here and now. He stood alone and wondered where Bill Jones and the car were. Slowly a rather battered-looking silver car emerged from the visitors' carpark and drew up beside him.

'Greg?' the driver enquired, and Greg nodded. 'I'm Bill,' the driver continued, 'chuck your bag in the back, and we'll get going.'

As Greg got into the front passenger seat, Bill held out his hand to him. Greg was momentarily taken aback. He hadn't shaken hands with anyone for a long time.

'It should take us about two hours to get to Mulchester, depending on the traffic, of course,' said Bill, 'and I'll phone Charlie when we're nearly there. She wants to meet you at your flat.'

Greg wondered if he'd heard correctly. 'So Charlie is a woman, is she?' he asked.

Bill gave a hearty guffaw.

'She most certainly is,' he said with a grin. 'Sorry, I'd forgotten you don't actually know her.'

They drove on in silence for a while, with Greg mentally readjusting to the prospect of having a woman supervising him. He gradually came to like the idea, having lived in a predominantly male environment for so long.

* * *

Unknown to Greg, his release had been watched.

Frank Purvis-Brown was enraged to see a fit-looking Gregory Mortimer emerge into the sunshine and to witness him being driven away by a man in a silver car.

I bet he's on some protection scheme, Frank seethed, *and he's being taken to a "safe house" somewhere. The bastard doesn't deserve that!*

Frank had planned that he wouldn't follow whatever car picked Mortimer up. He just noted down its number, for future reference. His contacts would tell him the details of Mortimer's destination, just as they'd given him the date of his release. Frank could always find someone to grass on a criminal. Everyone has their price.

His feelings were still running high as Frank drove off in the opposite direction from the silver car.

'He shouldn't be out…' he shouted in his car, 'that's not bloody justice!'

Frank was unaware that he, too, was being watched.

Thirty-Five

Attendance at the next day's briefing meeting, chaired by DCI Ray Couzens, wasn't optional. He expected a full exchange of information between all his officers, as limited resources didn't allow for duplication of effort. He also required all aspects of the case to be covered.

The DCI now had the local media on his back, he said, and he was to attend a press conference later, so external pressure for progress was mounting.

DS Clive Meadows and DC Sharon Page reported on their work to date, focusing particularly on Marie Wilkinson's connections with convicted sex offender Gregory Mortimer and with Lucy Flynn, freelance reporter. Nothing had emerged from their investigations so far to suggest that Marie Wilkinson intended to commit suicide. A search of Marie's home had led to the removal of her laptop and other devices, and these were now being examined.

Clive also reported on their visit to the petrol station and café a few miles from the scene of Marie's accident. The café proprietor had located CCTV footage from that afternoon, which she recalled clearly due to the atrocious weather. She also remembered the woman who had taken refuge in the café and seemed to be doing some work on an electronic device. The proprietor said that she'd been concerned when the woman left to resume her journey.

Clive anticipated that forensics would have retrieved the device and hopefully the data would still be usable for analysis. He reported that CCTV footage from the petrol station was also made available to them. There was a car parked on the far side of the forecourt, with the driver sitting in it. The images were far from clear, but could perhaps be enhanced, suggested Clive. The driver didn't either buy fuel or go into the shop, but just sat in the car, from where there was a direct view of the exit from the café. A matter of seconds after Marie Wilkinson's car left the café carpark, the unknown car also set off, in the same direction, perhaps twenty or thirty yards behind. So both sets of footage were now with the data technicians.

'I accept,' said Clive, 'that the second car may be irrelevant to our investigations, but it needs to be checked out.'

The DCI had been listening intently. His officers were aware of his astute, analytical mind, although his facial expressions usually gave little away about what he was thinking.

'Thanks, Clive,' he said. 'Can you add anything from the forensics team's perspective, Richie?'

Richie McCleod looked up from his notebook.

'Well, sir, as you know, we've been fast-tracking this case, as requested,' he replied in his soft Scottish brogue.

Sharon looked across at him. She hadn't met Richie before, and she was immediately annoyed with herself for being attracted to his voice.

Feelings don't belong at work, she reprimanded herself, *and it's only his voice, after all!*

Richie was continuing, 'The team's initial investigations reveal nothing mechanically wrong with the car which would cause it to swerve off the road. We've carried out a series of diagnostic tests, and there is no indication of anything having been tampered with or badly maintained. The tread on all four tyres was within legal limits too. But,' he said, his voice a little louder now, 'there was damage to the rear end of the car. This could have been historical, so to speak, or it may have been caused as a precursor to the car entering the water. This requires further investigation, as do the tyre marks at the scene of the incident.'

'So, in your professional view, was Wilkinson's car shunted off the road by another vehicle?' asked the DCI, anticipating that Richie wouldn't firmly commit himself. And he was right.

'As I say, sir,' Richie had reverted to his quiet voice, 'it's too soon to be definitive.'

'But it's at least a possibility,' continued the DCI, 'if the forensics confirm this, that Wilkinson's car was pushed by another vehicle, causing her to end up in the river, and it's also a possibility, again if the forensics support this, that the second car was the one in the CCTV footage. I know this is only one of a range of hypotheses at the moment, and we must all remember that.' He paused. 'If the evidence leads us in that direction, though, was it, or was it not, a deliberate act by the second driver?'

* * *

Half an hour later, Sharon and Clive were returning to Clive's office, via the coffee machine, to discuss the meeting. He got his biscuits out of the desk drawer and offered them to Sharon.

The phone rang. Clive answered it and gave Sharon a thumbs-up signal. She was intrigued. Clive's end of the conversation gave her few clues as to the identity of the caller, so she wandered over to the window and waited.

'Hmm…' he said enigmatically, after replacing the phone, 'more progress perhaps.' He leaned back in his chair and grinned at Sharon.

'That was Richie,' he said, 'and while he was in the meeting with us, his team had been analysing some paint found on the back of Marie's car, and from that they've identified the make of car, but not the actual model yet. It's only a tiny step, but at least it's progress.'

He punched the air.

'Right, Sharon, let's have a look at our boards,' began Clive. 'Is interviewing Lucy Flynn near the top of the list?'

Thirty-Six

Two weeks passed, and Joanna heard nothing from Mike.

But he said he'd be away for three to four weeks, and that he'd be unable to contact me, she reminded herself. *So I've either got to accept this weird situation, or I forget about him… and I don't want to do that!*

Sophie, Marcus and Leonie had met Mike briefly at the restaurant, when Joanna had last seen him. The following morning at the gym Joanna wondered what her friend would say about Mike. She knew that Sophie had reservations about her relationship with Mike, (*if you can call it that,* she reflected ruefully), as far as his reliability and elusiveness were concerned.

After a strenuous workout, Joanna and Sophie were sitting relaxing in the café.

'Mike seemed to be very pleasant and friendly,' remarked Sophie, unsure whether or not to mention him. She tried to gauge her friend's reaction, but, to Sophie's relief, Joanna just smiled and nodded.

'So do you know where he's working this time?' Sophie continued tentatively.

Joanna's facial expression changed to one of wistfulness.

'No,' she replied, 'he's done his usual disappearing trick, and it may be weeks before I hear from him. I know it all seems very strange to you, but it doesn't seem like that to me when I'm with him. But when I try to look at it all objectively, which is hard, it *is* a bizarre situation. There's no physical relationship between us, yet he comes across as being very fond of me, and he takes a huge interest in me and my future, without revealing anything about himself. He's even left me a task to tackle while he's away!'

Sophie looked bemused. What on earth was she talking about?

'Yes,' Joanna laughed, a little embarrassed, 'I have to do some serious job-hunting and report back, when I next see him!'

Sophie didn't reply immediately. She was clearly thinking about what her friend had just said.

'Jo,' she eventually said, 'I know we think differently in many ways, but I really don't want to see you being hurt any more. You've had some dreadful experiences in the recent past. I just wonder…' she hesitated, 'and you may not like me saying this… but I wonder if you realise how vulnerable you are, and therefore open to being exploited.'

'Oh, come on, Sophie,' scoffed Joanna, 'being exploited is a bit extreme, isn't it? Yes, I certainly misjudged Steve, and I'm still paying the price for that, but you're not suggesting that Mike is in a similar category, are you?'

Sophie gave her friend a kindly look.

'Well, Jo,' she said, 'you've told me in the past that there was a power imbalance in your marriage to Steve and that was the root of many of your problems. Well, as an outsider admittedly, I wonder if you should take a closer look at your friendship with Mike. Who calls all the shots now?'

* * *

Joanna had spent the following two weeks scouring journals and the internet for potential jobs. She found few inviting possibilities.

But she continued looking, trying to convince herself that the job-hunting was *her* idea, and not Mike's.

Sophie's more astute than I usually give her credit for, she conceded, lounging on the sofa at home, *or am I just horribly naïve and easy to flatter? Is Sophie right, and Mike is exploiting his power over me? He certainly calls all the shots, as she put it!*

* * *

Another week passed, and there was still no word from Mike.

At the start of the fourth week, Joanna arrived home from work with an Indian take-away meal and a bottle of wine. She collected her mail, threw it on the kitchen worktop, and settled with her meal in front of the television. She watched a programme about antiques being sold at auction, idly wondering if she could re-train as an auctioneer. That looked like an interesting job.

She took her dirty plate back to the kitchen, feeling mellowed by two glasses of wine. She picked up her mail and took it with her to the lounge. One envelope caught her interest. It was hand-written, while most of the others were printed circulars. Much to her relief, the handwriting was not Steve's.

Inside was a card with the simple message, "Miss you", in swirly mauve script on one side. On the reverse was written, 'Hope you're OK. Found this, and thought you might be interested!' An internet link followed, and the card was signed 'Mike'. There was an afterthought, 'See you soon'.

Joanna felt elated. Mike hadn't forgotten about her. He'd even been job-hunting on her behalf, or so she guessed from the message.

Why did I doubt him? she asked herself, and then she recalled Sophie's reservations.

Joanna opened her laptop and followed the link Mike had sent. She stared at what she found. It was one of the briefest job adverts she'd ever seen.

"Personal assistant/researcher required for writer. Graduate level. Based in northern England. Accommodation provided. Further details available by email."

Joanna was intrigued. Why did Mike think that this would appeal to her? It would mean a total change in her life.

Or is this his way of getting me out of his life? she asked herself despondently.

After a few moments, she decided to email for further details.

Why the hell not? she thought, and poured another glass of wine.

Thirty-Seven

Greg Mortimer's new home was a small, rather shabby, sparsely furnished first-floor flat in a cul-de-sac on the edge of a housing development in Mulchester. Compared with his cell, though, this was a great improvement. He had a key to his front door, he had windows he could open, there were no bars on the windows, he could come and go as he pleased, and he could choose what food he bought and when he cooked it.

The transition from prison to community wasn't easy, though. Bill, the driver, had tried to help during their journey together. He suggested that they stop at a supermarket as they approached Mulchester, so that Greg could buy some groceries.

'I'm sure you'll want to make yourself a cuppa, at least,' said Bill jovially.

But Greg had felt self-conscious, even in a large supermarket in a town where he was a stranger. He'd feared that people would realise he was a newly-released prisoner. Gradually, though, he convinced himself that no one knew that, nor gave him judgemental looks. It was all in his own mind.

Bill had phoned Charlie Johnson, Greg's community supervisor, while they were at the supermarket, and she was waiting outside the flat when they arrived. Greg had been apprehensive about meeting her, but first impressions were reassuring.

Charlie was in her fifties, or so Greg guessed, rather overweight and cheerfully business-like. He accepted that he would have conditions attached to his supervision and that Charlie would be an influential person in his life for quite a while.

'Honesty and mutual respect will be the fundamentals of our relationship,' she told Greg, with a smile. That sounded fine to him.

She gave him a map of the area, highlighted where her office was, noted down her phone number, and arranged an appointment for him at her office in two days' time.

* * *

Greg had been contemplating his release from prison for several weeks, unconvinced that it would really happen, especially with the spectre of new charges hanging over him. But it *had* now happened, and he felt very alone. It took only a matter of minutes to unpack his holdall and his small bag of groceries.

But at least I'm not in a hostel with a lot of strangers, and I've got everything I need for now. I've got to find positives in this situation, he told himself.

It was a long time since Greg had cooked a meal for himself. In the supermarket he and Bill had bought some eggs, mushrooms and potatoes, so Greg made a passable mushroom omelette and some mashed potato. He realised that he hadn't bought any salt or other seasoning, so it was rather bland. He found a scrap of paper and started making a shopping list for tomorrow, aware that his discharge money wouldn't stretch far. But he had satisfaction in cooking his first meal in his new home.

* * *

Lying in bed that night, Greg was struck by how quiet it was. Constant noise had been an integral part of prison life, but now he was surrounded by unaccustomed silence. Just occasionally he heard a car door slam outside, or the voices of people walking by in the street below.

Just one of the re-adjustments I've got to make, he thought.

He lay there, pondering the future.

First thing, he decided, *must be to find a job, any job. I'll ask Charlie's advice about that. I must have something to do during the day. And I'll change my appearance, let my hair grow, and have a trim beard.*

Amid his late-night positivity, though, Greg remained haunted by the events which had completely altered his life. He tried not to be bitter, but it was all still beyond his comprehension.

Why, oh why, did a girl, whom I hardly knew, concoct such a web of lies and stick to her story? he wondered, bewildered. *And who the hell is this woman who's invented yet more allegations? I couldn't face another prison sentence.*

Greg tried to divert his thoughts from this horrendous possibility. He'd witnessed the worst of human nature in prison, but also experienced friendship. Kieran, who was unlikely to leave that debilitating environment for many years yet, and who had committed an offence sufficiently serious to earn him a life sentence, had watched out for Greg when others had openly despised him. Kieran had been Greg's only friend.

Suddenly an image of Marie Wilkinson came unbidden into Greg's mind. He'd only met her once, but she'd been easy to talk to, allowing him a brief oasis of near-normality in an otherwise desperate world. And Greg had hoped that she might visit him again. But this hope had been cruelly dashed.

Was it really a dreadful accident? Could her death have been connected somehow with her visit to me? I doubt if I shall ever know, he thought sadly.

Thirty-Eight

Zak Lewis was enjoying an early evening run. He'd had a fraught day at work, sitting for hours in front of a computer screen, and the best way to relax was to go for a strenuous run. His favourite six-mile route took him along winding country lanes and then onto tracks alongside fields to the woods. That way he didn't go towards the river. He still felt uneasy running near the weir, where he'd found the submerged car.

It was a still evening, and the wispy white clouds were outlined in orange-pink from the glow of the setting sun. Zak turned into the woods, when suddenly there was an almighty noise, like an explosion. A flock of startled birds flew up out of the trees, squawking loudly. Then Zak saw flames, perhaps a couple of hundred yards ahead of him, among the trees. He had run along this track many times before, and he couldn't think of any landmarks which might have caught fire there.

He unclipped his phone and rang 999 for the fire service. Zak ventured a little nearer the fire, which was continuing to blaze fiercely. It had spread to surrounding undergrowth and the lower branches of trees. And then he realised what was on fire. He could hardly believe that he'd stumbled across a second car, the first sunk at the weir, and this one a blazing inferno. He prayed that there was no one in this car, as there'd been in the first one.

The emergency services were quickly at the scene. For a second time, Zak sat in a police car giving them details of what he'd heard and seen.

* * *

Clive Meadows and Sharon Page were standing on Lucy Flynn's front doorstep, waiting for her to answer their knock, when Sharon received a message on her phone. She called back. There were crime scene officers about a mile from where Marie Wilkinson's car had been spotted in the river. Now a burning car had been found by a member of the public, secreted in the woods. The same man had found both cars.

Sharon immediately told her boss. There was still no reply to their knocks on Lucy's door, so they hurriedly returned to their car and headed towards the new crime scene.

'Any bodies in this car?' asked Clive, as he wove in and out of the slowly moving traffic.

'That's not known yet,' replied Sharon. 'Apparently it was one helluva blaze, and the officer didn't think much of the car would survive it, let alone a person. It makes me wonder what sort of forensic evidence they'll be able to find, too.'

Clive looked across at Sharon briefly and said, with a chuckle in his voice, 'Well, perhaps you'll have to spend some time with Richie, learning more about forensic science. Off-duty, of course!'

To her annoyance, Sharon could feel herself blushing.

The boss doesn't miss a thing, does he? she thought.

Clive was quiet for a few moments, before commenting, 'I'm not a betting man, but the odds against coming across two cars in suspicious circumstances, within a mile or two of each other, and in a short timescale, must be huge, mustn't they? I have to say, that I thought Zak the runner was absolutely genuine and truthful, but perhaps we'll have to re-assess him now. Or else he's just very unlucky,' he added.

'It's possible, though, Sarge,' said Sharon, having recovered her composure, 'that the second car is nothing to do with the Wilkinson murder. Maybe it was just some joyriders larking about in a stolen car, and it got out of hand.'

'True,' replied Clive, 'and you're right, coincidences *do* occasionally happen. But let's keep open minds, eh?'

* * *

They drove past the weir and along the road with the river not far below them on the left. They came to the village where Zak Lewis lived, turned left over the bridge and through the main street. It wasn't difficult to find the woods and the burnt-out car. Blue and white crime-scene tape cordoned off a large area and officers in white overalls were meticulously searching the scene.

Several villagers had come to see what was going on, including young boys on muddy bicycles. Officers were trying to keep them all at bay, explaining that evidence there must not be compromised. Some of the boys were trying to distract officers and egg each other on to go closer.

Sharon nudged her boss's arm and said quietly, 'Look over to your right, Sarge. No wonder she didn't answer her front door.'

Clive glanced over, and there stood Lucy Flynn, engrossed in all that was happening.

Thirty-Nine

Mike had now been away for four weeks, and Joanna had heard from him only once, and that had been a card enclosing an advertisement for a potential job for her up in the north of England.

So what sort of message is that supposed to give me? she asked herself, disconsolately. *I've obviously been deluding myself, and now I feel like a complete idiot!*

That morning she'd received an email in response to her request for further details about the job. The advert had aroused her curiosity, but the "further details" didn't enlighten her a great deal. There was no indication of who the writer was, or why she or he required a personal assistant/researcher, or what the writer's topics of interest were. Joanna concluded that no specialist expertise in scientific or medical fields could be required. The applicant must be "graduate level" and preferably have post-graduate research experience too. The salary would mean a drop in income for Joanna, but accommodation was provided. Joanna thought she could rent out her apartment and have extra income from that. The job was apparently based in a rural area, where there was only limited public transport. The more Joanna thought about it, the more appealing the job sounded.

What is there to keep me in Blakesford? she reflected. *My current job hit the buffers ages ago, and there's no sign of Tony moving on. My abusive ex-husband is somewhere in this area and doesn't seem able to let go of me, for whatever distorted reasons. My apartment is too small, but I can't afford a larger one. And the only man I'm interested in behaves weirdly, and I don't know where I stand with him. My sister's in Canada, so that just leaves Sophie, but she's content, living in the lap of luxury, and she won't miss me, other than at the gym.*

Joanna soon convinced herself that she should apply for the mysterious job.

A new challenge would be fun, she decided.

The application required only a curriculum vitae and a covering letter initially. So that evening she dug out her most recent CV, which needed updating, and composed an enthusiastic letter expressing her wish to be considered for the job. This activity was accompanied by a couple of glasses of wine.

Should I read it through again in the morning, when I'm sober, or shall I send it off now? she asked herself.

Another thought suddenly flashed through Joanna's mind, and that decided her. She pressed the send key, and the application had gone.

Earlier in the week the police had contacted her again. Steven Hearnden, she was told, had been charged with assault on another woman. He had also admitted assaulting her, Joanna, as shown in the pictures still circulating on social media. The court case would be heard locally, and Joanna fervently hoped that it would be too insignificant to be picked up by the media. But this thought reinforced Joanna's decision to move to a new area.

Now she would just await the outcome of her application.

Forty

'Ms Flynn,' called out DS Meadows, 'could we have a word, please?'

Lucy Flynn was hurrying back to her car, wanting to get her story about the blazing car filed as quickly as possible. She stopped and looked round. The two police officers had almost caught her up.

'I'm in a rush,' she said breathlessly. 'I can't really stop now.'

She set off again towards her car, which was parked in a nearby layby.

'We won't keep you long,' persisted Clive. 'We called at your home earlier, as we think you may be able to help with our investigation.'

By now Lucy had unlocked her car remotely. They were walking towards the front of it, so Sharon discreetly surveyed it for any suspicious marks, but there were no dents or damaged paintwork to be seen.

'Have you just come from Falkenside Prison?' asked Sharon, much to Lucy's surprise. 'It's not far from here, is it?'

'No, I've never been there,' replied Lucy, 'why should I have been?' She was beginning to feel defensive.

'You have an interest in the case of Gregory Mortimer, don't you, so I wondered if you'd been to talk to him,' continued Sharon.

Clive was watching Lucy closely, and he could see her neck becoming red... a sign of anxiety?

'Didn't Marie Wilkinson manage to elicit everything you wanted from him?' asked Clive. 'Didn't he cooperate with her?'

By now Lucy's eyes betrayed real unease, but she tried to appear calm.

'What's this all about?' she asked. 'I haven't heard anything from Marie. She promised to tell me about her visit to Mortimer, but she didn't do it. I've rung her, texted her and been to her home, but I can't get a response from her.'

Clive and Sharon looked at each other, wondering if Lucy was really unaware that Marie was dead. Clive decided to change tack.

'Why are you here today, Ms Flynn? Why is this burning car of interest to you?'

Lucy explained that she had been pursuing a story in the area ('No, nothing to do with Falkenside'), and she'd heard the explosion. So, being a journalist, she decided to investigate and hopefully be the first to report on it. But that wouldn't happen if the police delayed her.

Lucy agreed to go to the police station the following afternoon to speak with the two officers. Clive advised Lucy that Marie had died and that she'd been among the last to have contact with her. The police needed to discuss this with her. Lucy blanched visibly, and her hands were shaking.

'Shall we drive you home, and you can collect the car another time?' asked Sharon.

Lucy shook her head, and said, 'No, I'll wait a few minutes. I'll be fine.'

'See you tomorrow, then,' replied Sharon. 'Drive carefully.'

* * *

Sharon was driving them back to the station.

'What did you make of Lucy then, Sarge?' she asked. 'Did she really not know that Marie's dead?'

'She's a good actress, if she did,' he replied. 'I reckon that was genuine shock, and I suspect she'll spend the evening ferreting around trying to find out what happened to Marie, so that she feels more prepared when she sees us tomorrow. She was taken aback, too, when she realised how much we know about the link with Greg Mortimer.'

'So you think she'll turn up tomorrow, Sarge?' asked Sharon.

'I'm certain she will... anything to get a scoop!' laughed Clive. 'But seriously, Sharon, I spotted you giving her car the once-over, so anything to report on that?'

'Not a scratch or dent anywhere, as far as I could see. And I can't imagine that car shunting Marie's bigger car into the river without significant damage. And it wasn't similar to the suspect car on the CCTV footage, was it?' said Sharon.

'And talking of damage to cars, what are your thoughts on the burnt-out car?' asked Clive.

Sharon cursed as the traffic light at some lengthy roadworks turned red. She'd already worked a long day and missed meeting up with a friend, and she felt hungry and tired. She could do without roadworks as well!

'Well, Sarge,' she said, focusing her thoughts again, 'until forensics have examined it closely, I don't think I can come to any conclusions. As we've said previously, we've got some coincidences, like the location being not far from Marie's accident, and that runner chap finding both vehicles, but until we know the registered owner, and whether or not it's stolen, I'm not sure what I think. It was well-hidden, and I guess some sort of accelerant must have been used, because they made a thorough job of the fire. Someone didn't want much of it left.'

The traffic light at last turned green and Sharon set off again.

'But sometimes,' she continued, 'pyromaniacs wait to see the blaze, don't they? I'm afraid I didn't look to see who else was there, once I'd noticed Lucy Flynn. I just kept my eye on her. How about you, Sarge, did you notice anyone suspicious?'

'I quickly scanned the onlookers but, like you, watched Ms Flynn,' Clive replied, 'but perhaps some house-to-house calls will yield results.'

They drove on, and when they had nearly reached the station, Clive looked across at Sharon and said, 'Ring Richie tomorrow, before Ms Flynn arrives, and see what he has to say about today's car, will you?' He gave her a sideways smile.

Forty-One

Sharon had an update for her boss. She'd taken the call in the carpark and was now hurrying to Clive's office. He looked up wearily from his computer screen when she came in.

'Sorry to disturb you, Sarge,' she began, 'but I've just received a call about Bronwen Smythe.'

'Who?' asked Clive, looking mystified.

'Bronwen Smythe,' repeated Sharon, 'the woman who's made the historical abuse allegations against Gregory Mortimer.'

Clive now appeared interested. He stood up, stretched his back and walked over to the window. He leaned his back against the sill, saying, 'Fire away then, Sharon, I could do with some positive news.'

Sharon explained that a police colleague, in the area of Wales where Bronwen Smythe now lived, had called her to say that Ms Smythe had been to the police station again. She claimed to have additional information to give the police. She stood by her original allegations but had remembered more details.

Sharon outlined the substance of Ms Smythe's allegations, much of which she and Clive already knew. Ms Smythe alleged that Mortimer sexually abused her when she was eleven years old. He'd been a peripatetic music teacher who came to her school once a week to rehearse the school choir, of which young Bronwen was a member. Rehearsals were after school, and Mortimer had given her a lift home a few times, and that's when the abuse happened. None of the other choir members knew about this, she thought. She didn't tell anyone, because she was scared and didn't think she'd be believed. And anyway, it was a secret between her and Mr Mortimer. He'd insisted on that.

'And do our colleagues find her allegations credible?' asked Clive. 'Has she told them why she is disclosing all this now? And has she given the police any other new information?'

Sharon drew breath.

'Well,' she went on, 'it seems that she's now recalled more details, like the names of some other girls in the choir, the type of car that Mortimer had, where the secluded spot was that he parked in when he abused her, which day of the week the choir practice was held, and other facts like that. Our colleagues were surprised by the amount of detail she came up with, which she hadn't remembered at the first disclosure. So they're following it all up. Her manner concerned them too. Her account was very matter-of-fact, lacking much emotion. So, Sarge, do they find her disclosures credible? After this new interview, they seem less certain. What are *your* thoughts?'

'I think we wait until they contact us again, but if they conclude that her allegations wouldn't stand up in court, and there should be no prosecution, then Mortimer will be one very relieved man,' said Clive.

'But why would she invent such a story?' asked Sharon. 'There must surely be some connection between her and Mortimer, even if the allegations are untrue, mustn't there? I know that he tried to assure us, when we went to Falkenside, that her allegations are complete fabrication, so what's the link?'

Clive grinned at her. 'And therein lies the crux of good detective work, Sharon… find the missing links. So get to it!' He laughed, and Sharon couldn't help but join in.

'Just before you go, though,' said Clive, looking more serious, 'you should know that Mortimer is out. He's in a "safe house" away from here. There were anonymous threats made against him, both while he was in prison and regarding his safety in the community, which were sufficiently plausible to warrant protective action. So he's not as easily accessible as he was.'

'Well,' replied Sharon, 'I hope that's the case, if someone's intent on harming him.'

Clive hadn't viewed the situation in quite that way.

How long will it take, he asked himself, *for Sharon to become as cynical as me?*

'And don't forget we're seeing Lucy Flynn this afternoon,' he called out, as Sharon left the office. She nodded.

* * *

'Thanks for coming in, Ms Flynn,' said Clive.

Lucy sat opposite Sharon and Clive, across the table.

'Are you feeling OK now, after the shock of hearing about Marie Wilkinson?' asked Sharon.

'It certainly was a shock,' replied Lucy. 'What happened? I feel awful for cursing her for not contacting me.' Lucy looked down at her hands in her lap.

'So, when did you last hear from her?' asked Clive.

Lucy held her head up and looked him straight in the eye.

'It was a text from Marie, and I'm sorry, but I forgot about it when I spoke to you yesterday. I can show you,' and she took her phone out of her jacket pocket. She found it and read out, "Seen GM. Will send report tomorrow. Adult victim is Bronwen Smythe. M."

Lucy turned her phone round and showed the text to the officers. Clive nodded.

'After that, I didn't hear anything, and no report arrived...

and now I know why. Poor Marie,' concluded Lucy, looking on the verge of tears.

'So, how did you and Marie know each other, and why did she go to Falkenside?' asked Sharon, immediately regretting that she'd asked two questions in one. But Lucy was willing to answer each.

'We were both at Gregory Mortimer's trial,' she said. 'I was in the Press seats and Marie was in the public gallery. I nobbled her afterwards, outside the court, because I got the impression that she was as surprised by the verdict as I was. She didn't want anything to do with me to start with, but we met later, and eventually she agreed to visit Mortimer in prison, if he would talk to her. We were both concerned about a possible miscarriage of justice, and that's a topic I've been researching for some time. I asked Marie to go, rather than me, in case he recognised me as a reporter from the court. I hoped he would open up more to her. Marie's interest in the case arose from her having been the girl's teacher in the past, and it didn't all add up for her.'

'Oh hell,' she added, with a gasp of horror, 'he won't know that his visitor has died, will he?'

'Don't worry, Ms Flynn, leave that to us,' said Clive.

Lucy put her phone back in her pocket.

'You told us yesterday,' said Sharon, 'that you happened to be in the neighbourhood when you heard the car explode in the woods, and you went to investigate. Do you mind telling us what you were doing there? You were very near to where Marie died, weren't you?'

Lucy looked shocked, and the colour drained from her face.

'The truth is,' she began, 'that I was visiting someone in the village close by, and I left in a hurry when I heard the noise. I… I thought there might be a story in it.'

Sharon and Clive were thinking about what Lucy had told them, when Clive broke the silence.

'Ms Flynn, have you had reason to hire a car recently, or borrow one?' he asked quietly.

With an expression of surprise on her face, Lucy immediately replied, 'No, why would I? I've got a perfectly good car, small but nippy. Why do you ask?'

'Sometimes people need another car if theirs is in for servicing, or something like that,' said Clive, deciding to change tack. 'So, did you manage to file a report on the blazing car? It was quite spectacular, wasn't it?'

'No,' said Lucy, 'I was too shaken up by Marie's death. I still can't believe it. Are you thinking that it was linked to her visit to Falkenside? I couldn't sleep last night for wondering if there was a link, and that something might happen to me too. Or was it a ghastly accident, with nothing sinister behind it?'

'We're working on the answers to those questions,' said Sharon. 'Is there anything else you want to tell us?'

Lucy shook her head. 'But I'll call you, if I think of anything.'

* * *

Clive went to the coffee machine, while Sharon escorted Lucy back to the reception area and thanked her for coming in.

'How useful was that?' asked Clive, as he handed a cup of coffee to Sharon.

'Well, two things stand out for me,' replied Sharon, after a sip of coffee. 'Firstly, I suspect that she's busily searching out information about Bronwen Smythe, as I don't think she'll let her interest in Mortimer wane, even without Marie's report. And I think, Sarge, that we should pressurise the tech team to give us all the info from Marie's laptop and phone as soon as possible.'

Clive nodded.

'And secondly, I'd like to know who Lucy was visiting yesterday when she heard the explosion. I just had the impression that she didn't want us to probe that. An illicit rendezvous, perhaps?' speculated Sharon, with a grin.

Clive laughed. 'Hmm, you could well be right. But don't let's go there at the moment, eh?'

Forty-Two

Gerry and Penny Thorncroft were sitting in the plush surroundings of The White Horse hotel and restaurant in Snaysby. They were having a champagne celebration. Not only was it their thirtieth wedding anniversary, but they had also completed the sale of Hotheby Farmhouse that afternoon.

Things don't get much better than this, do they? thought Penny contentedly.

'A penny for your thoughts, Pen,' said Gerry, looking lovingly at his wife, 'and then we'll toast the next thirty years!'

'I was just thinking how lucky we are,' she replied. 'I certainly didn't envisage all this thirty years ago. We were so happy then with our first little flat, and you setting out on your police career, and I was a lowly clerk at the local council. And look at us now! We've got a beautiful house, well, some of it is beautiful, idyllic surroundings, and Carruthers! Oh yes, we've got Mrs T too, mustn't forget her!'

'Hmm…' agreed Gerry, topping up Penny's champagne glass and sharing her sentiments. 'But moving here is best, even if we won't now be lord and lady of a huge house! Renovating that place would've taken us forever, and I'm happy enough in Ivy House. The sale has given us money, but also time.'

'But you'll soon be expanding your empire into a luxury

caravan site, as well as the holiday cottages, so we're not going to be idle!' laughed Penny.

'You and I were not designed to be idle,' said Gerry. 'So, let's raise a glass to the next thirty years!'

They clinked their glasses.

* * *

While at the solicitors' office that afternoon, Gerry had asked what the buyers' plans were for Hotheby Farmhouse. He knew it was none of his business, but he decided to ask anyway.

Apparently, the barn was to be completely renovated and transformed into a high-spec home, screened from the farmhouse, with parking and a small, landscaped garden. The farmhouse itself had restrictions, as Gerry knew, on what structural alterations could be done. So, the emphasis was to be on renovation only on the ground-floor. The back extension, on the first-floor, was to become a granny-annexe, a self-contained small flat.

Gerry and Penny had listened with interest. They were pleased to think that Hotheby Farmhouse was going to be a family home. What a lovely environment to grow up in! Penny wondered, though, whether the barn might become a holiday-let, in competition with their cottages. But Gerry didn't envisage that a high-spec barn conversion would attract the same clientele as their humble little cottages.

'Well,' he said, 'it'll be interesting to see how long all that work takes. And I hope we can have a Mrs Thwaites-style grand tour before the new owners move in!'

Forty-Three

The full four weeks had now passed, and Joanna had heard nothing more from Mike since his card. She felt thoroughly dispirited.

A few days later, though, she received a letter inviting her for a job interview. She hadn't really expected that her slapdash application for the unusual job would result in an interview. She wished that she could contact Mike to tell him the exciting news, but she couldn't. The interview was scheduled for two weeks hence, so perhaps they'd have met up again by then, she hoped.

Sitting in the train on her way to the central London hotel, where the interview was to take place, Joanna thought wistfully about her last train journey. Mike had scrambled clumsily into the slowly moving train as it drew out of the station, his foot landing heavily on hers. She smiled to herself.

Well, she told herself, while looking out of the train window at the towering blocks of flats as they approached London, *it was great while it lasted, but my hopes were obviously far too high. And I can't cope with being left dangling all the time.*

She sighed and decided to think about the impending interview, reminding herself that this might be a welcome escape from the other unsatisfactory parts of her life, too.

* * *

The interview lasted an hour. It was conducted by a man and a woman from a London agency, on behalf of their client, Simon Northam. They disclosed little about Mr Northam, but Joanna decided that she could look him up on the internet later and find out about his research interests, now that she knew his name.

It wasn't until Joanna had left the hotel and was sitting in a station café, waiting for her train home, that she realised just how much of the interview had focused on her as a person, rather than on her skills. There had been questions about her past research experience and knowledge of research techniques, which she'd hopefully bluffed her way through, but the interviewers deftly probed Joanna's views on lone working. The position would be a fairly isolated one, they explained. Joanna had honestly admitted to some reservations about this, as it would be a new experience for her.

Well, she thought, as she sat in the train returning home, *now I have two weeks of waiting to find out if they've recommended me to this chap Northam. I wish I'd met him… I really don't need another elusive man in my life!*

* * *

On Friday evening Joanna's favourite television programme was interrupted by the sound of the intercom buzzer. She answered it, hoping it might be Mike, and dreading that it might be Steve. It was neither.

'DC Don Jackson, Ms Hearnden, may I come up and have a word with you?'

Joanna's heart sank. *Now what?* she wondered.

'Yes, of course,' replied Joanna politely, and she buzzed the police officer in. She quickly pressed the record button on the remote control and switched the television off.

'Apologies for disturbing you, Ms Hearnden,' began DC Jackson, sitting down on Joanna's settee, 'but there are one or two things I want to inform you of, in respect of the assault on you by Steven Hearnden.'

Joanna listened as the officer explained that Mr Hearnden had been charged with assault on another woman, at the home they had been sharing. Joanna tried not to betray her surprise. He would appear in court next week, when a "Guilty" plea was anticipated. His admission of the assault on her, Joanna, would be taken into consideration when he was sentenced. DC Jackson asked if she would like to talk to a victim liaison officer, but Joanna declined.

She had begun to panic, though.

Was DC Jackson wanting her to attend the hearing? To come face to face with Steve? She'd told the police before that she didn't want to press charges against him.

The police officer assured her that this visit was just to update her on the situation.

But when DC Jackson left, Joanna had concerns about how Steve would react to being publicly labelled as a domestic abuser. Would she be at risk again?

* * *

After their workout at the gym the following morning, Joanna told Sophie about her visit from the police. She'd had an email exchange with her sister, Zoe, late the previous evening, so she'd worked through her initial emotions about it. And Joanna wanted Sophie to hear about Steve's court appearance from her, rather than via the golf club's grapevine.

Sophie seemed surprised that Joanna had no intention of attending the court hearing.

'I'll come along with you, as moral support, if you'd like me to,' Sophie offered, but Joanna was adamant that she would stay away.

'So, do you know who this other woman is?' asked Sophie.

Joanna shook her head and said nothing.

That'll be the aspect of all this that the club members will be most interested in, she surmised. *Come to think of it, Jane Denton, or whatever her name really is, said that she'd been a victim of domestic violence, so I wonder if it's her.*

Sophie decided to change the subject. It was clear that Joanna had said all she intended to on the subject of Steve.

'Any word from Mike yet?' she asked tentatively.

The doleful expression on Joanna's face gave Sophie her answer.

Forty-Four

DS Clive Meadows came into the office just as Sharon was finishing a long phone call. He looked harassed and made straight for the drawer where he kept his stash of chocolate biscuits. Sharon had a lot to tell him, but she decided to wait a few minutes, until her boss seemed calmer.

'Well,' began Clive, a tone of annoyance in his voice, 'let's just say that DCI Couzens was less than complimentary about our progress.' He thumped his fist on the desk in frustration. 'I won't give you his exact words, as I don't use language like that to colleagues. But the gist of what he said was this… we've got an unsolved murder of a woman who'd just been visiting a convicted paedophile in prison, who himself faces more abuse allegations, a suspicious burnt-out car nearby, and a young Miss Marple of a newspaper reporter sniffing around, so what the hell are we doing about it?'

'Didn't he mention the fact that Mortimer is now a free man?' asked Sharon, laughing. 'He surely didn't forget that little nugget, did he?'

Clive choked on his biscuit as he sniggered at Sharon's response. She had a knack of keeping difficulties in proportion, and he appreciated it.

'Well,' said Sharon, 'to cheer you up, I've just had a long call with our colleagues in Wales about Bronwen Smythe, which may give us some new leads.'

'Great,' said Clive, 'but I need a coffee first. What about you?'

Sharon nodded and stood up to go and fetch them, but Clive motioned to her to stay in her seat.

* * *

A few minutes later Clive returned with two coffees and some sugar-coated doughnuts.

'Right, Sharon, fire away,' he said, and took a large mouthful of doughnut sending a cascade of white sugar down his shirt. 'Sod it,' he muttered.

'Well, Sarge,' she began, 'Bronwen Smythe seems to move around a lot and hasn't actually been in their part of Wales for very long. So they've been liaising with other forces who've had more contact with her. The bottom line is that she's a seasoned drug-user who's been in and out of various rehab facilities. She has spells of being drug-free, when she's law-abiding and can hold down a job, but if something triggers her addiction, she's back in trouble again. She has convictions going back years, but they're all minor, mainly thefts from shops.'

Sharon drank some coffee.

'So are they thinking that she's clean of drugs nowadays, or does she have a different source of income?' asked Clive. 'If she had a chaotic childhood,' he continued pensively, 'but of course we don't actually know that, it's possible that she was abused then, I suppose, but why disclose it now?'

'She could be motivated by the hope of financial compensation, perhaps,' speculated Sharon.

She drank some more coffee and took a bite of doughnut.

'Right, Sharon, what else did our Welsh colleagues tell you?' asked Clive.

'Well, Sarge, it seems that she did actually go to the school where Mortimer sometimes worked, but they're not sure how long for. The school records seem to be incomplete about that. But the names of the other girls she mentioned are genuine, too. So that's all being followed up.'

Sharon paused, while she consulted the scribbled notes she'd made during the phone call.

'Oh yes,' she continued, 'this bit's interesting… the last rehab Bronwen went to was over in Sharnden, only forty or so miles from here, and that was two years ago. It was following a court order for an offence of drug-driving. I haven't known of many of those, Sarge, have you?'

There was no response from Clive.

'Anyway,' continued Sharon, 'that's her latest recorded conviction.'

'Start another wallchart please, Sharon,' said Clive, 'with Bronwen at the centre. I want to visualise the various links.'

Sharon stood up and methodically compiled a chart of people, places and timelines, highlighting their connections with Bronwen.

'Did our colleagues comment on whether they believe that Bronwen was drug-free at the time of first making the allegations against Mortimer, and if she's clean now?' asked Clive.

'Well,' replied Sharon, 'her drug history has only emerged since she made the allegations and her background has been investigated, so I would think, and sorry, boss, but this is only conjecture, that she gave them no reason to suspect drug-use. But I'll get back to them on that.'

The phone rang and Sharon answered it.

'Hello, Sharon, it's Richie from forensics. I've some progress for you, if you could come over here for a wee while,' he said. 'It's about the burnt-out car.'

Sharon gave her boss a thumbs-up and told Richie that she'd come to his office straightaway.

'That was Richie,' she told Clive, 'there are developments on the burnt-out car.'

'You'd better get over there, then,' said Clive with a grin.

Forty-Five

The two new caravans were now in situ in the paddock a hundred yards beyond Mrs Thwaites' cottage. Some local builders had laid the concrete bases in readiness for them, and the necessary amenities were in place, too. Sam Thwaites and Gerry had planted shrubs and small trees to give the potential holidaymakers some shelter and privacy. And the potholes in the track leading to the paddock had been filled in.

'It all looks pretty good, don't you think?' asked Gerry.

Sam beamed with pleasure and agreed. He liked working for Gerry, who was always appreciative, and the extra money certainly came in handy. He'd been concerned that Gerry might not need him once the two holiday cottages had been finished, but then the work on the caravan site had come along. And now Sam was responsible for keeping the cottages and the caravan site in good order, together with the land around them. Sam was so pleased that his aunt had recommended him to Mr Thorncroft.

'Now we have to hope for lots of bookings,' said Gerry, 'but with these beautiful views and smart caravans, who could resist a holiday here?'

He chuckled contentedly.

* * *

That afternoon Gerry and Penny decided to take Carruthers for a walk to Little Cragworth. They both wanted to see how the work on Hotheby Farmhouse was progressing, just out of curiosity.

Immediately after the sale was completed, the buyers had started on the renovation of both the farmhouse and the barn. Gerry and Penny were surprised at the speed with which the work was being done. They hadn't met the owners yet, but they'd spoken occasionally with the site foreman, who showed them the plans for the barn.

Carruthers ambled along behind them, as Gerry and Penny walked up the track which led from the lane to one side of the barn. Safety barriers had been erected at the end of the track, but even from there they could see the extent of the renovation. The shell of the barn had been strengthened, so that the exterior could remain unchanged, except for a new, large opening at one end, at first-floor level.

'Presumably that's for the massive window we saw on the plans,' said Penny, 'and the views from it will be spectacular. It faces roughly west,' she continued, 'so just imagine the sunsets!'

Gerry held his wife's hand and smiled.

'You're not regretting that we sold this place, are you?' he asked.

'Not really,' she replied, with a rueful smile, 'it's been quite enough getting Ivy House and the holiday-let business sorted out. And the money these people are investing in all this would be way beyond our means. No, I hope they enjoy their new home. But do you think they'll lure Mrs Thwaites away from us... and Sam?'

Gerry guffawed.

'I certainly hope not,' he said. 'We'd have to start cooking for ourselves again!'

As they couldn't walk any further up the track, they called Carruthers, who was lying patiently on a sunny patch of grass nearby, and set off down the hill to Little Cragworth.

* * *

The following morning a police car drew up in front of Ivy House. Penny was outside, planting geraniums and trailing lobelia in the window boxes. The two officers got out of their car and greeted her cheerfully.

'Good morning, Mrs Thorncroft,' said the officer who'd been driving. 'I'm PC Craig Asher and this is PC Chris Caldecote. Is Mr Thorncroft about?'

Penny was taken by surprise, and asked, 'Is something wrong?'

'Don't worry,' said PC Caldecote, 'this is just a courtesy call, to introduce ourselves. Is Mr Thorncroft here?'

Gerry appeared from behind the house, where he was repairing some fencing. He'd heard the car arrive.

The officers repeated their introductions and explained that there'd been a spate of thefts from outbuildings in the area, so they were visiting properties which might be targeted.

'We're increasing patrols around the area,' said PC Caldecote, 'so you may see us around. We'll leave you a leaflet about rural security, and there's a phone number on it, if you have any concerns. We're off to Hotheby Farmhouse now, as we've noticed there's a lot of work going on, and they could be vulnerable to thefts overnight.'

'Nice to have met you,' he added, and the two officers drove off.

'Well,' said Gerry, 'they must have more resources than we used to have! Good to have the warning, though. And it reminds me that we must install proper security systems here. We discussed it ages ago, but I think we now need to take action. We'll soon be having strangers staying on our property, so we can't be too careful!'

'Oh Gerry,' replied Penny, looking alarmed, 'you're not suggesting that our holidaymakers will pinch the family silver, are you?'

Gerry laughed, and gave his wife a reassuring hug.

'I certainly hope they won't… just the odd teaspoon perhaps, by mistake! But the officers do make a serious point about ensuring security. I'll go into Snaysby tomorrow and talk to the home security company in the High Street. I'll see what they can suggest.'

'Good idea,' said Penny, 'and while you're there, you could go to the wine shop. Our stocks are getting low!'

Forty-Six

Sharon listened attentively as Richie McCleod talked her through the meticulous forensic examination of the burnt-out car. Although she didn't understand all the science involved, she was excited by their findings. Richie explained that there was definitive evidence that paint samples from the burnt-out car exactly matched those from the car found in the river by the weir. And, equally importantly, said Richie, there was evidence that the damage to the front of the burnt-out car coincided with that on the rear of the submerged car.

'So, I would certainly conclude,' said Richie, smiling at Sharon, 'that there was an impact between the two cars at some stage.'

'But did that impact cause Marie Wilkinson's car to end up in the river?' asked Sharon, fearing that this would be disputed by lawyers.

'I thought you might wonder that,' continued Richie, 'and I have more for you. Even though the weather was more than inclement on the day the car slid down into the river, there were sufficient tyre-marks at the scene to identify two distinct sets. Take a look at these photos...'

Richie showed Sharon the pictures on his laptop. She craned forwards to get a closer view and was conscious of Richie's face close to hers. She immediately remonstrated silently with herself, telling herself not to be so childish, as he was just trying to help her.

'This shows where the first car came off the road and slid down the bank into the swollen river. These tyre-marks are a definite match with the submerged car. But if you look at this picture, you'll see another tyre-mark showing that a different car came off the road surface, just a tyre's width, and then, within a metre or two, re-joined the tarmac. Then the next picture shows the muddy tyre-mark and the angle at which it came back onto the road,' said Richie.

'But in view of the second car having been set on fire, can we be sure that the tyre-marks are a match with it?' asked Sharon.

'Trust me on that one… we have our ways and means,' said Richie, chuckling softly. 'Whoever set the car ablaze may have made a spectacular job of it, but it wasn't as thorough as he'd have liked it to be! And the fire service did a good job, too.'

That seemed to be the end of Richie's feedback, so Sharon smiled and thanked him for sharing the forensic findings.

'So, do you know the owner of the second car yet?' he asked, as she stood up to leave.

'We're still working on it,' answered Sharon. 'As we speak, various bits of CCTV footage are being scrutinised, which we hope will clarify that.'

'Well,' said Richie, 'keep me posted, and I'll help in any way I can.'

Sharon was walking towards his office door, when Richie said diffidently, 'Sharon, I don't wish to sound presumptuous, but would you care to go for a meal with me sometime?'

Sharon could hardly believe her ears, but, trying to hide her elation, she replied, 'I'd love to, Richie, thank you.'

'Would next weekend suit you?' he asked, and Sharon nodded. Richie smiled at her.

* * *

Clive looked up from his computer screen as Sharon came into the office.

'Well,' he said, 'you look pleased with yourself. Good news?'

Sharon could scarcely conceal her happiness, so she immediately told her boss succinctly about the forensics results, hoping that would camouflage her feelings. Clive was pleased with the progress, too.

'Tina Dawson has been watching hours and hours of CCTV footage for us, and we have some interesting findings from her as well,' he said. 'We've got the number and owner's name of the burnt-out car. It was stolen two months before the incident and reported to the police by the owner. There's no reason to believe that he was involved in its subsequent use. So that makes things more complicated. Who stole it, and where's it been in the meantime?'

Sharon sighed. Detective work constantly seemed to be two steps forward and one back, so she reminded herself to focus on the forward steps.

'I had a thought, though,' continued Clive, 'and asked Tina to follow it up. How long had the second car been following Marie Wilkinson? We pick it up at the petrol station, but had it actually been tailing her right from Falkenside? So one of Tina's colleagues has been to the prison to view their relevant footage, and my hunch was right. It shows Marie Wilkinson driving out of the prison visitors' carpark, and not long afterwards our suspect car follows her. There were no images of the driver, unfortunately, but the registration plates tally. So, I've spoken to the security manager at Falkenside, and he's agreed to review their records of the day to try and identify the driver. He thought it would be a long shot, though.'

'But we now have evidence of the car, which forensics show as having shunted Marie's car, tailing her from the prison. So that points to intent, doesn't it, Sarge?' asked Sharon.

'But *why* did the driver intend to hurt or kill Marie, if that theory is correct?' mused Clive. 'Good progress today, but still a long way to go.'

Hmm... thought Sharon cheerfully, *more progress than you realise, Sarge!*

Forty-Seven

Cheryl answered the phone on the library's front desk. She beckoned to Joanna, who was talking to a member of the public close-by. Joanna saw Cheryl give her a mischievous wink as she handed her the phone.

'Hi Jo,' said Mike's voice, 'how are you?'

Joanna had almost given up all hope of hearing from him again. She'd resolved to take the new job, if offered it, and make a completely fresh start. She would park both Steve and Mike firmly in the past. But, once again, Mike had surprised her and unsettled her equilibrium.

'Hi Mike,' she said, trying to sound calm, 'it's been a long time.'

'Yes, it has, and I'm so sorry,' he replied.

Joanna raised her eyebrows. *Here we go again, more apologies,* she thought, but waited for him to say more.

'I've been away working, and I've just been unable to contact you,' Mike continued, 'so can I make it up to you? How about dinner on Friday evening? I want to hear how everything's going for you.'

Joanna had been caught off guard by his phone call and reacted spontaneously.

'OK,' she replied, 'what time?'

'That's great,' said Mike enthusiastically. 'I'll call for you at seven-thirty. Look forward to it.' With that, he hung up.

Cheryl looked across, giving her a knowing smile.

Joanna was cross with herself for succumbing so easily to Mike's charms. She decided that Friday evening would be her last with this totally impossible man!

* * *

On the way home Joanna bought an Indian take-away dinner, including an enormous Peshwari naan. She couldn't be bothered to cook, but she hadn't had any lunch and felt ravenous. She had a partially-drunk bottle of white wine in the fridge, so she decided to finish that off with the meal. Joanna felt content.

She picked up her post and threw it on the table. Then she settled down to enjoy her meal, whilst watching a film.

Later on, she looked through her post and found an envelope with the recruitment agency's logo in one corner. She ripped it open, expecting to read that she'd been rejected for the strange job. But, on the contrary, the agency was saying how impressed they had been with her at interview, and that they'd recommended her for the post to Mr Northam. He wished to follow their recommendation and hoped that she would accept the job. He sent his regrets that they hadn't yet met in person but hoped that wouldn't influence Ms Hearnden's decision.

The letter then gave details of the location of the job, the accommodation which went with it, the salary, and so on. It was regretted, though, that the starting date could be no sooner than three months hence, as Mr Northam would be unavailable until then. They requested that Ms Hearnden let them know when it would be convenient for her to commence after that, if she wished to take the job.

Well, well, thought Joanna, *it continues to be unorthodox and mysterious, but I've convinced myself that I want a fresh start, and here's a brilliant opportunity! Do I want to accept the job? Of course, I do! I'll email Zoe straightaway and tell her I'm going for it!*

She pressed the send key, and wondered how long it would take Zoe to respond.

Telling Sophie, though, had greater ramifications. Did she want to risk Steve hearing that she would be moving away? She decided to leave it until nearer the time.

And then there was Mike, whom she would be seeing on Friday. He'd been the person who found the job advert, and he was sure to ask her about it. If she was resolved to have no further contact with him, did he need to know? Perhaps she could just say that she still awaited the outcome of the interview. But lying convincingly didn't come easily to Joanna.

One thought did amuse her, though, and that was the prospect of Tony Stoneman's reaction to her resignation from the library!

Forty-Eight

Joanna was surprised by her sister's email. She'd anticipated words of caution from Zoe, but her sister seemed enthusiastic about the proposed move.

'You've always been more adventurous than I have,' she wrote, 'so go for it! If it goes pear-shaped, you can always get another job with your qualifications. You need to put distance between yourself and Steve, and this strange new bloke. If you rent your flat out, you'll have security there for the future. Why don't you put your notice in, stay at work for two more months, and then come over here for a few weeks? It would be great to see you, and the kids would love it.'

Joanna had doubts about Zoe's final claim, as Armand and Delphine sounded fairly independent now, and she thought that a visit from an aunt, whom they hardly knew, wouldn't interest them. But a seed had been sown in Joanna's mind, and another opportunity was opening up. She warmed to the idea of a trip to Canada and some time with Zoe.

* * *

Joanna spent the next couple of evenings researching how best to rent out her apartment. She eventually decided that she would put it in an agency's hands and let them deal with everything. She would just have to pack up anything she intended to put into storage, until she had seen her new home.

She also searched online for cheap flights to Montreal, none of which seemed cheap to Joanna. And the longer she left her choice, the more expensive the flights became, or so it appeared.

But you can afford it, she told herself, *and a chance like this won't come along again in a hurry.*

She emailed Zoe again, before she could change her mind, to say that she would be coming to Canada.

That just left two letters to write, the first to accept the job with a starting date in three months, and the other to submit her resignation from her job at the library.

* * *

Friday evening arrived, and Mike was punctual as usual. He greeted Joanna with the smile which had so attracted her initially, and a fleeting kiss on the cheek.

'I've found a restaurant with good reviews in a different village, so I hope you'll approve. And, with a bit of luck, Sophie and her family won't be there!' said Mike, walking with Joanna to his car which was parked nearby.

Joanna felt apprehensive. Would she be able to carry through her resolve to end this unsatisfactory relationship? She enjoyed Mike's company so much, but she just couldn't cope with the lack of openness and mysterious disappearances. She'd spent many hours thinking about the pros and cons, and now she had to be strong.

The pub, which Mike had chosen, proved to be one that Joanna had eaten at with Steve several times, but she kept quiet about this. She just prayed that Steve wouldn't appear there this evening, with another woman.

'So how have things been with you, Jo?' asked Mike, while they were waiting for their meals. 'Any progress with the job-hunting?'

Well, thought Joanna, *nothing like getting straight to the point! So, in for a penny...* She took a deep breath.

'Actually,' she replied, 'I responded to the job advert you sent me, and I got it! I start in three months.'

Mike was watching her closely, and, after a moment's hesitation, he said, 'Well done, Jo, that's brilliant. You must be really pleased with yourself. Tell me all about it.'

But Joanna didn't want to talk about the job. She had other things to say to Mike, and if he was not to be part of her new life, away from Blakesford, she decided that he didn't need to know the details of it. In the past he'd shown an uncanny capacity for seeking her out, anyway.

'I have some more exciting news, too,' she said. 'I'm off to Canada soon, to stay with my sister.'

'Good for you,' began Mike, smiling and patting her hand. 'You certainly haven't been letting the grass grow under your feet, have you? The future seems to be panning out well for you, doesn't it? That's great!'

'Thanks,' said Joanna. 'I'm certainly looking forward to a fresh start, and to being with Zoe.'

'You deserve it all, Jo,' replied Mike warmly.

Joanna was in a quandary. Mike seemed genuinely pleased for her, and unfazed by no mention of himself in her plans. Did he assume that their friendship would continue as now? Or did he accept that he would no longer be part of her life? Joanna just couldn't read him, but that had always been the case.

Their meals arrived, and they ate in silence for a while.

'Please tell me I'm wrong, Jo,' said Mike, looking into her eyes, 'but I'm picking up that your future life has no place for me... is that right?'

Joanna fought back her tears, thinking how best to respond. She had planned beforehand what to say to Mike, but now the time had arrived, she couldn't find the right words.

Mike reached across and gently held Joanna's hand.

'I'll take that to mean "yes", then,' he said softly. 'Believe me, I'm grateful that you've put up with me for this long. I wish that circumstances were different, and perhaps, one day, they will be. I've grown very fond of you, Jo.'

Joanna was distraught. This was the last time she'd see Mike. There'd been no drama, just quiet acceptance of the situation.

Forty-Nine

With Charlie Johnson's encouragement, Greg applied for several jobs in Mulchester, but his lack of recent employment always seemed to count against him.

'I really don't mind what sort of work I do,' he insisted to Charlie. 'I'll try my hand at anything. I just want to spend my time usefully and have some financial independence.'

Charlie had seen similar problems many times before. She knew how difficult it was for released prisoners, especially when, like Greg, the disclosure of imprisonment for sex offences often closed doors. But Greg was determined, and he pursued any suggestions she made. Charlie knew the local area and where potential jobs might be.

Eventually Greg was offered a probationary period working in a warehouse on the opposite side of Mulchester from where he lived. Charlie managed to find a second-hand bike for Greg, to save on transport costs, and he agreed to pay for it by weekly instalments. It wouldn't take many weeks. Charlie had confidence that Greg would both abide by this agreement and make the most of his job.

* * *

Much to Greg's relief, his work in the warehouse required that he was constantly busy. He found it monotonous, but it was physically strenuous, so he was always tired by the time he'd cycled home each evening. The only opportunity for any social interaction with the other workers was at lunchtime, and then the main topic of conversation was sport. The turnover of staff at the warehouse was fast, and no one was interested in what jobs people had previously had. So Greg was accepted at face value, like all the others, and no difficult questions were asked.

He settled into a routine of going to work six days a week, and to Charlie's office one evening per week. At the end of his third week, with his wages in his pocket, Greg stopped at the local fish and chip shop. The enticing smell had wafted out of the shop each evening as he cycled past, so on this evening he decided to treat himself.

This may not mean much to most people, but for me it's another step back to normality, he told himself, putting his wrapped fish and chips into his rucksack. *And I'm going to enjoy it.*

Back at the flat, Greg sat on his settee eating his fish and chips out of their paper on his lap, and a can of beer out of the fridge was on the floor beside him. He listened to music on his phone.

Life's OK for now, he thought, *but soon I'll have to start thinking about the longer term, as Charlie has said. This job's an adequate stopgap, but I'm capable of much more, and all my musical training is wasted at the moment. But teaching children will never be an option again, and I've got to accept that. It's desperately unjust, but I'm stuck with it. The only person who shared my sense of injustice has died in an accident, or that's what the police have told me. I wonder if her reporter friend will pursue it... but she'll never be told where I am.*

Greg finished off his fish and chips, scrunched up the wrapping paper and put it in the kitchen bin. He'd really enjoyed the meal, but he wondered why it had needed four or five sheets of paper to wrap it.

He picked up his phone, got another beer out of the fridge

and went into the bedroom, where he lay on his bed, listening to music. The light was fading outside, and Greg felt more at peace than he had for years.

* * *

He must have fallen asleep, as he didn't hear the intruder. Nor was he aware of a figure bending over him, with a weapon raised above his head. There was a muffled thud, and Greg lay silent and still.

The kitchen bin, full of crumpled fish and chip paper, was moved to one corner of Greg's bed, close to the covers. Before the intruder left, some fuel was poured into the bin, and then it was lit.

* * *

A few minutes later, a neighbour happened to be arriving home and noticed the flames in Greg's flat. She immediately called the emergency services and waited outside on the pavement, fearful of going any closer. The woman was very relieved when she heard the sirens approaching. She told a fire officer that a man lived alone in the burning flat, but she didn't know his name.

Fifty

Sharon was finishing a long telephone conversation when Clive came into the office. He knew that she'd been having difficulty contacting Charlie Johnson, Gregory Mortimer's community supervisor. They'd received intelligence this morning that Mortimer had been attacked in his home, and they wanted the details. They were still investigating the historical abuse allegations against him.

'Well, Sarge,' Sharon began, 'if it hadn't been for swift action by a member of the public, we might've had another murder investigation on our hands.'

'You managed to get hold of Mortimer's supervisor then, did you?' asked Clive.

'Yes, eventually,' said Sharon, 'and although she's clearly shocked by it all, she was more than cooperative. Apparently, Mortimer's in an unnamed hospital, or she doesn't know it at least, and in a life-threatening condition. But, as I said, someone rang the emergency services fairly soon after the fire started, and he was rescued alive. From what I was told, we won't be able to interview him for quite a while, though.'

'Did Charlie Johnson have any thoughts about what might've happened, or why?' asked Clive.

'She seemed to feel very guilty about whether or not she could've done more to protect him. He'd been given that accommodation because of prior threats against him, and he was meant to be safe there. He's only been out in the community for a few weeks, so Charlie doesn't know him very well yet. She gave me a couple of names of people who have threatened harm to him, but they're still in prison. From the discussions she's had with Mortimer, she thinks that the person he knew best in Falkenside was a Lifer called Kieran. He apparently watched Mortimer's back when he could. Charlie doesn't know any more about Kieran, though, other than they worked together in the prison library.'

'Has Charlie talked to Mortimer about the historic allegations?' asked Clive.

'Yes, Sarge,' replied Sharon. 'He continues to insist that they are complete fabrication, and he's non-plussed by them. He also continues to deny the offences for which he was sentenced. She has the impression that he's scared of another prison sentence. Apparently he was given a hard time in Falkenside.'

'Anything else from Charlie?'

Sharon continued, 'She told me about his current employment, at a warehouse in Mulchester, but there didn't seem to be any problems there. She said that few ex-prisoners she's supervised have been so determined to find work. She thought he was re-adjusting well to life after prison.'

'Right, Sharon,' said Clive decisively, 'I'll fetch us some coffees, and then we'll sort out a new plan of action and put it to the DCI.'

* * *

An hour later, Clive outlined their strategy to DCI Couzens, and it took only a few minutes to convince him that a visit to HMP Falkenside was justified. There were two main lines of enquiry. The first involved speaking with the head of security about the known threats to Mortimer while he was in prison, and secondly, they wished to view any prison CCTV footage of Mortimer's release. The latter was speculative, but Clive stressed to the DCI how informative CCTV footage was being in the Wilkinson enquiry. Clive also sought the DCI's views on whether they should interview Lifer Kieran, if he would cooperate.

Much to Clive's surprise, the DCI immediately rang Falkenside's head of security, Karl Percival, succinctly explained their requests, and, with profuse thanks, ended the call.

'Right, Clive,' said DCI Couzens, 'you and DC Page are to report to the head of security at four o'clock this afternoon. I'm unlikely to sanction any more visits, so go there well-prepared.'

Clive left the DCI's office thinking, *well, that was more painless than I expected!*

Fifty-One

Joanna and Cheryl were having a lunch-break together in the library's staff kitchen. They'd each had a busy morning and were relieved to sit down for a while.

'One of Darren's friends held a party at the golf club at the weekend, so we went along. I don't know if you want to hear it, but there was a bit of gossip going around about your ex,' began Cheryl. 'Just tell me to shut up, if you'd rather not hear it.'

Joanna wasn't surprised that stories were still circulating. She thought she'd prefer to hear the gossip from Cheryl, who was unlikely to embellish it too much, than from anyone else.

'You might as well tell me,' replied Joanna, 'as I expect that my name was mentioned, wasn't it?'

'Once or twice,' agreed Cheryl, 'but mostly it was about Steve and his court appearance.'

She told Joanna that Steve had apparently been living with a Jade something, possibly Henton or Henson, and that she was a police officer.

'So he was thought to be totally stupid to hit her,' continued Cheryl, 'and she was the person who took the photos of you being assaulted. Apparently, she'd been following him for some reason and then witnessed the incident with you. That backed up her allegation that he can be violent. But he chose the wrong woman to mess with. Sorry Joanna, I don't mean any offence to you.'

Joanna just smiled at Cheryl. She was mentally piecing the picture together. She had obviously misheard Jade's name as she drove away. She'd also mistakenly assumed that Jade was referring to the prison, not the police station, when she'd said that she worked at the local "nick". Joanna felt reassured. At least there was nothing sinister about Jade. It all fitted.

* * *

That afternoon Joanna handed a copy of her resignation letter to Tony Stoneman. She hoped that head office had received the original by post that morning.

Tony's reaction amused Joanna. He tried to quiz her about the new job, as she had put no details of it in her letter. But Joanna disclosed as little as possible, without appearing too secretive.

Tony doesn't need to know the ins and outs, she persuaded herself, *and I'm not interested in his views anyway. He'd highlight all the negatives, like he always does with my ideas, and I don't want to hear them. The move is right for me!*

By now, Joanna had been working with Tony for four years. He'd found her both indispensable and a threat. Joanna's departure would be a testing time for him, but also an opportunity to recruit someone a little less forthright, perhaps more malleable, someone who would appreciate his ideas. But he also knew that he would miss Joanna's ability.

Fifty-Two

'I really wouldn't want to work in there every day,' said Sharon with feeling, as she and her boss walked back to the prison's carpark.

'I tend to agree with you,' replied Clive, 'but we've had a productive visit. We'll talk it through on the way back to the station. But first, I just want to note where the security cameras are which cover the carparks here.'

Sharon walked on, unlocked the car and sat in the driver's seat.

'Right,' said Clive, getting into the passenger seat a few moments later, 'let's go.'

* * *

Neither Clive nor Sharon spoke until they had passed the stretch of river where Marie Wilkinson had drowned in her car. But each was thinking about the events there.

Clive was the first to break the silence.

'The security manager, Karl Percival, had prepared well for our visit, hadn't he? The CCTV footage was exactly what we hoped for. We now have firm evidence that the car leaving Falkenside, immediately after Marie's car, was the same one as seen at the petrol station not long afterwards, which then followed her again.'

Clive paused, and then continued, 'It would be good to know where the car went after following Marie. The next sighting we have is when it was set on fire. But at least our friend, Richie,' Clive cast a quick glance towards Sharon, who ignored him, 'has linked Marie's car and the burnt-out car.'

'We don't yet know, though, who stole that car or was driving it,' Sharon reminded him.

'True,' conceded Clive, 'but the other interesting CCTV was of Mortimer's release from prison. We know from Charlie Johnson that he was collected on the morning of release by Bill Jones, and we've seen that car on the CCTV. Of more relevance is the car which left the prison not long afterwards. It came from the area where staff usually park, and Karl Percival confirmed that it belongs to a prison officer. As he said, though, cars go in and out of the parking areas regularly, so it could just be coincidence. So, Sharon, we need our traffic colleagues to check whether the second car was seen on cameras near Mortimer's home in Mulchester on that day.'

'That would fit with Kieran Mulholland's description of Mortimer's treatment by a particular prison officer. Pity he wouldn't give us a name, but understandable, I suppose,' said Sharon.

'Yes,' agreed Clive, 'but we've got the name of the car's registered owner, anyway. So what did you make of Mulholland?'

Sharon let out a deep sigh, as the lights at a railway crossing flashed red and the barriers descended. They had to wait for a train to pass through.

'Well, Sarge,' she said, 'my first thoughts are that he's a level-headed, intelligent man who is wasting his life. But, of course, I don't know what crimes he committed to warrant his sentence. There's obviously some good in him, though, judging from the way he tried to shield Mortimer. I think he was genuine in that, but perhaps he fooled me. I had the impression too, that he was angry at Mortimer being attacked in the community when he'd managed to survive in prison.'

Sharon was drumming impatiently with her fingers on the steering wheel, as they waited for the train to pass.

'That won't speed the train up, Sharon,' chortled Clive. 'But I agree with you about Mulholland. Whatever people think about paedophiles, he didn't like the treatment Mortimer was handed out in prison. From his account, Mortimer suffered quite a few bruises, and worse. It's probably too risky for Mulholland to grass on a prison officer by name, but at least we know who he was talking about.'

The barriers at the level crossing finally lifted, and they resumed their journey.

'It was helpful too,' said Sharon, 'that Karl Percival had identified the two inmates on Mortimer's Wing who were most likely to have assaulted him. They both have a history of violence against sex offenders, and often end up in the Segregation Unit. But they're both serving long sentences and won't be released for years yet, so I think we can discount them in our current investigations, don't you, Sarge?'

'I agree,' replied Clive. 'We'll see what we can find out about Prison Officer Raynaud and his movements on that day, though, and whether his car has been caught on camera in Mulchester.'

* * *

Back in the office, Clive had a call from Josie, one of the tech team.

'Brilliant,' shouted Clive, giving Sharon a thumbs-up, 'send it all over, please… and thanks, Josie.'

A few minutes later, Clive and Sharon were poring over the transcribed contents of Marie Wilkinson's tablet and phone. Josie had located Marie's history of calls with Lucy Flynn, and the notes which Marie had emailed to herself from the café, not long before she died. They gave a detailed account of her conversation with Gregory Mortimer in Falkenside. The notes had the heading, "Edit before sending to LF".

'There's a real poignancy about these notes, isn't there?' commented Sharon sadly. 'Marie had no idea what was about to befall her, nor that the police would be examining her private notes. It all feels horribly intrusive, but I know we have to do it.'

'I appreciate what you're saying, Sharon,' responded her boss, 'but we have to focus on the job in hand, which is to establish who killed Marie and why, and who attacked Gregory Mortimer and why... and what the link is, if any. We can't bring Marie back, but we'll hopefully bring some form of closure to her nearest and dearest. And we need to prevent any more attacks on Mortimer. We really don't want any more violent incidents to investigate right now, do we?'

Sharon nodded in agreement, silently wishing that she hadn't betrayed her feelings to her boss.

Fifty-Three

The following morning Sharon was rushing into the office, carrying a large mug of freshly-brewed coffee. She'd heard the office phone. As she was lifting the receiver, she spilled steaming coffee over her hand and cursed.

'Oh, sod it,' she exclaimed, trying to put her mug on the desk without spilling any more.

'I hope that's not a comment on my phoning you,' laughed a familiar Scottish voice.

'Oh hell, I'm so sorry, Richie,' replied Sharon, 'I was just cursing my clumsiness. Anyway, it's nice to hear your voice. What can I do for you?'

'Well, we may have made a minor breakthrough, which I hope will interest you. We've been examining the bits of debris gathered up around the incinerated car, fragments which were dispersed in the explosion. And one of my team has found some DNA, which might link to your investigation. Would you like to come over for a chat?' asked Richie.

* * *

Sharon didn't need a second invitation. She hurriedly washed the coffee off her hands and sleeve, and made her way to Richie's office. She hadn't spoken to him since their dinner date at the weekend.

'Thanks for coming over, Sharon,' said Richie. 'I suppose I could have explained everything perfectly well over the phone, but I wanted to see you. I hope you don't mind, but I so enjoyed our time together on Saturday.'

'Me too,' said Sharon, 'and I look forward to the next time. But we're at work now, so don't keep me on tenterhooks. Whose DNA have we got?'

Richie seemed taken aback by Sharon's business-like approach, but he reminded himself that they'd agreed to keep work and their personal lives discreetly separate.

'Well,' said Richie slowly, 'we've actually found two distinct lots of DNA, but we've only found a match for one, so far.'

'OK,' said Sharon impatiently, 'so whose is it?'

'We ran it on the national database several times, just to be sure,' continued Richie, in his customary measured way, 'and it matches a known drug-user, Bronwen Smythe. But we must be careful, Sharon, as this points to a connection between her and the car, but in no way indicates that she was the driver of it. We need to do more work on that. So, does the name Bronwen Smythe mean anything to your investigation?'

'It most certainly does,' replied Sharon, grinning broadly, 'and you're an absolute gem! We'll have to bring her in for a chat.'

Sharon couldn't help herself, flung her arms round Richie and quickly kissed him on the cheek.

'Let me know when you identify the second DNA, please… and thanks again,' she called out as she left his office, eager to tell Clive about the latest development.

Richie watched her go, with amusement and affection.

* * *

There'd been no difficulty finding Bronwen Smythe when the police were initially investigating her allegations against Gregory Mortimer, but now she was being elusive. Clive wondered if she'd reverted to taking drugs, or was in a rehab somewhere.

Further intelligence had been gathered relating to Bronwen's history and the reliability of her allegations. In the DCI's view, it was increasingly unlikely that these would form a credible case to put before a court. There were inconsistencies in her allegations over time, and her versions of events appeared to be rehearsed, rather than spontaneous. Her story would be torn to shreds by a skilled defence team, he thought. But the police were persevering with their enquiries, and Gregory Mortimer remained under suspicion.

Bronwen was now a suspect too, though. The forensic evidence suggested that she was linked to the car which had caused Marie Wilkinson to plunge to her death. Her situation had taken on a new level of seriousness, and the DCI wanted her brought in immediately for questioning.

* * *

The following morning Bronwen was sitting in an interview room opposite DS Meadows and DC Page. She had returned to her home the previous day and been arrested. She looked tired and haggard.

A local lawyer, Evie Trueman, sat with Bronwen throughout her interview, making notes and prompting her client. Her primary advice was to give "No comment" answers. She'd had little time to consider the case.

Bronwen looked stunned as the realisation dawned that she could be facing a charge of murder.

Making abuse allegations against someone is one thing, but taking the rap for a murder is totally out of order, she thought, panicking. *This is all going too far.*

But she couldn't say that to the stranger sitting by her side, and she was very scared of the repercussions.

The interview continued, and Bronwen remained unforthcoming. Eventually it was terminated, and she was taken to a police cell. Bronwen would be given time to think about her situation.

* * *

She slept little that night. She couldn't think clearly, and she desperately craved some drugs. How long would they keep her here? She tossed and turned on her hard bed.

The questioning resumed the following morning, and Bronwen refused to have the lawyer, Evie Trueman, to advise her. Clive stressed the seriousness of her situation, but Bronwen was adamant that she would represent herself.

But as the interview proceeded, Bronwen became increasingly distressed. She was sweating and trembling uncontrollably, and her speech became slurred. The DCI was observing through the two-way glass, and he called a halt to the interview. He phoned for medical assistance, and Bronwen was soon in an ambulance on her way to hospital, with a police escort.

Fifty-Four

'Our pace of life here is so much more leisurely,' said Penny Thorncroft contentedly, 'and yet things still happen suddenly.'

Her husband laughed. Penny was right. Only a few days after posting an advertisement online for their holiday-let caravans, the first enquiry was received. It came from a man coming alone to work in the area for a few days, and, as he wished to be based around Hotheby specifically, the caravans were ideally located.

The following Monday, just after noon, Rob Ellsman knocked on the front door of Ivy House. Gerry welcomed him heartily and suggested that they go together to the caravan. During the short drive, Gerry asked what work brought Mr Ellsman to the area, and he was surprised by the answer.

'I'm here to view the renovations being carried out at Hotheby Farmhouse, and to oversee the choices of various fixtures and fittings,' said Rob Ellsman. 'And I'll be talking to a design company in Snaysby about the interior of the barn. But you know all about those buildings, don't you? Weren't you the previous owner?'

Gerry laughed.

'You've done your homework, then!' he replied. 'Yes, we decided that Hotheby Farmhouse was one project too far for us, and we're very happy in Ivy House. So, who will be living up there?'

By now they'd arrived at the caravan furthest from Mrs Thwaites' cottage. Gerry gave his guest the key, and gestured to him to go in.

'Give us a shout if you need anything,' said Gerry. 'Oh yes, one other thing I must mention. There's an older lady, Mrs Thwaites, living in one of the cottages we passed. She's very kindly and an extremely good cook. She also likes to know about people, so you may find yourself being quizzed.'

Rob Ellsman looked amused.

'I'm sure I'll be able to handle the interrogation,' he said, 'but thanks for the warning. I'll see you around then.'

Gerry gave him a wave, as he left to walk back to Ivy House.

* * *

'Well,' asked Penny, 'what do we know about our first guest?'

'Not a lot,' replied Gerry, 'but his work's the interesting part,' and he told Penny about the Hotheby Farmhouse connection.

'Wow,' she said, sounding impressed, 'designers coming over from Snaysby, eh? They're certainly spending a huge amount on that place. Perhaps by Friday we'll know a bit more about who's going to live there. I'm sure Mrs T will do her best to find out!'

* * *

Early each morning, Rob Ellsman drove slowly past Ivy House, and he didn't return until mid-evening. But Gerry happened to meet him in Snaysby one afternoon. On impulse he invited Mr Ellsman to dinner with them on Thursday, his last evening in the caravan. Gerry felt sure that Penny would not object to the arrangement. It would be an opportunity to hear about the renovations at Hotheby Farmhouse.

Mrs Thwaites was asked to prepare one of her speciality chicken and vegetable pies, and a cheese and broccoli quiche, in case Mr Ellsman preferred vegetarian dishes. She suggested making a plum crumble and custard for pudding, and Penny was relieved at not having to make a dessert herself. Gerry had the impression that Mrs Thwaites would have liked to serve the food at the table, too. He stressed, though, that this was to be an informal meal.

'Don't worry,' said Mrs Thwaites, 'I can do all the clearing up on Friday morning.'

* * *

On Thursday evening, over dinner, Mr Ellsman described the progress being made at the farmhouse. All the period features on the ground-floor were being retained, which Penny was pleased about. A new central heating system had been installed, as it was anticipated that it was probably a cold house, situated as it was on an exposed hill. One of the reception rooms had been transformed into a study with fitted bookshelves along one wall, in a style in keeping with the house. And the kitchen had been extended and modernised.

'Perhaps it's best not to tell Mrs Thwaites about that,' laughed Penny. 'She apparently ruled the roost in that part of the house, and I'm not sure that she would approve of modernisation!'

Mr Ellsman smiled and said, 'Well, she makes an excellent pie, whatever sort of kitchen she works in.'

'She'll be delighted to hear that you enjoyed it,' replied Penny. 'But do you know who our new neighbours are to be?'

Penny decided that a direct question would be the only way to find anything out.

'Unfortunately, I'm not in a position to tell you, as I haven't yet met them,' replied Mr Ellsman, 'and I don't know when they hope to move in, either.'

'Are they perhaps overseas at present?' persisted Penny.

'I'm really sorry, Mrs Thorncroft, but I'm not privy to the details of these matters,' said Mr Ellsman.

Gerry was beginning to feel uncomfortable about Penny's determination, so he thought it was time to offer them all some cognac. And he changed the topic of conversation to their plans for the caravan site, and asked Mr Ellsman if he would kindly be the first to post a review of the site and its facilities on their website.

Fifty-Five

Sharon was sitting in her boss's office going through Marie Wilkinson's notes of her visit to Gregory Mortimer with a fine toothcomb.

'How's it going?' asked Clive, arriving back from a meeting with the DCI.

'Well, Sarge, I accept that Lucy Flynn is a campaigning journalist with particular axes to grind, but reading through Marie's version of her meeting with Mortimer, I really do wonder why he didn't appeal against his conviction,' Sharon replied.

'So are you saying that the police, the prosecution and the jury all got it wrong?' asked Clive, a surprised look on his face.

'I wouldn't go that far… yet,' said Sharon, 'but I appreciate why Lucy thinks she could argue a case for it. But, before you remind me, Sarge, I also accept that Lucy, and perhaps Marie too, were looking for things to reinforce their beliefs, rather than taking a more detached and objective view.'

'And Lucy may still be doing that,' said Clive. 'We can't discount it, even though she was severely shaken up by Marie's death.' He paused for a few moments. 'In fact,' he resumed, 'it may increase her impetus in digging around. And I'd bet that Bronwen Smythe is top of her list to follow up. So what did Marie say in her notes about Bronwen? I seem to recall that Mortimer gave her Bronwen's name, and Marie texted it to Lucy, shortly before her death.'

'That's right,' replied Sharon. 'According to Marie's notes, Mortimer was adamant that he had no recollection of a Bronwen Smythe, or any other Bronwens. He told Marie that he had indeed worked at the school during the years mentioned, but he went there only one afternoon per week, and only for two hours at most. He rehearsed the girls' choir ready for concerts, but someone else conducted those. Marie thought he was being honest about his short time working at the school. He apparently seemed totally bewildered by the allegations and why they had suddenly surfaced recently. He admitted to Marie that he felt paranoid about it all, and couldn't figure out why some unknown person was apparently being so vindictive towards him. He'd wondered if an inmate at Falkenside had set it all up, but he couldn't figure out how anyone could've got hold of all the details. Mortimer accepted that there was a lot of hostility to him there, because of his conviction. He knew that threats of violence had been made against him, and he'd got bruises to show for it.'

'So, in brief, Marie found Mortimer's version of events quite convincing,' summarised Clive, and Sharon nodded. 'But presumably they talked about his current conviction… after all, that's what prompted Marie's and Lucy's interest in him. So what do her notes tell us?'

'Marie says that Mortimer was much more emotional when talking about this,' said Sharon. 'She describes his demeanour as "confused and depressed", and Marie thought they were genuine feelings.'

'But we both have experience, Sharon, of offenders whose apparent depression stems from the fact that they've been caught, rather than from remorse or claims of wrongful conviction,' commented Clive, wondering if his DC was retaining her objectivity, 'and Marie wasn't a professional in this field.'

'Point taken, Sarge,' said Sharon, 'but I'm simply reporting what Marie wrote.'

'Quite right,' said Clive, 'carry on.'

'Mortimer acknowledged that he knew Louise Purvis-Brown as a member of his children's choir in Hadley St Giles. She was a quiet girl, who didn't seem to have friends in the choir, and whose parents didn't take much interest in her singing. He told Marie that he'd driven Louise home a couple of times after rehearsals, as no other parents had offered her a lift, and the evenings were cold and dark. She reportedly didn't say much during the short journey, but thanked him politely when they reached her home. He stated that he never saw her anywhere except in the context of choir rehearsals. Mortimer did say to Marie, though, that he thought Louise was an unhappy girl, but he didn't know why. And he still couldn't fathom out why she made the allegations.'

'Well,' said Clive, 'he certainly opened up to Marie, didn't he? But perhaps he thought he had nothing to lose now, and a lot to gain.'

'I wonder what Lucy would have done with all this information, had Marie sent it to her as she intended,' mused Sharon, 'because all she's got is Bronwen's name and the fact that she made the historical abuse allegations against Mortimer.'

'I suspect,' replied Clive, 'that'll be enough to keep her busy for a while. She'll be like a terrier with a rag doll.'

Sharon smiled at the mental image.

'While you're sifting through Marie's report a bit more, I'll fetch us some coffees, and then I've got some other updates for you,' said Clive, heading for the office door.

* * *

'The DCI rang the hospital, while I was with him,' began Clive, 'for the latest on Bronwen Smythe. I got the impression that he'd been worried we were heading for an unexplained death in custody. Thankfully, though, the medics have sorted her out and she's on the mend. She'll be discharged this afternoon, if there's no recurrence, and brought back into custody here. I'm relieved to say that DCI Couzens had nothing critical to say about our interviewing of her. But we may have to apply for more time to keep her here.'

'And the other update?' asked Sharon.

'The DCI also had a report on Mortimer's condition,' said Clive. 'It's expected that he'll pull through, but he's badly burned, particularly on his face and hands. There are concerns too about damage to his legs, so months of various operations and therapies are envisaged. The DCI doesn't anticipate that we'll be able to talk to him for quite a while. But at least the poor man's going to survive.'

'I know I shouldn't express sympathy for Mortimer, but I want to,' said Sharon. 'I know you expect me to remain objective, but I'm human too, Sarge.'

'Don't worry, Sharon, I'm pleased you are,' replied Clive with an understanding smile. 'Now, one last update. The DCI made another call while I was in his office, and that was to Karl Percival, the security manager at Falkenside. He explained our interest in Officer Raynaud. It seems that Raynaud's been disciplined a few times for inappropriate behaviour towards sex offenders. But, more importantly for us, Karl Percival confirmed that Raynaud was not rostered to work on the day Mortimer was released.'

'But even if he was driving the car which followed Bill Jones' car, there's no evidence that he went to Mulchester, is there?' asked Sharon.

'Not yet,' replied Clive, 'but perhaps it's just a matter of time.'

Fifty-Six

At lunchtime on Joanna's final day at the library, Tony Stoneman insisted that the staff meet together in the kitchen to wish her well. Coffee and cakes had been organised, and Tony had prepared a short speech in appreciation of Joanna's contribution to the library's success. Cheryl had anticipated that Tony would turn this into a fairly dull gathering, so she'd brought along some bottles of prosecco. She realised that this was probably in contravention of some policy or other, but she thought Joanna deserved a cheerful send-off.

After a short while most of the staff drifted back to their jobs, but Cheryl and Joanna stayed in the kitchen, enjoying the prosecco. Cheryl was sad that her colleague was leaving, and moving away from Blakesford, but she could understand it. Steve had been ordered by the court to complete substantial hours of unpaid work under supervision in the community. The golf club still circulated gossip about him occasionally, so Cheryl appreciated Joanna's decision to put distance between herself and her troublesome ex-husband.

* * *

For the past two months Joanna had been putting everything in order for her holiday in Canada and her new job. The agency had a tenant lined up for her apartment. Beth McKenzie was a newly appointed teacher at a primary school in Blakesford, whose references were excellent, according to the agency. She was to move into the apartment a week after Joanna had left for the new job. So she'd sifted through everything in the apartment and decided what was to stay for the tenant's use, what could go to the local charity shop, what should be put into storage, and what Joanna would take with her. She decided that everything in the last category must fit into her car.

For a while, Joanna had wondered whether to contact Jade Henton, as she now knew her name to be. She concluded, though, that it might somehow filter back to Steve, and she certainly didn't want him thinking that she retained any interest in him. So she'd dropped that idea.

Her gym workouts with Sophie had continued, but their chats over coffee were less relaxed than in the past. Sophie seemed to be treading on eggshells, carefully not telling Joanna what she really thought of her hare-brained plans.

I know she thinks I'm daft, swapping security for a host of unknowns, but I wish Sophie could be just a little bit happy for me. It wouldn't suit her, but it's right for me, she thought.

When Joanna returned from her trip to Canada, there would be only one more Saturday workout before she finally moved.

* * *

During the week before her holiday, Joanna received a card from Mike. He wished her "bon voyage" and hoped that she would enjoy her stay with her sister. Joanna smiled to herself on reading it. She was pleased to hear from Mike, but also gratified that she remained resolved to cut the emotional ties with him from now on.

She was looking forward to being with Zoe.

Fifty-Seven

'It seems we may have underestimated young Lucy Flynn,' said Clive, as Sharon came into his office. She'd been helping a colleague watch some tedious CCTV footage, unrelated to her cases, and she was pleased to get back to her own work.

'What's she been up to then, Sarge?' she asked.

'Well, while we thought she'd be following up on Bronwen Smythe, she's also been busy finding out more about Gregory Mortimer,' replied Clive. 'I've just had a long call with an old friend of mine, who's now a DS in Mulchester. Kirsty is working on the fire at Mortimer's flat, and from the records she made the link with our investigation into the abuse allegations, so she called me. They're certain that the fire was arson, not an accident, but no fingerprints or shoe-prints were found at the scene, and no weapon. So they still have a long way to go.'

'So it sounds like a professional job, doesn't it?' asked Sharon.

'Kirsty was understandably circumspect in what she told me about the investigation, but she knew that Mortimer is now medically out of danger,' said Clive. 'Her call was actually prompted by the identification of a person and a car.'

Sharon looked intrigued.

'You're not saying that Lucy Flynn found him and possibly set fire to the flat, are you?' she asked in disbelief.

'Not quite,' said Clive, surprised by Sharon's train of thought, 'but it seems that she'd tracked him down, which in itself is worrying, to say the least. Kirsty's team were alerted by a neighbour of Mortimer's to a woman asking a lot of questions, a few days after the fire. She was accosting people in the area and trying to establish who lived in the flat, and how well they knew him. There's no CCTV coverage in the immediate vicinity of the flat, but there are cameras showing traffic entering and exiting the cul-de-sac in which Mortimer lived. One of Kirsty's eagle-eyed DCs spotted a car making several visits to the cul-de-sac on the same day. So they ran a check on the registration plate, and it wasn't a resident. In fact, it was Lucy Flynn's car. So Kirsty rang me.'

'This was all after the date of the fire, right?' checked Sharon. 'So it doesn't link her to the fire itself, but I take your point about it being concerning that she could find him. How the hell did she do that?'

'I think that's something we should ask her, don't you?' suggested Clive.

* * *

Lucy Flynn was at home, engrossed in some internet searches, when the front door bell rang.

'DS Meadows and DC Page,' said Clive, 'may we come in?'

Lucy looked very surprised to see them, but gestured for them to come in.

'Have you got friends in Mulchester?' asked Sharon, without any preamble, and smiling at Lucy.

'Why do you ask?' replied Lucy, trying to disguise her astonishment.

'The reason for our question is that a colleague in Mulchester informs us that you've been asking locals about an incident in a particular cul-de-sac there, and more specifically about the person involved,' said Clive. 'As this is an incident being investigated by Mulchester police, we need to know what your interest is. We realise that you're an investigative journalist, but what story took you that far off your usual patch? Hence DC Page's question about whether you have friends there.'

'Would you like a coffee?' asked Lucy, playing for time, while she decided how much to tell the police.

'No thanks,' said Clive, 'we don't want to keep you any longer than necessary. So why were you in Mulchester? Just to explain, we know that your car was in the cul-de-sac as it appears several times on CCTV.'

'I've no reason to deny that I went there. It's the only time I've been to Mulchester,' began Lucy. 'I've told you before that I'm researching possible miscarriages of justice, and you know that one of the cases concerns Gregory Mortimer. Well,' she paused briefly, 'I liaise with two other journalists who are doing similar work, covering different geographical areas. We occasionally exchange data. But, before you get the wrong idea, all the data we collect is already in the public domain. It just takes a bit of finding.'

Clive nodded and said, 'Go on.'

'Well, one of them discovered the name of the victim of the fire in Mulchester. He'd come across that sort of treatment being meted out to paedophiles before, so he checked the name against our combined data, and contacted me,' said Lucy. 'I went to Mulchester to try and get more information about the fire and about Mortimer, like his current whereabouts. But I don't know where he's in hospital, if that's of any reassurance to you.'

'And you say that you'd never been to Mulchester before then, and haven't been back there since?' asked Sharon.

'That's right,' said Lucy. 'Is Mortimer recovering OK?'

'We understand that he's still in hospital,' replied Clive, unwilling to comment further.

'And do you know whose car was set on fire yet?' asked Lucy, accepting that she would be given no information about Mortimer. 'Any link with Marie's death?'

But Clive and Sharon had no intention of being drawn into Lucy's agenda, thanked her for her cooperation, and left.

Fifty-Eight

Much had happened since the day of Joanna's unusual job interview, but the day now dawned of her move to her new home and her employment with Simon Northam. She'd received several "Good Luck" cards, but thankfully there hadn't been one from Steve. Joanna hoped that he knew nothing of her fresh start and that she would have no more to do with him.

So, with her car packed to capacity, she handed the keys of her apartment to the agent, and set off on her long journey north. She felt excited, mixed with a dash of apprehension. She pushed to the back of her mind that she would never see Mike again.

* * *

Two hours later she pulled off the motorway into a service area, needing to stretch her legs. She wandered around the few shops and many fast-food places, and decided to have a coffee and a scone. The enormity of her move suddenly struck her forcibly and, for the first time, she was in danger of losing her nerve. She'd cut all ties with her life in Blakesford, other than one or two email contacts, and she was heading to a place where she knew no one, to work for an employer she'd never met. And what would her new home be like?

Joanna sternly reminded herself that this was an adventure, which she had chosen. She finished her coffee and bought a few groceries in the tiny supermarket. At least she would have something to eat this evening. Then she returned to her laden car and resumed her journey.

* * *

After another half-hour, Joanna reached the junction at which she finally turned off the motorway, onto a more minor road. Gradually the landscape around her changed, and the afternoon sun lit up beautiful hills and dales. The doubts about her move were beginning to recede.

How could I not be happy living in these surroundings, she asked herself, *it's just stunning!*

By now she was driving along narrow roads following the instructions she had scribbled on a large piece of paper, in case the satnav didn't recognise the roads! She'd never really trusted her satnav. In any case, Joanna liked looking on maps and seeing the evocative names of villages and towns in the vicinity. But so far on this journey her satnav had served her well.

As the lanes became even narrower, Joanna was looking in wonder at the vista of fields hemmed in by dry stone walls and the craggy outcrops on the hills in the middle distance.

She was abruptly jolted out of her reverie by an angry-sounding car horn. Thankfully she was driving slowly, but the driver of the large truck, towing a trailer filled with tall trees and shrubs and coming towards her, was rightly concerned that Joanna's mind was not fully on her driving. He had slowed almost to a halt, knowing that there was too little room for the vehicles to pass without considerable manoeuvring. The car, though, seemed slow to brake, hence the blast on the horn. Joanna reacted swiftly, and her car skidded slightly and came to a halt just in front of the truck. She looked up, embarrassed, and saw a genial-looking, middle-aged man grinning at her, and a dog in his passenger seat.

She wound down her window and called out, 'I'll back up... there's a farm entrance not far behind me, so I'll pull off the road there.' She was blushing as she spoke, knowing that the error was hers.

'That's right,' shouted the man, 'that's where I want to turn in, so please back up just beyond it.'

'Fine,' replied Joanna, and she started reversing along the narrow lane, wishing that her back seat had not been piled up so high.

The other driver duly turned into the farm entrance and gave Joanna a cheerful wave. She set off again, determined to concentrate more on her driving.

* * *

A mile or so further along this lane, according to the directions given her, would be the entrance to her new home. Sure enough, seemingly in the middle of nowhere, there was an incongruous opening in the high hedges flanking the lane. On either side were curved stone walls which led to tall wrought-iron gates, which appeared to open electronically, but on this occasion stood wide open.

How strange, thought Joanna, *this entrance seems completely out of place... it belongs more in a city gated community.*

Then she found herself driving over a noisy cattle grid, which seemed more in keeping with the surroundings. The drive was actually a track, whose potholes had been periodically filled with hardcore. As she drove up the incline, there was a neglected apple orchard on her right, fringed with rambling brambles. On her left was a large expanse of lawn which sloped down to the lane she'd just left, shielded from it by a high unkempt hedge. The garden had seen better days, with straggly rose bushes and other shrubs fighting each other for space.

The house was not immediately in view, as a splendid old yew tree and a dilapidated farm building hid it until Joanna followed the drive round to the left. Here it broadened out, revealing the stone farmhouse. Its façade was original, and there were high sash windows on either side of a huge oak front door, which was sheltered by a porch with wooden benches and a variegated creeper clambering up outside over the slate roof.

Wow, what a gorgeous place, thought Joanna as she parked and walked over to the front door. Having rung the bell, she turned and looked away from the house. Beyond the downward-sloping lawn was a simply breath-taking view. Hills, valleys, fields and trees in multifarious shades of green as far as the eye could see, with just the occasional glimpse of a village. And it was so quiet too.

Just then, Joanna's musings were interrupted by the door behind her being opened.

Fifty-Nine

It was the name of the school which caught Lucy Flynn's attention. She was scrolling down her usual news sites when she gasped in horror. The headline read, "Schoolgirl, 15, killed by train." That was horrendous enough, but then Lucy read that the victim of the accident was a pupil at Dorlingsworth School. It couldn't possibly be Gregory Mortimer's accuser, could it? That would surely be too coincidental. She read the article more closely.

"Tragedy struck in the usually quiet town of Whiteleigh today, when a pupil at nearby Dorlingsworth School was killed by a fast through-train on the unmanned level crossing near the station. An eye-witness, George Bryce, 42, saw the tragedy unfold as he waited on the nearby station platform.

'I saw the young girl put her schoolbag carefully on the ground against the fence near the crossing. The barriers were down across the road and the red warning lights were flashing, but there were no cars about. She waited a few moments, then opened the pedestrian gate. I shouted at her to stop, but my voice was drowned out by the noise of the oncoming train. She looked straight ahead of her and walked, quite deliberately, into the path of the fast train. The driver had no chance of reacting. For me, it all seemed to happen in slow motion. It was horrific. I've got a daughter about the same age. I shall never forget it.'" The reporter went on to say that the police had issued

a statement about the accident but had not disclosed the victim's name, as the body had not yet been formally identified. But the report stated that she was named locally as Louise Purvis-Brown.

A tear rolled down Lucy's cheek. She had never met Louise, but she'd heard her timid voice in the courtroom at Gregory Mortimer's trial. What had driven the girl to commit suicide? What was she so troubled about? Lucy sat in a state of shock, staring vacantly into space.

* * *

Sharon answered the phone. She'd had a succession of calls, several of which were of little consequence, and she was becoming irritated. She didn't want any more interruptions.

'DC Page,' she said, scarcely concealing her impatience.

'It's Lucy Flynn here,' said the caller in an uncharacteristically reticent way, 'and I've just read a report about Louise Purvis-Brown, Gregory Mortimer's accuser. I wondered if you knew about it?'

Sharon was fully alert now, sensing that Lucy might have something important to say.

'What are you referring to, Lucy?' asked Sharon encouragingly.

'Well,' replied Lucy, 'she's apparently killed herself. She's reported to have thrown herself in front of a train… the poor girl… it must be the same girl.'

Sharon was thinking quickly, as Lucy read out the report with sadness in her voice. Lucy's call sounded genuine. So had someone been putting pressure on Louise in some way about her allegations? Was there any link with the fire at Mortimer's flat? Or was it something completely unconnected with their investigations? She needed to find out more.

'Lucy,' she said quietly, 'please send me the link to this report, and anything else you find in relation to it. And take care of yourself… you sound quite shaken up. And thank you.'

Sharon ended the call, hoping that she would now have some space to think through the implications of what Lucy had told her, and waited for the link to arrive.

I wonder whether there was anything significant in Louise's schoolbag, which she carefully placed against the fence... that sounds strange to me, she pondered.

* * *

Clive arrived back in the office just in time for a full team briefing called by DCI Couzens. Sharon had phoned the Dorlingsworth police several times, but still had no answers about the contents of Louise's schoolbag, and her father had not yet been to confirm the identity of the body. No one was in any doubt, though, that the suicide victim was Louise. Sharon hurriedly updated her boss on the latest developments as they made their way to the meeting room.

'Does this mean that protection needs to be put in place for Mortimer's current accuser, Bronwen Smythe, then?' asked the DCI, despondently envisaging yet more of his valuable resources being taken up by the Mortimer case.

Clive hadn't had an opportunity to discuss this with Sharon, so both of them were thinking on their feet.

'We don't yet know, sir,' replied Clive, 'whether or not the girl's suicide was connected at all to her role as Mortimer's accuser. And we have nothing to indicate that Mortimer holds a continuing grudge against his accuser. His attitude seems to be one of bewilderment about all that happened, rather than vengeful in any way. We have no knowledge of any networks, either in prison or in the community, who would pressurise the girl on his behalf. And why would he? He's trying to put all that behind him, although, of course, he still has the current allegations to answer.'

'Right,' said DCI Couzens, 'so what more have we got on this reporter woman, Lucy Flynn? Her name seems to be cropping up rather a lot. Has she perhaps visited Dorlingsworth School at some stage and talked to Louise? I recall that she busied herself around Louise's previous school before Mortimer's trial. And she attended the trial, didn't she? And later she turned up at the site of the burning car. So where does she fit in?'

Sharon was always impressed by the DCI's memory and his ability to cut to the chase. She found it intimidating. How many cases and details could he recall at any given time? She hoped that one day she might develop similar skills, but without intimidating anyone.

Clive looked across at Sharon, indicating that she should answer.

'Well, sir,' began Sharon, 'the notes which Marie Wilkinson made shortly before her death have been retrieved, and also a brief email she sent to Lucy Flynn at the same time. In that she stated who Mortimer's current accuser is, as Mortimer had told Marie the name, which is, of course, Bronwen Smythe. We anticipated that Lucy Flynn would be searching around for information about Bronwen Smythe. But she also found out about the fire at Mortimer's flat in Mulchester and drove over there. There's CCTV evidence of her car entering and leaving the cul-de-sac where he lived, a few days after the fire. She admits having been there and trying to elicit information from his neighbours.'

Sharon paused, and the DCI asked, 'Anything else, Sharon?'

'Well, sir,' she continued, 'to answer one of your questions, we have no evidence of Lucy Flynn seeking out or making contact with Louise Purvis-Brown at Dorlingsworth School or anywhere else. I have the impression that her immediate attention is focusing on Bronwen Smythe rather than Louise.'

The DCI's phone pinged.

'Right,' he said, 'next meeting tomorrow at the same time. For now, Bronwen Smythe is downstairs, apparently well enough to be interviewed again.'

Sixty

'Ah,' said the elderly woman who opened the heavy oak front door, 'you must be Mrs Hearnden.' She smiled at Joanna. 'We've been looking forward to you coming to Hotheby. I do hope you've had a good journey, you've come such a long way.'

The woman hardly drew breath, and continued, 'Mr Northam is sorry that he can't be here to welcome you today, so he asked me to get you settled in and show you where everything is. I'll just get your keys and take you over to your new home. I do hope you'll like it.'

She left Joanna standing in the porch, but quickly returned with a bunch of keys.

Joanna realised that she hadn't yet spoken to the woman, so she smiled and said, 'Yes, I'm Mrs Hearnden, but please call me Joanna. I'd much prefer that.'

'And I'm Mrs Thwaites,' said the older woman. 'I do lots of the cooking for Mr Northam and general house-keeping. But what a lovely afternoon it is, so you're seeing Hotheby at its best. It's not always like this, you know. We get such gales and strong winds sometimes, being up on a hill, but today it's lovely and sunny to welcome you here. Look, take your car round to the barn, just follow this track, and there's a place to park round the back. I'll walk over and open up for you.'

* * *

Joanna drove the short distance to the converted barn, which was to be her new home. Initially it was partially hidden by another huge old yew tree, but then she saw a large building covered in dark wooden cladding and flanked on one side by tall, swaying trees. Her first impression was of a forbidding building, standing along one side of what had originally been a vast farmyard.

But the inside is much more important, Joanna told herself.

She parked and walked round to where Mrs Thwaites was standing by the front door. Joanna noticed that newly planted climbers were being trained up trellises on this side of the barn, and she hoped that they would be fast-growing varieties, as it would soften the austere appearance of the barn's exterior.

'Do go in, Joanna,' said Mrs Thwaites. 'I won't stay long, 'cos I'm sure you'll want to look around by yourself and get unpacked. I've put a few bits and pieces in the fridge for you, just a few basics until you can get to a shop. Mr Northam asked me to do that. Oh, and I made a chicken casserole for you. It just needs heating up. So that'll do for this evening, if you fancy it, won't it?'

Joanna was quite overwhelmed by Mrs Thwaites' thoughtfulness, and told her so.

'Don't be silly,' she responded, 'we all look after each other round here. That's what neighbours are for, isn't it? Now, Mr Northam has written you a letter, it's over there on the coffee table. So, if you come over to the farmhouse tomorrow morning, whenever you're ready, I'll show you where things are. The key with the green tag opens the side entrance, opposite you when you open your front door. That's the best door for you to use.'

She handed the large bunch of keys to Joanna and said, 'I'll see you tomorrow then,' and left.

* * *

Joanna stood alone in the cavernous barn, taking it all in. She could hardly believe her good fortune. The interior was stunning, and compared with her flat in Blakesford the barn felt enormous.

The front door was halfway along one of the longer sides of the rectangular barn. As she walked in, her eyes were drawn immediately to her left. That end of the building seemed to be just one huge gothic-style window, looking out onto a view similar to the one she had admired from the front door of the farmhouse.

I can't believe my luck, thought Joanna, *even Sophie would have to approve of this! I must send some pictures to Zoe tomorrow.*

Joanna realised that the window was actually only the central part of the far wall. An open staircase led up to a mezzanine gallery which overlooked the living area in which she was standing, and this allowed views from the first-floor level, too. Opposite the staircase, on the upper-floor, the gallery led into a small bedroom with a steeply slanted ceiling and two skylights. On the ground-floor the bedroom was supported by three stone gothic arches. These created a cloister-like area, with two long, narrow windows facing the old yew tree. The cloisters were in fact a well-equipped office.

So I guess this is where I'll be expected to work sometimes, she thought. *What a contrast to the grotty facilities in the library!*

Turning her back on the huge window, Joanna saw that the large space beyond the front door was divided, more conventionally, into rooms on the ground- and upper-floors, to which another wooden staircase led. Upstairs was the main bedroom, with a vaulted ceiling and an en-suite shower room. The bathroom and kitchen were situated below. The whole barn was beautifully furnished, and Joanna was captivated by it.

Wow, she said contentedly to herself, *I really have landed on my feet here!*

Then she noticed two bottles of wine on the coffee table, with an envelope leaning against them. She had a sudden flashback, recalling unwelcome envelopes from Steve.

Don't be so stupid, she told herself sternly. *Mrs Thwaites said that Mr Northam had written me a letter, so this must be it.*

Joanna picked up the envelope and sank onto the comfortable settee.

"Dear Joanna, (if I may),

Welcome to Hotheby Barn!

I hope you like your new home. I'm sorry not to be there to welcome you in person, but I'm aiming to be home in two or three days.

Until then, I'm sure Mrs Thwaites will do all she can to assist you. She knows everything about Hotheby and its environs, so do ask her.

It would be very helpful if you'd spend some time unpacking the many boxes of books which are sitting on my study floor. I'm taking advantage of your librarianship skills! Please sort them out and get them systematically onto the empty bookshelves. It's an eclectic mix of books, which I've gathered up in the past.

But don't spend all your time working! Get to know the area too.

I look forward to meeting you soon.

Kind regards

Simon Northam"

Joanna leant back on the settee, looking at the letter.

Well, she thought, *I can't imagine Tony Stoneman ever writing a welcoming letter like that! This chap seems very laid-back, which suits me just fine! Overall, I'm very pleased with my move… so far!*

221

Sixty-One

Bronwen Smythe sat in the interview room looking listless and pale. She had again refused to have the lawyer with her.

'Right, Bronwen,' began Clive, 'just for the tape, we'll recap where you stand. There are two separate but linked issues, aren't there? You're the complainant against Mr Mortimer, but you're under suspicion regarding the death of Marie Wilkinson. And we're holding you in custody in relation to the second issue. Do you understand all that?'

Bronwen nodded slowly, without raising her head.

'And you don't want a lawyer with you, is that correct? Please answer for the tape,' said Sharon.

Softly, Bronwen replied, 'Yes.'

'So,' said Clive, in an authoritative tone, 'tell us how your DNA came to be in the car which was found burned out.'

Bronwen seemed to gain strength momentarily, as she realised the seriousness of her situation.

'I stole that car,' she said, 'that's all.'

'Even though you're banned from driving?' asked Sharon.

Bronwen muttered, 'Yes. I knew I shouldn't be driving, but I had to steal it… you don't understand.'

'So help us to understand, Bronwen,' said Clive.

Bronwen sat and picked at the skin around her fingernails,

shifting nervously in her seat. Her eyes were fixed on her lap, and her willingness to talk had evaporated.

'Did someone put pressure on you to steal the car?' asked Sharon.

Bronwen suddenly looked up, fear in her eyes.

'So who was it?' asked Clive, leaning slightly towards Bronwen across the table. 'I bet they wouldn't hesitate to name you, if they were here instead of you, would they? Why do you want to protect them?'

'No comment,' replied Bronwen, recalling her lawyer's earlier advice. 'I can't tell you anything.'

'Well, Bronwen,' said Clive decisively, 'we've been granted more time to keep you here, so we'll take you back to your cell now, but it's in your interests to think about what we've asked you. Have a long, hard think about it, and we'll see you in a short while.'

Bronwen meekly stood up, a bewildered expression on her face, and was led back unsteadily to a cell.

* * *

'While Bronwen is cogitating on what to tell us,' said Clive, 'we've got time to go over and talk to Prison Officer Neil Raynaud. I checked, and it's his day off today, so let's hope he's spending it at home.'

Surprised, Sharon grabbed her jacket and followed her boss out of the office. They discussed their tactics during the journey and were now sitting in Neil Raynaud's front room, while he was making tea for them in the kitchen. Lying on the floor opposite them, alert and with his ears pricked, was a menacing German Shepherd dog guarding the door.

Not a dog I'll try to make friends with, decided Sharon.

She looked around the room, seeing if there were any clues about the character or interests of Neil Raynaud. But apart from the overwhelming flatscreen television facing her on the wall, and two framed photographs on an otherwise empty shelf, there was little to see. The photos interested Sharon. One showed Raynaud in a military uniform, standing to attention, and the other was of Raynaud in his prison officer's uniform.

Hmm, she wondered, *uniforms as symbols of power?*

The door was pushed open, and Raynaud came in with three mugs of tea. The dog shifted slightly and lay down beside his master, still watching the visitors.

'So what's this all about?' asked Raynaud, with scarcely disguised contempt in his voice.

'We're following up some intelligence concerning your movements on the day of former prisoner Gregory Mortimer's release,' replied Clive, keeping steady eye contact with Raynaud.

'Don't know what you're on about,' retorted Raynaud, snappily.

'Well,' continued Clive, 'for starters, we have CCTV evidence of your car following the car which picked Mortimer up at eight o'clock that morning. Why were you following him?'

'And what proof have you got that I was driving the car, even if it was my car?' asked Raynaud aggressively.

'Was it you driving it?' countered Clive.

The dog seemed to sense that Raynaud was losing his cool and growled throatily. His master lifted one finger, and the growling ceased.

'Look, Mr Raynaud, that's not a difficult question, and the sooner you answer us, the sooner we'll be gone,' said Sharon, calmly.

Raynaud gave Sharon a surprised look, as it was the first time she'd spoken. He seemed to come to his senses.

'The truth is,' he began, 'it was my day off, and I'd heard that he was being released that morning, and I was mad about it. People like him should serve much longer sentences. I just watched to see if it really happened. OK? I couldn't stand him.'

'Is that why you tried to kill him later?' asked Sharon, pointedly.

Raynaud leapt out of his chair, a venomous expression on his face. The dog jumped up, barking wildly. Sharon and Clive remained in their seats, outwardly calm, hoping this would take the heat out of the situation. They waited.

Raynaud eventually grabbed the dog's collar and motioned to him to lie down, and the dog obeyed. Raynaud tried to hold his own emotions in check and sat down.

'What are you playing at?' he asked, his voice and hands shaking in anger. 'How dare you accuse me of trying to kill Mortimer? Why would I risk life imprisonment for scum like him? But I wouldn't care if someone else killed him.'

'Well,' said Clive, 'the easiest thing would be if you just tell us where you went after following Mortimer away from the prison.'

Raynaud decided reluctantly that he had no alternative.

'If you must know, I drove over to my mum's house, about five miles away and had breakfast with her. It was her birthday and I wanted to surprise her. She'll vouch for me,' he said.

Clive and Sharon exchanged sceptical glances.

'Right,' ordered Clive, 'call her number now please, and hand the phone to me. It won't take a minute to check this out… and no silliness, OK?'

The phone call was made, and Raynaud's mother unquestioningly confirmed her son's version of events and added that they'd later gone out for a lovely lunch together, too. He was such a kind son to her.

Bit of a Jekyll and Hyde, perhaps? wondered Sharon. *I can't picture him being kind to anyone, except himself.*

'And will it stop all these questions,' asked Raynaud, 'if I tell you that I don't know or care where Mortimer lives, and I have no intention of looking for him. I see enough filth like him every day.'

Clive and Sharon both stood up, and so did the dog.

'Well-trained dog, you've got,' remarked Clive, and Raynaud gave him a triumphant smirk.

'Thank you for your cooperation, Mr Raynaud,' said Sharon, and they left.

Raynaud seemed relieved to see them go.

* * *

'What a charmer,' remarked Sharon sarcastically, as she and Clive drove back to the station. Clive laughed.

'Not your type, then?' asked Clive with a grin. 'Perhaps he lacks the finesse of, say, Richie McCleod, but we know from his mum what a kind heart he has.'

Sharon decided to ignore Clive's comment about Richie.

'Did you take note of the number he called?' asked Sharon. 'I couldn't see it, but I thought we should cross-check it, just to be sure he really was calling his mum.'

'What a superbly suspicious mind you have,' replied Clive, 'and yes, I have memorised it, but I feel certain it was genuine. It was in the memory as "Mum". We'll get it checked, though. So, what did you make of the man?'

'His attitude towards some prisoners concerns me a great deal,' replied Sharon, choosing her words carefully. 'I suspect he's devious in his dealings with them, and ensures that he rarely gets caught. Although we know that he's been disciplined in the past in relation to his treatment of sex offenders. Did you notice the photos of him in uniform? I think he revels in the power a uniform gives him. I bet he adopts a real swagger in front of prisoners, especially men like Mortimer. And he's certainly got a short fuse. And when he hasn't got a uniform to give him power, he uses his dog. A lot of latent aggression in him, I'd say.'

'You may well be right in all your assessments, Sharon, but where do you stand as far as possible involvement in the attempted murder of Gregory Mortimer is concerned?' asked Clive. 'Is there any evidence which connects him to it?'

'None at all, as far as I can see, Sarge,' replied Sharon. 'He despises Mortimer, but that's not an offence. I doubt he has the contacts, the know-how, or the guts to set out deliberately to kill someone, not even a sex offender, knowing that he might end up on the wrong side of the prison fence. I think he was right when he said he wouldn't risk his own liberty.'

'I agree with you,' said Clive, 'but we had to rule him out... for the time being, anyway.'

* * *

They drove back to the station as fast as the traffic would allow, hopeful that Bronwen would now start spilling the beans.

Sixty-Two

It was Joanna's fourth evening in her new home, and she was feeling content with life. On her first night she'd been disturbed by unaccustomed sounds, as the trees' swaying branches tapped on the barn's roof in the wind. She thought she heard an owl hooting. But the more pervading quiet was alien to her, as there was no traffic noise or human voices outside.

It's just so peaceful here, she thought, *and once I start making some friends, it'll be perfect, apart from not having Mike in my life. I wonder where he is... but he probably wouldn't tell me anyway!* She smiled ruefully.

But today she had met Simon Northam for the first time. She'd been forewarned at the interview, which now seemed a lifetime away, that Simon had been badly injured in an accident several months ago, and had been undergoing extensive surgery and physiotherapy ever since. She was determined, in theory at any rate, to look beyond any disfigurement he might have.

When she let herself into Hotheby Farmhouse this morning, she found Simon sitting in a wheelchair behind the enormous desk in his study. He looked up at Joanna, and a welcoming smile spread across his scarred face. His forearms were resting on the desk, and Joanna noticed that some of his fingers were crooked into his palms and seemed immobile.

Almost immediately, Mrs Thwaites appeared, carrying a tray of coffee and biscuits. She placed an adapted mug in front of Simon and poured coffee into a china cup for Joanna. Then she disappeared back to the kitchen.

'I'm so pleased you're here, Joanna, and thank you for sorting out my books. I want to say a few things, though, before we talk about the work I'd like us to do,' he said hesitantly, 'as obviously it's an unorthodox set-up here, and I need you to be sure that you want to stay. There'll be no hard feelings, if you don't.'

Joanna was taken aback. She hadn't anticipated her new boss pointing out the drawbacks of the job and giving her the option of resigning straightaway.

'You have a very expressive face, Joanna, if you don't mind my saying so, and I've come to read people's reactions quite well since the accident,' said Simon, with a kindly smile. 'I know I'm not a pretty sight nowadays, and I'm still annoyingly helpless in some situations, and I can get horribly grouchy at times, so I want you to have a realistic picture of what you're letting yourself in for. We're living in a fairly remote area, although there are villages nearby, and I gather that Snaysby is quite a bustling town, so you'd have to go out to find any sort of good social life. We have some helpful neighbours, and I gather that you've already met one of them, Gerry Thorncroft.'

Joanna looked blank, and then the realisation hit her. He must be the chap whose truck she nearly drove into in the lane, when she first arrived in Hotheby.

Word spreads fast around here, she thought.

Simon's eyes were twinkling.

'Yes,' he said, 'you can't sneeze around here without everyone knowing! So, Gerry told Mrs Thwaites about his close encounter with you, and she told me. So, be warned!'

'Well,' replied Joanna, laughing and trying to cover her embarrassment. 'I'll just have to commit all my misdemeanours well away from Hotheby, won't I?'

'D'you know, Joanna,' said Simon, 'you've made me smile more in the last ten minutes than I've done in a long time, but I'm serious about you knowing the score here, and if you want to change your mind, after you've given it more thought, I'll completely understand. I'd be sad, but I'll understand.'

Joanna nodded slowly, drank some coffee and took a biscuit.

'My problem is,' she said, after a few moments' pause, and with a jocular expression, 'if I left, I'd want to take the barn with me!'

Simon smiled again.

* * *

While sorting through Simon's books and journals, Joanna had set herself the challenge of identifying what topics she might be asked to research. He seemed to have a wide range of interests, though, from the history of art and architecture, to biographies, to wildlife, to modern novels, and a lot more. Joanna was at a loss to know what research themes Simon had in mind.

'Now then, Joanna,' began Simon, 'what do you know about lychgates?'

Joanna was perplexed by the question.

'I don't think I've ever given them any thought!' she answered with a laugh. 'Why do you ask?'

'Well,' replied Simon, 'that's what our initial research will be into. I've been commissioned to write a chapter for a book, and I'm hoping it will kick-start my writing again. For obvious reasons, I haven't done much writing lately, and I'm not at a stage where I can do it all without help yet, so that's where you come in. Penny Thorncroft, Gerry's wife, came here for a couple of days and helped me put together a folder for you. This contains the original research proposal and an outline of the fieldwork, parameters, timelines, and so on. I'd done a lot of the preparatory thinking and submissions before the accident, but now, of course, I can't get out to do interviews, which are central to the whole thing. The folder is actually quite hefty, so I suggest you take it over to the barn and get to grips with it all there. There's a short bibliography in it, so that should give you some starting points.'

Joanna looked pensive.

'So, is there much to say about lychgates? As I say, it's not a subject I've ever really thought about,' said Joanna, beginning to have concerns that this job might be short-term.

Simon seemed to read her thoughts.

'To reassure you, I'll give you a quick potted history,' replied Simon. 'They were erected from about the mid-fifteenth century onwards, and the word "lych" seems to be of Saxon derivation and means "corpse". It may be linked to the German word "Leichnam", a dead body. So, the lychgate was really the corpse entrance to the churchyard. Some theories say that part of the funeral service was conducted in the shelter of the lychgate, and others suggest that the body was just put there until the clergyman arrived for the service. Others say this was a sort of resting place for the body immediately before the final farewell of burial. But as well as their purpose, we'll be looking at the architectural styles of various lychgates. These vary enormously, depending on what materials were available to builders of the area and times. Are you any good with a camera, Joanna?'

'I'm no expert,' she replied, 'but I'll certainly have a go.'

'Excellent,' said Simon, 'and now I'll outline the part of the whole project which interests me most. I've long been fascinated by World War I and its legacy on towns and villages, especially when a large proportion of their menfolk didn't return home. Lots of communities re-built or renovated their local lychgates, turning them into memorials to the missing or the dead. And this was at a time when they didn't have much in the way of resources. So I want you to identify and visit lychgates within our specified geographical area, which have memorials incorporated into them. These may be to individuals or groups. And, if possible, it would be helpful to follow up some of the stories behind the people involved. So, that's it in a nutshell,' concluded Simon. 'I hope I haven't put you off!'

Joanna smiled confidently, a smile which belied her apprehension.

I wanted a new start, she reminded herself, *well, nothing could be newer than this!*

'Once you mentioned the WWI connection,' she beamed, 'I was hooked! I went to northern France once on a school-trip, and we spent quite a bit of time visiting the war graves and memorials there. It made a lasting impression on me.'

She hesitated.

'I won't pretend I'm not a bit daunted by the whole project, but I'll give it my best shot,' she said.

'I can't ask for more than that,' replied Simon quietly. 'I'm so pleased.'

Sixty-Three

'You're still under caution,' Clive reminded Bronwen Smythe, who nodded disconsolately.

'You admitted to us, earlier, that you stole the burnt-out car, in which your DNA was found,' said Sharon, 'and you said that you had to steal it, but we wouldn't understand why. So, what's that all about?'

'He'll kill me if I grass on him,' whispered Bronwen, a scared expression on her face.

'Who will?' continued Sharon, coaxingly.

'I can't tell you,' said Bronwen, 'I'm scared.'

Clive decided to change tack.

'You know that you're the second person to make allegations of sexual abuse against Gregory Mortimer, don't you, and that he went to prison as a result of the first allegations?' began Clive. 'Well, sadly his first accuser has died. Did you know that? We can't give you any details, but it's sad, isn't it?'

Bronwen's face blanched.

* * *

After a few minutes' vacillation, Bronwen burst into tears and then began to tell her interviewers her version of events. She wasn't far into her story, when Sharon interrupted.

'Are you sure, Bronwen, that you don't want a lawyer with you?' she asked. Bronwen remained adamant that she did not.

Her account was that she'd been instructed to steal that particular car and to take it to a specified carpark two days later. She had to leave the keys out of sight on the top of the rear offside tyre. She insisted that she didn't know what the car was to be used for. Sometime after that, she was picked up in the same car and driven to the woods where it was set alight. She was then left to get away from the scene however she could.

Clive and Sharon listened as Bronwen told them this, at times incoherently and backtracking to correct herself.

'So who instructed you to steal the car? And why?' asked Clive, beginning to sound exasperated. 'The car was used as a murder weapon,' he continued, 'so why are you protecting that person? Why should we believe that someone else was behind it? Give us a name, Bronwen.'

But Bronwen hung her head, and she was visibly trembling. Fearing a repeat of her earlier hospitalisation, Clive halted the interview, offered Bronwen some water, and gave her ten minutes to compose herself. He and Sharon withdrew, leaving a uniformed officer in the interview room with Bronwen.

* * *

'Everyone has their Achilles heel,' said DCI Couzens, who had been listening in on the interview. 'With Smythe, it must be her drug addiction. There's got to be something in her past or present that's holding her hostage, so to speak. She's very scared of that, and she knows she's potentially facing a murder charge now, so press her harder. And make a link with her allegations against Mortimer. Is the same person behind those?'

Clive and Sharon had grabbed a quick coffee during the break, while discussing the interview with the DCI. With a strategy in place, they returned to the interview room.

* * *

Bronwen appeared calmer and agreed she was ready to resume the interview.

'Your record for possession of drugs goes back a long way, doesn't it, Bronwen? And your convictions have become progressively more serious, haven't they?' commented Sharon. 'I know that you've been in rehabs a few times, but then there've always been relapses, haven't there? So your addiction makes you vulnerable in all sorts of ways, doesn't it?'

Bronwen looked up at Sharon and nodded, almost imperceptibly. Clive noted it for the tape.

'That makes people take advantage of you, doesn't it?' asked Sharon, quietly.

Again, Bronwen gave a slight nod.

'Has someone in particular got a hold over you at the moment?' continued Sharon.

A third nod of the head.

Clive could almost feel the DCI urging them to "go for the jugular… now!" but he decided that their strategy was working and would be more productive. He hoped so, at any rate. He let his DC continue to take the lead for now.

'What sort of hold has that person got?' asked Sharon gently.

'He knows I've been dealing drugs,' replied Bronwen, her voice quivering.

'And is he threatening to report you, if you don't do as he instructs you?' asked Sharon.

Bronwen nodded again.

'So, are you talking about a serious quantity of hard drugs, if he can threaten you like that?' continued Sharon. 'Is he a user too?'

Bronwen suddenly straightened up and looked Sharon straight in the eye.

'No, you've got it all wrong,' she blurted out, in a surprisingly strong voice, 'he's not a user, he's one of your lot.'

She slumped back down in her seat, looking scared again.

Then she reverted to "No comment" answers, and Clive terminated the interview.

They had the potential breakthrough they were hoping for.

Sixty-Four

Joanna was feeling more content and relaxed than she'd done for a long while. Her traumatic marriage to Steve, which had initially been so idyllic, was now firmly consigned to the past. She was confident that he would not seek her out in Hotheby.

She loved her new home, with its wonderful views. Each evening she sat on a large beanbag on the gallery, a glass of wine in hand, watching the circling birds and the ever-changing sky. She had only one lingering regret, no matter how much she tried to banish it. Every now and again, Mike would appear in her mind's eye. She told herself angrily that she hadn't known him very well, and perhaps the relationship wouldn't have worked out, but she nevertheless wished that she could see him again.

As far as her new job was concerned, Joanna had thrown herself wholeheartedly into Simon's research project and was enjoying all aspects of it. She was constantly encouraged by Simon, whatever new approach she suggested, and they had stimulating discussions.

What a contrast to good old Tony Stoneman, she thought. *I'm appreciated here, and Simon's got a wicked sense of humour. And yet he must have been through so much.*

Joanna's enthusiasm for her new life was shared by her sister, Zoe. She was very relieved that Joanna had ditched Steve and the new enigmatic man, who seemed to be leading her sister a merry dance. Joanna hadn't been entirely honest with Zoe about her residual feelings for Mike. But the sisters were now in more regular email contact again, and they were both enjoying it. Joanna had no other family, so it was good to have news of her nephew and niece in Canada, too, especially since her recent visit to them.

* * *

There was a loud knock on the barn's front door. It was the first time Joanna had had a visitor, other than Mrs Thwaites, and this was definitely not her tentative knock.

Joanna got up from her desk, and opened the door, to find two uniformed policemen standing there. She must have looked startled, as one of them laughed, and said, 'Sorry to disturb you, Joanna, we've just come to introduce ourselves. I'm PC Craig Asher, and my colleague is PC Chris Caldecote.'

Hotheby is certainly full of surprises, thought Joanna, *and they even know my first name!*

'We're regularly on patrol round here, and we call in at the farmhouse, just to make sure all is well. There've been a lot of thefts recently from outhouses locally. You're lucky, because a lot of security measures were installed here when all the renovations were carried out,' said PC Asher, 'so you'll be safe. We hear that you're not used to living in the country, though, so here's the number to call if you think something suspicious is going on.'

He handed Joanna a card. While he was talking, PC Caldecote seemed to be checking on the various security cameras which were placed discreetly on the side of the farmhouse and the barn. Joanna hadn't noticed them before, but it was reassuring to know that they were there.

'Well,' said PC Asher, 'I expect we'll see you out and about. I gather you know Gerry Thorncroft already, and he and his wife will keep an eye on you too, I'm sure. Bye for now.'

And with that, the two policemen returned to their blue and yellow car.

Joanna then realised that she hadn't actually said a word to them.

But I'm sure that Blakesford police don't make "welcome to our patch" visits! she thought, chuckling.

* * *

Joanna turned off her laptop and put it in her bag. As she locked the front door, she thought about giving the nearest security camera a wave, but told herself not to be so childish!

She planned to spend the day in Snaysby Library, particularly perusing their local history section. Then, if she had time, she thought she'd visit the parish church and have a look at the lychgate, if it had one. At four o'clock she was due to meet with Simon, to discuss her progress so far.

She found a parking space quite easily and was walking across the market square to the library, when she heard a booming voice call out, 'Joanna!'. Her immediate reaction was one of dread.

Surely Steve can't have followed me here, can he? she asked herself.

But, much to her relief, she looked to the left and saw Gerry Thorncroft coming towards her.

'Good morning, Joanna, nice to see you,' said Gerry, a little out of breath, 'have you come to sample the delights of Snaysby?'

'Not quite,' she replied, 'I'm here to do some work in the library. But you're right,' she continued, 'it does look like a delightful town.' She paused, before saying, 'I'm very sorry about the way we first met, I haven't had a chance to apologise.'

Gerry guffawed, and a grin spread across his bearded face.

'Think no more about it,' he replied, 'but I'm afraid most of our little community knows about it. Don't worry, the next amusing thing will happen soon, and your daydreaming will be forgotten! So how are you getting along with our gem, Mrs Thwaites? She used to work for us, but Simon stole her,' he laughed. 'But we accept that he needs her more than we do, so it's worked out well. She still comes and stocks our freezer with home-cooked meals, so we often see her. She lives in one of the farm cottages near us.'

'I can understand why you value her,' said Joanna. 'I only have to walk into Simon's study and she appears with coffee and biscuits.'

'That sounds like Mrs T!' laughed Gerry. 'But I'd better let you get to the library. And I'm meant to be collecting some wine. Good to see you. Pop down to Ivy House, when you have some spare moments. Penny would love to see you.'

And they went their separate ways.

Sixty-Five

'He's on compassionate leave,' announced DCI Couzens, walking into the briefing meeting, 'because of his daughter's death. He's apparently not at his home, and his colleagues don't know his current whereabouts. I get the impression that he's not well-liked by them and certainly not close friends with anyone at work.'

Ray Couzens sounded irritated.

'Perhaps he's gone to stay with relatives, sir,' suggested Sharon. 'It must be a difficult time for him. Do his colleagues know anything about his family?'

Clive was momentarily concerned that his DC had seemed to imply a lack of sensitivity in the DCI. But it hadn't been interpreted in that way.

'Quite right, Sharon,' replied the DCI. 'I was told that his first wife, Louise's mother, died some years ago, and his current wife left him within the last two or three years. No one seemed to know anything about any other relatives or friends. He is regarded as a bit of a loner and hard to get on with. So I haven't made any headway with where he might be now.'

'I have some progress from a forensics perspective, sir,' came a quiet Scottish voice from the back of the room, 'if this would be the right time to tell you.'

'Go ahead, Richie,' replied the DCI, 'if it's something positive, let's hear it.'

Sharon turned her head slightly towards Richie. She hadn't realised that he was present.

'Well,' he began, in his customary thoughtful way, 'I have two news items. Firstly, the second DNA has now been confirmed as that of police officer, Frank Purvis-Brown.'

An appreciative murmur spread round the meeting, and even the DCI looked pleased.

'You'll recall, sir, that this DNA was found in the incinerated car, which is also linked to the car in which Marie Wilkinson drowned. The newly identified DNA was found in the driver's area of the car. I realise that it doesn't prove that he actually drove the car, though,' continued Richie, 'but am I right in thinking that the man you referred to earlier in the meeting might be this man?'

'Quite so, Richie,' said the DCI, 'and thanks for your excellent work. I know that you've been fast-tracking the tests for us. But you said you have two news items, so what's the second?'

'It's about the suicide of Louise Purvis-Brown, or, more precisely, about the contents of the bag she placed by the fence bordering the railway track,' reported Richie. 'As you know, sir, the death did not occur on our patch, and the forensic investigation was not strictly our province, but because of the Mortimer connection we had a legitimately shared interest.'

DCI Couzens was usually amused by Richie's ponderous style, but today he was willing him to get to the point more quickly.

'Was something in the girl's bag of particular importance then, Richie?' he asked.

'Yes, sir,' replied Richie. 'Louise left a suicide note and her phone in the bag. The suicide note took the form of a letter to Gregory Mortimer. And the technicians are still analysing the contents of her phone.'

There were several audible gasps around the room, as well as horrified looks. The DCI now had an expression of concern on his face.

'There's no doubt that it was Louise who wrote the letter, as specialists in that area have confirmed. And her prints are all over it, too. But having established those facts, it's the content which is significant to you all, I think.'

Clive and Sharon looked at each other, and Sharon closed her eyes and took a deep breath. They both feared they knew what they were about to hear.

'I will, of course, send you the full evidence,' said Richie calmly, 'so perhaps a brief synopsis will suffice now, sir?'

DCI Couzens nodded at Richie.

'In essence,' Richie continued, 'Louise retracts all her allegations against Gregory Mortimer. She states that they were all lies. She was pressurised into making them by her father, and he had schooled her into the performance she gave as a prosecution witness. Her sexual abuser was in fact her father. The abuse had begun when her mother died, and Louise hated him for it, but she felt trapped. But she came to hate herself for the way she had ruined Mr Mortimer's life, and couldn't live with herself any longer. The letter contains heart-wrenching apologies to Mr Mortimer.'

Everyone in the briefing room was silent while Richie related the contents of Louise's last letter. And the silence continued, when he'd finished.

The DCI was the first to speak.

'Thank you, Richie,' he said. 'Even though many of us have dealt with equally devastating scenarios in the past, each new one arouses a range of feelings. But this will reinforce our efforts, firstly to locate Frank Purvis-Brown, and secondly to address the aftermath for the survivors of all this. We'll close this meeting now, but, Clive and Sharon, we need to talk further. So, my office in ten minutes, please.'

Clive acknowledged the instruction, and went to fetch some coffees for himself and Sharon. Just time for a caffeine boost before the next meeting.

* * *

'Right,' said the DCI, 'we've only got a few hours before we either charge or release Bronwen Smythe. That's so, isn't it?'

Clive and Sharon had just arrived in the DCI's office.

'Correct, sir,' replied Clive. 'At present she admits to the theft and assisting in the destruction of the car which sent Marie Wilkinson to her death, but nothing else. She denies knowledge of, and involvement in, the death. And she's terrified of the consequences to herself of Purvis-Brown thinking she grassed on him. She hasn't named him yet, but she will, if we press her harder. She says that he has a hold over her in relation to drug dealing, and he's been using that to force her into other criminal activities.'

'One final push, then,' said the DCI. 'If all else fails, and assuming the prosecutors concur, we'll take her before the court tomorrow only on charges concerning the stolen car. But bear in mind that she may well be in danger from Purvis-Brown, if he hears about all this. You'll need grounds to oppose court bail, if necessary.'

Clive and Sharon left the DCI's office, and quickly planned their interview with Bronwen.

'And if Louise's allegations were false, perhaps Bronwen's are too,' said Sharon, 'and she's been wasting police time, as well as causing Mortimer even more distress.'

Clive nodded in agreement.

Sixty-Six

Clive and Sharon were making their way, via the coffee machine as usual, to the DCI's office. They had just spent an hour interviewing Bronwen Smythe again, and they were feeling elated and relieved. At last the different threads were coming together.

'Do you remember me asking you, a short while ago,' began Clive, 'if you thought that the police, the prosecution and the court had all got it wrong in respect of Mortimer? I'd got the impression then you thought his conviction might be unsafe.'

'Hmm,' replied Sharon, watching her cappuccino fill the mug, 'but it was only a gut feeling. It was the first time that I thought Lucy Flynn might actually be onto the truth.'

'Well,' said Clive, smiling at his colleague, 'next time you have a gut feeling, I shall listen carefully, as it might save us a lot of time and effort! We now have confirmation that you were right.'

The DCI was also pleased at the outcome of their interview. They were running out of time to keep Bronwen in custody, but now they had a coherent case for bringing her to court, in respect of the stolen car at least. Bronwen had decided to wipe that particular slate clean, whatever the consequences for herself. Clive and Sharon were in no doubt that she was scared, but perhaps the prospect of a prison sentence was preferable to any retribution which Frank Purvis-Brown might deal out. She remained adamant that she didn't see the stolen car between leaving it in the carpark as instructed, and being taken in it to the woods, where it was set ablaze. Clive was inclined to believe her, and they had no evidence to prove otherwise.

Whilst initially still reluctant to name the person she had referred to as "one of your lot", Bronwen soon realised that her interviewers knew his identity. It took more probing, though, to persuade her that it was in her interests to disclose the nature of Purvis-Brown's stranglehold on her. He'd arrested her previously, she said, for possession of hard drugs, but on one occasion he caught her supplying them... and it was a large quantity of drugs. She'd be going down for a long stretch, he'd told her, so he offered her a deal. If she made sexual abuse allegations against Gregory Mortimer and stuck with her story until he got a longer sentence, then he wouldn't take her drug dealing any further. She decided she had no option but to agree. He told her what to say to the police about Mortimer. But then he wouldn't leave it at that.

'So,' asked Sharon, 'did you know Gregory Mortimer? Had you ever met him?'

Bronwen shook her head, looking pleadingly at Sharon.

'No,' she muttered quietly, 'all I knew was that he was in prison for abusing that bastard's daughter.'

'So,' continued Sharon, 'did you know his daughter?'

Bronwen shook her head again, and whispered, 'No.'

'And you're now telling us that all the allegations you made to the police against Mr Mortimer were complete lies, from start to finish?' asked Clive, trying to keep calm.

'Yes, lies, all lies,' replied Bronwen, suddenly raising her voice and staring at Clive.

With that confession on tape, Sharon decided to move the interview on.

'You said just now, Bronwen, that Purvis-Brown wouldn't leave it at that. What do you mean?' she asked.

'He just kept turning the screw, like next I had to steal that car, and it had to be that one,' she replied. 'A bit later, like I told you, he drove me in it to the woods, where it was set on fire. But the sod just left me there, while someone else picked him up and drove him away.'

'And did he tell you to do anything else?' asked Clive.

'Not yet,' was the reply.

* * *

The DCI also had progress to report.

'Our colleagues on Purvis-Brown's patch have tracked down his estranged wife, Beverley Purvis-Brown, and interviewed her,' he told Clive and Sharon. 'She claimed to have no idea where he might be, and she felt certain that he would not seek her out. But she did talk about Purvis-Brown's abuse of his daughter. She had caught him one night, sneaking into Louise's bedroom. He was wearing no pants, and he had an erection. Louise was lying in bed, cowering against the wall, gesturing for him to leave her alone. That'd been enough for Beverley, and she immediately packed a few belongings, got into her car and left. Afterwards she texted Louise to tell her to ring the police, but she doubted Louise would do it. She felt bad about leaving her, she said, but she just needed to get away. Her revulsion at what she'd seen was too much for her.'

'And would she be willing to repeat all that under oath in court?' asked Clive.

'She said she would,' replied the DCI. 'They had the impression that she is racked with guilt at having abandoned Louise, especially when she was told that the girl had killed herself. She was absolutely distraught apparently.'

* * *

'But where does all this leave Gregory Mortimer?' asked Sharon, when she and Clive had returned to the office.

'Well,' replied Clive, 'at the moment, we literally don't know where he is, but I realise that's not what you mean.'

'When you think about all the ways he's been victimised, Sarge,' said Sharon, 'it's appalling. And whilst he'll eventually get his conviction quashed, hopefully, and he won't face any new abuse charges, his future's pretty much ruined, isn't it? And we still don't know who set fire to his flat, do we?'

'We can hazard an educated guess, though, can't we?' asked Clive.

Sharon gave her boss a faux-shocked look.

'But Sarge,' she replied, laughing, 'we need evidence, that's what you always say to me!'

Clive laughed too.

'It's gratifying that you listen to me... so let's get on with finding it!'

Sixty-Seven

Simon had mentioned a couple of reference books, which he thought would be helpful to Joanna. She'd forgotten to bring them over to the barn, so she decided to go to Hotheby Farmhouse to find them.

She quietly unlocked the side entrance door, hoping not to disturb Simon if he was working at his desk. To her surprise, though, she was greeted by a tall, athletic-looking man in his forties, who was going through files in one of Simon's cabinets.

'Hello,' he said with a smile, 'you must be Joanna. I wondered when we'd bump into each other.'

Joanna must have looked bemused, as the man laughed and explained.

'I'm Rob Ellsman,' he said. 'I live in the flat upstairs in the back extension. By the expression on your face, I guess that Simon has forgotten to mention me to you... right?'

'I'm afraid he has,' replied Joanna, and Rob laughed.

'Once Simon starts talking about his work,' said Rob, 'he forgets about everything else! Anyway, I'm his physiotherapist, nurse and general dogsbody.' He laughed again. 'I came here while the renovations were being done, to make sure that Simon could live as independently as possible, both now and in the future. I stayed in one of the Thorncrofts' caravans and oversaw things from there. They're really kind people, and they keep an eye on Simon, if I'm not around.'

'So, are you here full-time?' asked Joanna.

'Yes, more or less,' replied Rob, 'but we have a brilliant rota of nurses who come in at weekends, so there's always someone on hand if Simon needs help. He's actually in the therapy room at the moment with one of the peripatetic staff, so you'll probably see other people coming and going at times. I'll show you the therapy room sometime, if you like. There's some basic gym equipment in there too… if ever you feel in need of a workout!'

'Sounds tempting,' said Joanna with a smile, 'but I only came over here to collect a couple of books, so I'd better get on.'

'Sorry,' said Rob, 'I didn't mean to detain you. We'll no doubt see each other around.'

Joanna found the reference books and returned to the barn, wondering why Simon hadn't mentioned Rob and the nursing team.

This whole set-up must be costing him a fortune, she thought.

* * *

Joanna's phone rang as she opened the barn door. She accidentally dropped the books she was carrying, while she fumbled for her mobile in her pocket.

'Hello, Joanna, I hope it's a convenient moment,' said a friendly woman's voice, 'this is Penny Thorncroft, from Ivy House. Gerry tells me that you met each other in Snaysby the other day, and he suggested you pop in sometime. Well, how about coming for an evening meal tomorrow? We'd love you to.'

Joanna thanked Penny profusely, and arrangements were made.

My first social outing, she thought contentedly.

Joanna stooped down to pick up the books. One of them had fallen open, with the front hard cover showing a name written on it, with a date. It reminded her of her schooldays, when she used to rummage around in second-hand bookshops. She remembered looking at the names which people had written in them, and wondering who they were, and why the book had ended up in the bookshop. Joanna had always treasured every book she owned, and she too had usually written her name on the inside of the front cover.

So Joanna looked at Simon's book. It had been published only a few years previously and didn't look like the second-hand books of Joanna's childhood memories. But it wasn't Simon's name on the cover. She opened the cover of the other book, and the name was the same.

Perhaps this person was a former colleague of his, she speculated. *I'll ask Simon one day if he knows who G Mortimer is... I don't suppose he'll mind.*

Sixty-Eight

The DCI was updating the briefing meeting.

'Right,' he began, 'it's imperative that we locate PC Frank Purvis-Brown quickly. We have watertight evidence of his abuse of his daughter, his connections with the car which was linked to Marie Wilkinson's death, and now Purvis-Brown's DCI has informed me of additional offences. They were granted a warrant to search his home. There were two main findings. Firstly, they believe that he hasn't been there for a while, and the neighbours confirmed that they hadn't seen him or his car recently. Secondly, a laptop and phone were removed from his loft, where they were hidden, and the contents have been analysed. The laptop contains thousands of indecent images of children. Attempts had apparently been made to delete these, but the technicians could still access them. No evidence has yet been found that he has been distributing the images, but nevertheless Purvis-Brown is stacking up offences and is assessed as potentially dangerous.'

'Sir,' interjected Clive, 'do we all agree on who Purvis-Brown poses the most immediate risk to?'

'Quite right, Clive,' responded the DCI, 'for clarity's sake, the consensus is, firstly Bronwen Smythe, who remains in custody at present, and secondly, Gregory Mortimer, who is in a "safe house". His third potential target may be Beverley Purvis-Brown. Does anyone disagree?'

No one had any names to add.

'And has anything emerged from his phone, sir?' asked Clive.

'They're still working on that, I understand,' replied the DCI.

'Sir, would it be appropriate to report on the findings from his daughter's phone, at this stage?' asked Richie McCleod. 'I've been briefed by the technicians who've been working on that.'

'Of course, Richie, go ahead,' said the DCI.

'Well, sir,' he began, 'there's a sequence of harrowing texts from Louise to her father, over the fifteen minutes or so before she walked out in front of the train. She writes how much she hates herself for lying about Gregory Mortimer in court. She tells her father how much she hates him for abusing her, when he had always said that he loved her. She says that his actions have ruined her life and she hopes that he rots in hell. As I mentioned, sir,' continued Richie, 'this was a series of texts, not just one.'

'Understood, Richie,' confirmed the DCI. 'Did Louise text anything else?'

'Yes, sir,' replied Richie, 'she told her father that she had written to Mr Mortimer, and she hoped the police would find the letter.'

'Thank you, Richie,' said the DCI, 'I'll get all the details over to Purvis-Brown's DCI immediately.'

* * *

'It makes me wonder,' said Sharon, as she and Clive left the briefing, 'what impact those texts would've had on Purvis-Brown's already disturbed state of mind.'

'Hmm,' was Clive's only reply. He was deep in thought.

As they reached Clive's office, the phone was ringing. Sharon answered it.

'DC Page, it's Lucy Flynn here. I'm wondering if you could tell me how Gregory Mortimer is? And whether Louise's suicide has shed any light on his case?' she asked.

Sharon was caught off guard by the phone call, but quickly gathered her thoughts.

'Hello, Lucy,' she replied, indicating to Clive who was calling, 'how are you? I know you were shocked by seeing the report of Louise's death.'

Clive flicked the switch so that he could hear both ends of the conversation. He signalled to Sharon to give no information to Lucy.

'I'm fine now,' said Lucy, 'but I'm wondering if anything has emerged which strengthens my hypothesis that Mortimer was innocent of Louise's abuse. And are you still investigating the subsequent allegations?'

'As you appreciate, Lucy, we can't disclose anything about ongoing matters. As soon as issues are in the public domain, that's different, and you can pursue them through your usual channels,' replied Sharon calmly.

'Well,' said Lucy, 'I'm aware that Bronwen Smythe, Mortimer's second accuser, was in court, charged with theft of a car and other driving offences, and she's now in custody. So how does all this tie together?'

'I'm sorry, but I can't comment. Sorry, Lucy, but I have another call waiting,' said Sharon, and she hung up.

'That one doesn't miss a trick, does she?' commented Clive. 'Well handled, Sharon.'

* * *

Clive was about to fetch some coffee for them both, when the phone rang again. He groaned.

Sharon answered and immediately handed the receiver to her boss, saying, 'It's Kirsty from Mulchester.'

Sharon fancied a sandwich as well as a coffee, so she went off to the canteen while Clive spoke to his former colleague. By the time she returned, carrying a tray, Clive had finished his conversation and was looking buoyant.

'More progress, Sharon,' he grinned, and punched the air.

'What did Kirsty have to say, then?' she asked.

'Well,' began Clive, 'it seems that the person who set fire to Mortimer's flat was over-confident… or bloody stupid.' He paused and took a mouthful of sandwich.

'Come on, Sarge,' laughed Sharon, 'you don't have to draw this out for dramatic effect.'

'Right,' spluttered Clive and finished his mouthful. 'Good choice of sandwiches, by the way!'

'Sarge…' began Sharon, showing exasperation.

'OK, OK,' said Clive. 'Forensics in Mulchester have analysed some DNA found on the edge of the pillowcase on Mortimer's bed. It was spittle, but not Mortimer's. From their various tests they've established that the person who hit Mortimer and then set fire to the bedclothes, also spat at him, and the spittle soaked into the pillow. Kirsty interpreted this as a sign of contempt on the part of the attacker, but that's, as I say, not based on science. She's probably right, though.'

'So, whose DNA was found?' asked Sharon, willing her boss to get to the important news.

'The DNA is that of Frank Purvis-Brown, and that seems to fit with Kirsty's unscientific theory too,' replied Clive.

'Thank heavens for forensics,' said Sharon exultantly.

Clive gave her a knowing smile.

'Well, the DCI needs to hear about this,' he said, standing up. 'It's one more nail in Purvis-Brown's metaphorical coffin!'

Sixty-Nine

Joanna was looking forward to supper with the Thorncrofts that evening. She'd been working in Snaysby Library for several hours and decided to call it a day, even though she still had some notes to write up.

Now, what did Penny say, she reminded herself, *wear old clothes because Carruthers tends to slobber over new friends! Well, that suits me fine. And any time after six o'clock… just whenever I'm ready. It sounds lovely and casual.*

As she was leaving the library, she remembered to go to the off-licence.

Hmm… she wondered, *what type of wine might they like?*

After a quick look at the off-licence's shelves, she decided on a Loire white, which was one of her favourites.

* * *

As she drove up towards Hotheby Farmhouse, it all looked very peaceful in the late afternoon sun. There was no sign of Rob Ellsman's car, and Joanna guessed that Mrs Thwaites had left by now. She chuckled to herself, wondering if Mrs Thwaites would be cooking their supper at Ivy House.

She parked round the back of the barn as usual. She'd decided to walk down to Ivy House, as it was such a calm evening, and it was less than a mile, and she'd take a torch, in case she needed it on the way home. After a quick shower, she put on a respectable pair of jeans and a casual top. Then she sat on the gallery and contentedly watched the birds for a while.

Just after six o'clock Joanna slung a jacket over her shoulder and set off towards Ivy House, the wine bottle in her bag.

* * *

Gerry was walking up from the caravan park as Joanna came through the farm entrance. He gave her a cheerful wave and quickened his step.

'Hello, Joanna, welcome to Ivy House,' he called out. 'Let's go in and find Penny.'

But it was Carruthers who came to greet Joanna next, and Penny had been right. His was a slobbery welcome, together with an excited bark. Finally, Joanna was introduced to Penny, who was busying herself in the large kitchen.

'Oh, a Loire wine,' exclaimed Penny, as Joanna handed her the bottle, 'that's just perfect. Gerry and I have had some wonderful holidays in that region, not to mention excellent bottles of wine!'

Joanna felt relieved. She also had a feeling that this was going to be her sort of evening.

* * *

After a delicious fish supper, followed by a raspberry pavlova, which Penny had prepared, rather than Mrs Thwaites, they went and sat in the drawing-room to have coffee. Gerry told Joanna about the renovations they'd done to Ivy House. It had been very dilapidated when they bought it, he said, but now it really felt like their home.

Gerry talked too about his years in the police, until Penny said they'd like to hear about Joanna, too.

Gerry took the hint, and asked Joanna, 'So how did you end up here in Hotheby?'

'Oh, honestly, Gerry,' scolded Penny, with a smile on her face, 'you make it sound as though Joanna is at the end of the line, like we are! She's chosen to come here, to this beautiful area, and who can blame her?'

Gerry laughed.

'Well,' said Joanna, 'a strange sequence of events brought me here actually, which I'll tell you about some other time, but I have absolutely no regrets. I have a gorgeous home, interesting work to do, an easy-going boss, you two just down the road, and a new friend in Carruthers... so I'm very content.'

Carruthers seemed to hear his name and waddled over to Joanna, slumping down by her feet. Joanna smiled at him and stroked his head.

'Now,' asked Gerry, 'who's for a game of cards?'

'Another time, perhaps,' answered Joanna, 'but I think I ought to go home, if you don't mind. I've got some notes I want to finish off before meeting with Simon tomorrow morning. I don't wish to appear rude, though. I've had a really lovely evening, thank you.'

'But you're very welcome to stay longer... we don't have to play cards. We're happy to sit and chat over a brandy, if you'd prefer,' said Penny, 'or you could stay over, and we'll run you back early, so you can finish your work then?'

'You're very kind, but no, I'd rather just get the work done before I go to bed, but thank you,' said Joanna.

'Then I'll walk up there with you. There's actually a short-cut to the barn which you may not have found yet, so I'll show you,' said Gerry, 'and I'm sure Carruthers would like to come too.'

* * *

The short-cut was indeed a quicker path back to the barn, so Joanna made a mental note of where to find the partially hidden entrance off the lane below. It led to the opposite side of the barn from the front door, near Joanna's parked car.

Gerry and Carruthers parted from her a short way before the end of the path, in order to return home. Joanna wandered round the barn to her front door and looked across at Hotheby Farmhouse, still and in darkness. She unlocked her door and went in, thinking about the work she needed to do.

She also thought about how hospitable Gerry and Penny had been... even offering her a bed for the night.

Seventy

Joanna was in her cloisters' office, when she suddenly remembered that the journal article, which she wanted to re-read before talking to Simon tomorrow morning, was in his study. She decided to go over and fetch it. It would only take a couple of minutes, and she wouldn't disturb anyone. She couldn't see any lights on in the farmhouse.

She picked up her keys, not bothering to lock her front door as she went out. She walked over to the side entrance, enjoying the quiet and solitude. It was the first time she'd tried to unlock the door in the dark, and she cursed herself for not having brought a torch. At last, the door opened. She fumbled around trying to find the light switch and dropped her keys.

Suddenly, there was a large, gloved hand over her mouth and a man's body close behind her, pushing her urgently towards Simon's desk. A whispering voice, next to her ear, told her not to make a sound. The words were more pleading than threatening. She was bundled into the well of Simon's enormous desk and squatted with her head against her knees. The hand was removed from her mouth, as the man also crouched under the desk. It had all happened so swiftly, that Joanna only now began wondering what the hell was going on. The man turned and signalled to her to stay silent. She nodded. In the gloom she could see that his face was entirely covered, apart from eye-slits, and he seemed to be wearing a flak-jacket. She thought it must be Rob Ellsman, as he seemed to be protecting her, and he'd called her by her name.

A man's voice rang out from a room towards the back of the house.

'Where are you, Mortimer, you cowardly bastard? Come out from wherever you're hiding…'

The man under the desk again signalled to Joanna to keep quiet and put his hand on her knee. She was now shaking with fear.

Mortimer, she thought, confused, *that's the name in Simon's books. And where is Simon? I hope he's safe.*

The man continued shouting obscenities about Mortimer, but in an incoherent, crazed way. Some of his outbursts sounded like uncontrolled rage, others like distress.

Joanna heard no other noises, just this madman going from room to room in the dark. She was terrified that he would come into the study and find her hiding. She had no idea who he was, but she sensed his potential for violence. Her protector put an arm round her shoulder, as much as the cramped space allowed. She closed her eyes and kept her head firmly against her knees.

A loud bang, quickly followed by another, caused Joanna to jerk her head up suddenly, hitting it hard, and noisily, on the desk above her. The pain was excruciating, and she felt sick.

After a few seconds, she realised that she was now alone under the desk. The noises she had heard were gunshots, and her protector was needed elsewhere. She stayed stock-still, in pain and bleeding, in her hiding place.

Meanwhile, there were sounds of orders being shouted, and another shot was fired. The shouting became more urgent. Joanna realised that there were many people in the house, all in a coordinated search for the gunman. And she had inadvertently walked into an armed operation.

Then she froze. Someone had come into the study, and she had no way of knowing if it was the gunman or one of the men searching for him.

'Come out, Frank, there's no escape, and we're armed too. This is a warning. We'll shoot.'

Joanna gasped in fear.

The gunman heard her and walked round the desk. He motioned aggressively with his gun for Joanna to come out. She began to move, while he continued to point the gun at her. She thought she heard someone else come into the room.

'Come any nearer, and I'll kill her...'

Another shot rang out, deafening and close.

She looked cautiously to her right, terrified, and saw a man's body slump, groaning, onto the floor only a few feet away. A gun lay beside him.

Joanna lost consciousness.

Seventy-One

The DCI hastily convened a meeting of all the officers involved in the Mortimer and Purvis-Brown cases.

'There've been developments overnight,' he began. 'Late yesterday evening there was a planned operation to arrest Frank Purvis-Brown, during which he was shot.'

DCI Couzens paused for a few moments, while a murmur of surprise spread round the room.

'Are you saying, sir,' asked Clive, 'that Purvis-Brown is dead?'

'My information is,' replied the DCI, 'that he was still alive when he was taken to hospital, but barely clinging to life. I'm waiting for a call to give me an update. But,' he continued, 'Purvis-Brown wasn't the only casualty. One of the undercover officers, who'd been watching him for a long time, apparently, was shot by Purvis-Brown, but thankfully he was hit in the shoulder, and not in any vital organs. He's in a different hospital, but he's expected to make a full recovery eventually.'

The DCI paused, allowing time for questions, but there were none.

'There was a third casualty, too. A young woman had recently been employed at the house where the stake-out took place, and she innocently walked into the whole operation. I understand that she was briefly held hostage by Purvis-Brown, who was threatening to shoot her. But one of the officers shot him first. She was checked over in hospital, but she refused to stay overnight and is being cared for locally by friends. She is also expected to recover fully.'

The DCI's mobile phone pinged. He read the text.

'Frank Purvis-Brown has been pronounced dead,' he said solemnly, 'so we all now need to think through the implications of that for our work. I'll be in my office if anyone needs me.'

* * *

'Phew,' said Sharon, when she and Clive were alone. 'I didn't expect that.'

'Start a new wallchart please, Sharon,' said Clive, 'with FP-B at the centre. It's the simplest way to see what we need to do.'

'I wonder what impact this will have on Mortimer,' said Sharon. 'And whose responsibility is it to tell him?'

The office door opened, and the DCI came in and leaned his back against Clive's desk. He looked at the beginnings of the wallchart.

'More news for you,' he said. 'Last night's operation took place in the "safe house" in which Mortimer lived. He was known there as Simon Northam.'

Sharon looked bemused.

'So how did Purvis-Brown find out where Mortimer was?' asked Clive.

'That's not known,' replied the DCI, 'but he bragged to an undercover officer, who he thought was his mate, that he knew where someone was and he intended to kill him. He didn't give a name, but there was enough detail for the undercover officer to put two and two together. And he even wheedled the timescale of his intended attack out of Purvis-Brown, so preparations were put in place.'

'So, have you heard whether Mortimer was injured during the operation?' asked Sharon.

'Mortimer was far too vulnerable to be left in the house, so yesterday morning he was secretly moved from the house to another location. Thankfully, it was just in time,' said the DCI, 'and the operation team took their places, and waited.'

'But then,' remarked Clive, 'this young woman, whoever she is, threw a proverbial spanner in the works.'

'Yes, Sarge,' remonstrated Sharon, 'but don't let's forget that she was also taken hostage… and injured.'

'Of course,' said Clive, smiling at his DC. 'I am rightly admonished.'

Sharon had to smile, too.

'I'll update you as soon as I hear anything more,' said the DCI, and he left.

Clive and Sharon returned to the wallchart. As the names and tragedies accumulated, Sharon sighed loudly and commented, 'How could one man create so much devastation and misery?'

Seventy-Two

For a couple of days Joanna lay in bed in the spare room at Ivy House, following the hospital's prescription of "complete bedrest". There was a dressing on her head-wound, and a thumping headache returned as the effect of the painkillers wore off. But by the third day, she felt well enough to persuade Penny to let her go downstairs and be among her friends.

Joanna sat on the comfortable old settee in the kitchen, with her legs up, and Carruthers lay on the floor beside her. Mrs Thwaites, who had been horrified on hearing of the events at Hotheby Farmhouse, scurried about the kitchen, pleased to be helping out there again. Initially she spoke to Joanna in hushed tones, but gradually she reverted to being her usual chatty self.

As the days passed, Joanna wanted to talk to Penny and Gerry about the topic which everyone seemed to be avoiding.

So, over dinner one evening, she asked, 'Have you heard how Simon is? Will he be coming back to Hotheby?'

The Thorncrofts had anticipated that Joanna would ask about him at some point soon, and they were honest in their answer.

'Simon is doing OK,' replied Gerry. 'He apparently wants to return to the farmhouse, but the people looking after him are recommending that he takes things slowly at the moment. He's been informed of all the events, but, I understand, they've raised personal issues for him which need to be sorted out. So the future's a bit unclear right now.'

Joanna looked relieved.

'I just want to be sure he's OK,' she said, 'he's such a lovely man.'

'Well,' said Penny, with a smile, 'I gather that he's been asking after you, too, and sent his best wishes. He hopes that you'll eventually work together again.'

Joanna smiled. It was her first happy smile since her injury.

* * *

There was a knock on the front door.

Penny came back into the kitchen and announced, 'You've got two visitors, Joanna,' chuckling as she spoke. She ushered in the local policemen, Craig Asher and Chris Caldecote.

Craig handed a colourful bunch of flowers to Joanna, grinning and saying, 'We've been worried about you, but we know you're in good hands here.'

Joanna thanked them, silently wondering where else in the world this would happen! It all felt a bit surreal.

The two men declined Penny's invitation to stay for coffee. Now that they were reassured that Joanna was recovering well, they would be on their way.

* * *

As Joanna's strength improved, she, Gerry and Carruthers went for short walks across the nearby fields. The views were not as spectacular as from the barn's gallery, but nevertheless beautiful. It was therapeutic, too, to be out in the fresh air and sunshine.

'Do you feel up to hearing a bit more about what happened at the farmhouse?' asked Gerry. 'If not, it can easily wait for another time.'

There was a rickety wooden bench at the edge of the field, and Gerry suggested that they sit there.

'I've been trying to piece things together in my mind,' replied Joanna, 'but it feels like a jigsaw with more than half the bits missing. So, if you've got some of them, I'd like to hear. But how do you know about what happened?'

'Well, Joanna, I think I've mentioned before, that in my pre-Hotheby life I was a high-ranking police officer,' began Gerry, 'and I was given privileged information about the situation at the farmhouse. It was renovated as a "safe house" for Simon Northam, but sadly things went very wrong.'

'But,' protested Joanna, becoming confused, 'I'm certain the gunman was shouting for someone called Mortimer, not for Simon. Was it really Simon that he wanted to kill?'

Tears began rolling down Joanna's cheeks, and Gerry wondered whether he should continue with the story.

'Shall we stop now, and I'll tell you more some other time?' asked Gerry gently.

Joanna shook her head.

'No,' she replied, 'I just get over-emotional when I think about it all... sorry... carry on... I'll be OK.

'Well,' continued Gerry, 'if you're sure. Simon and Mortimer are the same person. He changed his name to Simon Northam, on advice and for security reasons. So, sadly, it was Simon who was the gunman's target.'

Gerry paused, while Joanna processed what she'd been told.

'But Simon is such a kind and gentle person,' said Joanna. 'Why would anyone want to kill him?'

'It's a long story, but don't change your assessment of Simon,' urged Gerry, 'you're right about his character. But the man rampaging through the farmhouse was a violent and disturbed personality, waging an unjustified vendetta against Simon over a long period of time.'

'You said, he *was…* is he dead?' asked Joanna, hesitantly.

'He was shot by the police at the scene and died later in hospital,' Gerry clarified.

'I know that first part,' choked Joanna, looking ashen. 'He was pointing his gun at me when he was shot, and he fell down very close to me.'

Gerry put his arm around Joanna, apologising that he'd forgotten those details. She put her head on Gerry's shoulder, sobbing quietly. Gerry thought silently about the dreadful ordeal Joanna had gone through. Carruthers placed his head on Joanna's knee.

As they walked slowly back to Ivy House, Gerry said there was something else he wanted Joanna to know. He hadn't told Penny anything about his prior knowledge of the situation at the farmhouse. Her only involvement was that he had suggested that she persuade Joanna to stay overnight with them, when she came to dinner. Gerry had known that the operation was likely to take place then, and he wanted Joanna well away from the farmhouse. But Joanna had been determined to finish off some work at home.

Joanna recalled the invitation to stay. Had she done so…

They reached Ivy House, and Joanna turned to Gerry.

'Was anyone else hurt at the farmhouse?' she asked. 'I remember… at least I think I do… hearing more shots, before the gunman came into the study.'

'I'm told that one other person was hurt. He was shot in the shoulder, but not critically injured. He's apparently out of hospital now,' replied Gerry.

'Just one bit of good news, then,' said Joanna, as they went into Ivy House.

* * *

A couple of days later, Penny and Joanna were in a coffee shop in Snaysby, enjoying the sun on a terrace overlooking the river.

'The doctor was very positive about the way your wound is healing, wasn't she?' said Penny.

Joanna nodded.

'I just feel such an idiot, knowing how I did it!' she said.

'Oh, come on,' replied Penny, 'you couldn't have known that there were screws protruding under the desk, and hearing shots would be enough to frighten anyone into jolting upwards. Don't be so hard on yourself. The important thing is, that you're well and truly on the mend.'

Joanna leaned back, sunning her face and feeling content.

'Do you think you'd feel up to having another visitor this afternoon, Jo?' asked Penny.

'I reckon so,' she replied. 'Who is it?'

'Well, it's the man who pushed you into the well of Simon's desk, actually,' said Penny, concerned about Joanna's reaction. 'He contacted Gerry and said he'd like to meet you under different circumstances! He hoped you're recovering from your ordeal.'

'I have a lot to thank him for,' said Joanna, 'so, yes, I'd love to meet him and thank him in person.'

Penny gave Gerry a quick call, telling him to confirm the visit.

* * *

That afternoon, there was a knock on the front door of Ivy House, and Gerry brought Joanna's visitor into the kitchen.

She was completely taken aback, as she looked at the man, his arm in a sling.

'Mike!' she gasped.

Seventy-Three

Mike had forewarned Gerry that his reunion with Joanna might be awkward. And indeed, it was, for the first few minutes. But Gerry, jovial as ever, kept the conversation flowing, until Penny asked him to go out into the garden with her, as there were some urgent jobs to be done. So Mike and Joanna were left alone.

And now, a few hours later, they were sitting in the restaurant of The White Horse in Snaysby. Mike had suggested going out for a meal, in the hope that a neutral venue might lessen the obvious tension between them. Gerry offered to drive them to Snaysby, and he dropped them off at the restaurant.

They ordered their meals and an expensive bottle of wine. Mike hoped that a glass or two of wine might help Joanna to relax, as she was clearly not at ease yet.

'So what the hell were you doing at Hotheby?' she exploded. 'And did you know that I was here? What is it with you and secrecy?'

She looked tearful, and Mike felt confused. This wasn't how he'd wanted the evening to be. He tentatively put his hand on hers, half-expecting her hand to be withdrawn, but it wasn't.

'Jo, please, don't let's fight… I've so been looking forward to seeing you again,' implored Mike, 'and I'm happy to answer all your questions and tell you everything.'

Joanna looked sceptical.

'Everything?' she asked, and Mike nodded.

* * *

He was true to his word. During the meal, Mike explained that for several years he had been an undercover policeman, hence his frequent, unexplained disappearances. He tried to assure Joanna that he hadn't wanted to be secretive, but his job required it.

'So that'll never change, will it? You'll always disappear and reappear with no explanation,' said Joanna despondently.

'Not quite,' said Mike, with the disarming smile which Joanna hadn't seen for so long, 'because I've negotiated early retirement. As of now, I'm a free agent! I'll have to find a new job, but definitely not with the police. I'm now a wounded ex-policeman! What do you think of that, Jo?' He laughed.

Joanna was unsure what to think of it.

'So, tell me the truth about Hotheby,' she said. 'Did you know I was here?'

'Don't be cross with me, Jo, but of course I knew where you were… I encouraged you to apply for the job, didn't I?' confessed Mike. 'I've had news about you from Craig Asher occasionally, as he's one of Simon Northam's protection team.'

'And you were part of the operation at the farmhouse, to protect Simon?' she asked.

'That's right,' he said. 'I'd had the gunman under surveillance for some months, and he thought I was his mate.'

'But how could you let me get into danger like that?' asked Joanna furiously. 'I was very nearly shot by that madman!'

Mike could understand Joanna's anger, but he wasn't sure how to deal with it.

'Jo,' he said gently, 'please, listen to me. I tried to keep you away from the barn that evening. You were supposed to stay with the Thorncrofts, but they couldn't persuade you. We'd already moved Simon to another location. Whenever I could, I looked over towards the barn to make sure you weren't there, and it was all in darkness. Then suddenly I saw you coming across the yard towards the farmhouse. I waited by the side-door, and when you opened it, I grabbed you and shoved you into the desk-well. I tried to crawl in too, but there wasn't much room. Then, when the mayhem started, I had to get back to work. Soon after that, the bloke aimed at me, and the bullet hit my shoulder. It wasn't until afterwards that I heard what had happened to you. But honestly, Jo, I did all I could to protect you… and I'm so sorry that I failed.'

Joanna looked sad.

'And I haven't even asked you how your shoulder is. Sorry,' she said, quietly.

'I suspect there's a lot more that we need to say to each other,' said Mike.

He paused, and then asked, 'How would you feel about my staying in one of Gerry's caravans for a while, so we can sort things out?'

Joanna hesitated, then smiled and nodded.

'I'd like that,' she said. 'I'd like that very much.'

Mike looked relieved.

'But we need to take things slowly,' she warned.

'As slowly as you like,' replied Mike, putting his hand gently on hers.